# INVISIBLE WITNESSES

**Wayne Sheridan**

**Jeremiah 30:2 Publications**

**Bristol, Virginia**

*Invisible Witnesses*
Wayne Sheridan

Copyright © 2016 by Wayne Sheridan

Jeremiah 30:2 Publications
Bristol, Virginia

Library of Congress Control Number: 2016903066
ISBN: 978-1-944187-02-6



Publication services provided by Christian Self-Publishing Association, https://www.christianwriterhelp.com/service/publishing-packages/
Printed in the United States of America

# Acknowledgments

Thanks for the contribution of many homeless people that taught me about homelessness during my fifteen years as director of a homeless shelter in Bristol, Tennessee. Thanks to the Association of Gospel Rescue Missions that was instrumental in teaching me about homelessness, its causes, stereotypes and the challenges faced by those ministering with the homeless. For further information on homelessness, go to www.agrm.org.

Thanks to Lonnie Barrett, a friend with law enforcement experience who helped keep me in the realm of reality in regard to policemen and the way they work.

Thanks to Jim Kochenburger for his invaluable guidance through the publication process and for his contribution to this work through editing.

Most of all, I am grateful to my wife, Alice Sheridan, for her encouragement to pursue a longtime desire to write. She is a very helpful "reader" who helps me see the work from a reader's perspective. Thanks to her for performing the first edit on this book.

# Prologue

Staff Sergeant Richard Hawkins (Sarge) was four weeks from rotating out of Iraq to Kuwait, and then home. His five-foot ten-inch frame was packed with hard muscle. He was not only agile in body, but in mind. His quick thinking and accurate analysis of situations and conditions on the ground had made him a leader who enjoyed his men's trust. He had come to Iraq as part of the Surge in 2009 and was now a short-timer.

Hawkins had just received orders for an op that promised to be one of the most exciting he had experienced during his tour. It would also turn out to be the most dangerous of his tour. He called the platoon of marines to the briefing room at their forward operating base (FOB) in Fallujah to brief them on an exciting mission to rescue a valuable hostage.

He thought of the men who had become his family away from home. They were a melting pot of brawn and brain. These men came to the Corps with many differences in body, mind, and emotions. They had been melted and recast into a unified fighting machine, a family that would do whatever it took to complete the mission and to take care of each other. He felt secure in taking them out of the security of their FOB into the fury of almost certain action with the hostiles.

Red was first to arrive in the briefing room. He was always ready to go, and he chewed his gum rapidly, betraying pent up energy. "What's up, Sarge?" he called out to Sgt. Hawkins,

"We'll get to that in a moment. You ready for a little excitement?"

"Oorah!" bellowed out Red.

The marines had trained to not use their real names when on operations for fear the enemy would hear them and use the knowledge for no good. In previous wars, soldiers had heard their names used on enemy propaganda radio broadcasts. Combat nicknames were given by the group to new guys and used for all operational communications. Red was given his nickname due to his red hair. His given name was Rory McSwain.

The next man to walk in was Gabby, the radioman. The radioman is the platoon's connection to Command and Control. Billy Goat followed him. He had demonstrated a bent to leadership when under stress and had just been promoted to squad leader. Hammer and Max, the firepower, swaggered in right behind Billy Goat. Hammer would carry the grenade launcher and Max would carry the 30 cal. machine gun on the platoon's operations. Reggie walked in, still buttoning his camos and stumbling over a chair Max had purposely pulled into the walkway. He was a new guy, so he was the target of practical jokes. He didn't have his combat nickname yet.

Sarge automatically said a short, silent prayer that Reggie and all of them would make it through this tour of duty. Bones walked in, yawning. He had a phlegmatic personality, but the men respected his cool head in the midst of crisis and his knowledge of field first aid. Bones contributed significantly to the morale of the platoon because he gave them a sense of security—he was there to take care of them if wounded,

Hawkins listened to the typical jesting the men used with each other to lessen the anxiety of a pending operation. At last, all members of the thirteen-man squad were gathered and ready for the briefing.

Sgt. Hawkins yelled above the hum of chatter, "Marines, let me have your attention! We have an opportunity today to rescue a high value hostage that intel has located just south of Al Habbaniyah, about twelve miles from here on Highway 10. We will take two Humvees, proceed on 10, and then take the turnoff for the house where intel says the hostage is currently held. The house is on top of a rise about two hundred yards from the road. Intel believes there are three to five hostiles holding the eleven year old son of one of the government ministers. He was taken four weeks ago."

"We have not used 10 for much military traffic lately, so we do not anticipate any trouble on the way to the target. Nevertheless, wear your armor. We are not certain how many other hostiles in the area might come to the aid of the hostage-takers if things get hot. Any questions?"

"Sure," Billy Goat spoke up. "Do we have any backup?"

Sarge knew that Billy Goat was aware they always had artillery and Apache gunships available, should they get into a difficult battle. He assumed Billy Goat asked the question to help the new guy feel better.

"We'll have the usual artillery and gunship backup available, if needed," Sgt. Hawkins assured them. "Though you know the gunships are stretched thin in that area and might take a while to reach you. Be ready to leave in fifteen minutes."

While the marines moved toward the door, Sgt. Hawkins remembered one more thing and barked above the chatter, "Oh yeah, we'll have an interpreter with us . . . and Reggie, you need a nickname."

"Sarge, sir," Red called out. "I suggest 'Hawk.' I've seen him shoot and he's got a hawk's eye."

"Sounds good to me," Sarge responded. "Now let's go get it."

*******

It was only about thirty minutes' drive time to the house intel had pinpointed. In the brutal heat of Iraq, thirty minutes was long enough inside those mobile sweat boxes. Sweat beaded on their foreheads and caused expanding circles below their arms. Added to this was sweat from the anxiety of traveling on a road that had a history of IEDs (improvised explosive devices).

The two Humvees slowed near the turnoff that would take them to the target location. After drawing close, the plan was to leave the Humvees (and drivers) beside the road before moving cautiously uphill to the house.

When the lead Humvee crossed a culvert, a deafening explosion threw the occupants in both vehicles out of their seats. Only the close proximity of the Humvee seats, walls, and the men crowded inside kept them from all being thrown out of the vehicle. The marines' training kicked in and they immediately sprang into action.

Sgt. Hawkins pushed his way out of the second Humvee to get a better view of what had happened. His ears heard nothing but an internal siren. The first Humvee was completely overturned and filled with shrapnel. The tires were blown. He focused on the driver of the first Humvee as he picked himself up and reached back inside the Humvee. He struggled to drag a bloody fellow marine out. Sgt. Hawkins moved to help the driver. He could not tell if the other marine was alive or not. Some marines fled the vehicle as others helped out those left bleeding by the blast.

Sgt. Hawkins knew that this was likely the first blow, with more to come. A flashing question shot through his mind and he barely heard himself saying it out loud, "How did they know we were coming?" Then another question, "Why is this happening to me when I'm about to leave country?" He realized that hearing himself at all meant his hearing had begun to return.

"Get out of here and position yourselves in the ditch along this side of the road," he yelled with authority. He pointed to a ditch that would use the smoldering Humvees as cover. "Move it, marines!" The words had barely left his lips when, amidst the yells of his marines, when they heard the familiar sound of an RPG (rocket propelled grenade) being fired.

"RPG incoming!" Sarge shouted.

All the men had just reached the ditch, but were still thrown to the ground by the RPG blast as it penetrated the second Humvee and blew part of it into the surrounding desert. Though the Humvee was designed to be very stable and mobile, neither of the two had enough armor plating to stop an RPG round. The remaining part of the second Humvee had been blown onto its side. It rocked back and forth, threatening to fall over on top of them in the ditch. It slowed its rocking motion and came to rest on its side, leaving the threatened men to breathe a sigh of relief.

Sgt. Hawkins barked orders. "Gabby, get a message back to the FOB for support. Bones, get over there and check those men."

Bones was already on his way to check the wounded men in the first Humvee.

"Red, Billy Goat, Hawk, get up there behind that Humvee and check out the situation," he said, having observed all three were bloodied, but mobile. Sgt. Hawkins stooped and ran to the part of the ditch where the other marines were hunkered down. He noticed Hammer and Max were ready with their firepower, if needed. Later, he would learn that Max limped severely from a wound in his right leg that had only quit bleeding due to a tourniquet Bones had tied in place above it.

"Bones!" Sgt. Hawkins called out. "What's the status?"

"It's bad, Sarge!" Bones reported. "Jogger was killed outright by shrapnel to the head. Rag is in bad shape—got a big hole in his abdomen. He is losing a lot of blood. I stabilized him, but he needs to get to a surgical hospital, ASAP. Most of the men, including the interpreter, have wounds but can still contribute to the fight.

"Call in a medivac for the critically wounded," Sgt. Hawkins yelled to the radioman. Then he yelled to Red, "Red, I need a report!"

"Looks like three hostiles are moving slowly through the rocks toward our position," Red responded. "One has an RPG. I saw another hostile at the top of the rise."

"OK, drivers, stay with your vehicles and the wounded men. The rest of you move out. We are going to give it back to them now. The nine remaining marines moved out across the road and started up the gentle hill. To sit there would have made them sitting ducks. (Marines believe a good defense is to go on the offense.) Sarge ordered the men to spread out to avoid being a bunched target and move up the hill.

Three hostiles started firing at them. The marines answered with withering fire. Two marines threw grenades that hit one hostile and sent the other two running back up the hill. One was quickly hit by a barrage of bullets and knocked down, never to get up. The other made it to the top of the hill.

The marines moved further up the hill and cautiously approached the top where the hostiles had disappeared. They peaked over the crest, prepared to lay down withering fire and throw grenades. They saw no hostiles at first. A moment later, one of the hostiles ran from behind a boulder and_into the door on the front side of the house.

The squad moved toward the house and began taking fire from the one window on the front wall. Forty yards from the house, the firing stopped abruptly. Seconds later, the sound of a starting vehicle engine caught their attention.

"There's a road heading out behind the house," Hawk yelled from the far end of the spread out men. Sgt. Hawkins ordered three of his men to circle around the house with him. The others moved toward the house, and then went inside to clear it. Just as Sgt. Hawkins and his men came around the house, they saw a truck tear out ahead of them and start up the road.

"Take out the tires," Sgt. Hawkins ordered. "Don't shoot at the passenger area! I want him alive." He heard a barrage of bullets from Hammer's .30 caliber machine gun and saw the two left side tires blow away. The truck swerved and slid into a large rock before stopping suddenly.

"Move in!" barked Sgt. Hawkins.

The marines moved cautiously toward the truck. As they approached, two hostiles dragged a young boy out of the passenger side of the truck, away from the approaching marines. They then dragged the young boy with them up the hill. The boy slowed them down and the marines closed in on them, keeping an eye out for any hostiles that might pop up to help their buddies.

Billy Goat tackled one of the men, and Red tackled the other. The boy broke loose and started running out into the desert. Sarge ran after him to bring him back.

Just then, bullets started kicking up sand all around them. The fire was coming from further up the hill. The marines that had cleared the house began returning fire to help Billy Goat, Red, Max, and Sgt. Hawkins bring their prisoners back to cover.

Just as Billy Goat reached cover with his prisoner, a bullet slashed a deep cut across his left upper arm. The impact knocked him down, so he lost his grip on the prisoner, who started to run back up the hill. Hammer took him out.

Sgt. Hawkins barked an order, "Start working your way back to the road and set up a defense until support gets here. Red, you and Hawk keep an eye out behind us."

The platoon of marines with the boy and one prisoner moved down the hill to the road and took up defensive positions. There were no further actions by hostiles. Sgt. Hawkins thought they had hit and run once they lost their hostage. He assumed they were gone, but they would still be cautious. Rag was barely holding on. Sgt. Hawkins said a silent prayer for help to keep Mark alive, and for the medevac chopper to get to them in time.

The blend of clotting blood mixed with the pungent odor of burned diesel fuel, and the stench of anxiety sweat assaulted Sgt. Hawkins's nostrils. He looked around and saw that several of the men had minor wounds, mostly from shrapnel from the IED and RPG blasts. He had lost one man and could lose another. It really upset him when a man under his command was killed. It bothered him that so many were wounded. Sgt. Hawkins began thinking, *If only he had been more cautious, If only he had . . .*

The sound of approaching helicopters shook Sgt. Hawkins out of his thoughts. It was the medevac chopper with an Apache escort. They were really happy to see the Apache, as the enemy usually disappeared when an Apache joined the battle.

"The medivac pilot wants to know the status of the landing zone" the radioman called out to Sgt. Hawkins. The marines had marked a fairly flat area not far from the road as a landing zone, using a smoke grenade. Sgt. Hawkins knew the pilot was not interested in knowing the condition of the ground, but wanted to know if there were active hostiles that might fire at his chopper.

"Tell him we have had no action for about thirty minutes," Sgt. Hawkins called out. "But we can't guarantee there are no hostiles still in the area."

"Yes, sir," barked the radioman. He started repeating the answer as the medevac chopper descended toward the landing zone.

At least one of the hostiles had moved back to the top of the hill near the house. He had an RPG and wanted to be a hero. He took aim at the medivac chopper with the RPG, and fired the rocket. The Apache escort saw the rocket and started warning the medevac pilot to pull out quickly. The Apache moved in to take out the hostile that had fired the rocket.

Sgt. Hawkins heard the RPG fire. He yelled to his men to get down and dove to the ground himself. The chopper shuddered under the sudden command to turn and ascend away from the rocket. Then it lurched with the impact and explosion of the RPG that had entered through the open right side door. He saw a man who had been blown out of the chopper fall to the ground. The chopper seemed to hang in position, shuddering as it fought for life. Pieces flew from the failing, falling chopper. It all happened so fast that he did not have time to dodge a piece of the chopper that shot his way. He felt an instant of pain, and everything went black.

# Chapter 1

*The man shoved the woman against the wall, slapped her, and walked rapidly away, yelling to her, "Do what you have to do or I will settle it for you."*

Five Years Later

Doc was recovering his mind and strength after going on a third drinking binge in the last five years. He unconvincingly hoped that this dive into the pit of despair would be the last. The painful aching deep in his soul that had triggered past binges was still there, just pushed down below the surface again by the drugs he had received at the Veterans Administration (VA) program at Mountain Home in Johnson City, Tennessee. The VA transported him back to nearby Bristol, where he had been arrested for public intoxication.

December cold crept in through Doc's worn woolen sweater, given to him a few days earlier at the local homeless shelter. A homeless man could stay at the shelter in Bristol for five days without entering one of their special programs that allowed longer stays. He wasn't much for their programs, especially since he had just finished the treatment program for alcoholics. So after five nights, he left and found himself again on the streets of Bristol. It was Thursday evening, the stores were staying open late and people were shopping for Christmas.

Bristol has one downtown, yet is two separately incorporated cities: Bristol, Tennessee, and Bristol, Virginia. The city separation line is actually the same as the state border line. It is marked by brass markers down the middle of State Street. One side of the marker is labeled Tennessee and the other, Virginia (those on one side paid Tennessee taxes, while those on the other side paid Virginia taxes).

The two cities have their own governments and police forces. There is a mixture of cooperation and competition between the two Bristol city governments. Still, the cities are often seen as one. For instance, Johnson City, Kingsport and the two Bristols make up the region referred to as the Tri-Cities in upper east Tennessee. The two most notable facts about Bristol are that it is the home of the Bristol Motor Speedway, the fans most favorite track on the NASCAR circuit, and is the birthplace of country music.

It was the NASCAR race in August that brought Doc to Bristol. Word on the street was that they hired a lot of people, including homeless people, to clean up the track seating areas and parking lots after the race. The word proved good and he had worked for about a week at the track. He found the VA hospital in nearby Johnson City had a program for alcoholics. So along with his good feeling about Bristol, the program made it home for him for the fall and winter.

"Hey Doc, you got a light?" asked Jake, another homeless man who had lived on the streets of Bristol for several months. He smoked every discarded butt he could scrounge up, and he had one now. Jake never had his own light.

"Jake, you know I don't smoke. Why would I have a light?" Doc replied. Actually he had a used Bic he found in the gutter, but was saving its last couple lights for his own use.

Jake waddled off, mumbling, "I was just checking. Somebody has to have one for me."

Jake suffered from a mental illness. He told Doc the hospital called it bipolar disease, and it was from being a cocaine baby. But Doc knew Jake had abused drugs enough to cause any number of problems. Jake also talked about liking to smell gasoline, and had done that a lot while growing up. That might be why he seemed to have a learning disability. In any case, had Jake lived just a few decades before, his condition might have been considered severe enough to warrant admission to an inpatient mental facility. Now, to save costs, people with mental illnesses that can be managed through drug therapy were kept in the community are provided with a monthly payment for rent and living expenses, and a monthly appointment at the local outpatient mental health clinic. Though this seemed like a good idea, it was flawed. People like Jake could not manage their money and would periodically lose their housing, usually after quitting their maintenance medications. Doc believed Jake was basically harmless except that you had to know which pole he was in, depression or hyperactive, tared too long at women, and frightened some of them.

Doc had not smoked since being wounded in Iraq, and he couldn't smoke in the hospital. He decided he did not want to pick it up again. It was not hard to justify the need to quit smoking with the health knowledge he had obtained when training in at the Hospital Corps School in San Diego, California, before being assigned to the Marines in Iraq in 2008. He was perplexed at the thought that he could quit cigarettes but seemed unable to resist wine.

Doc used to keep his five-foot nine-inch tall body in great shape. That had fallen off since the tragedy, and he now seemed to constantly battle draining sinuses, an upset stomach, and occasional upper respiratory infections. The cold crept through his sweater, and he shivered in the twenty-eight degree temperature with enough breeze to make it feel like twenty degrees.

*******

Doc walked the three blocks to the shelter's kitchen that was his usual place for supper. On the menu that night was chicken patty with canned green beans, canned apple sauce, and a brown-n-serve roll. The food at the shelter was usually acceptable and warm when served. The best thing was, it was free and they asked no questions. Sometimes he stayed for the nightly chapel service that followed supper in order to enjoy the shelter's warmth a little longer.

Cookie dished his plate. As he handed it to Doc, he asked, "You staying warm enough, Doc? You know, if it gets in the low twenties, you can come back here."

"Yeah, I'm good. If it gets that cold, I'll check in."

Cookie and Doc could relate to one another. They were both veterans of Iraq, where Cookie had served in the Army and learned to cook for large numbers of people. His own battle with addiction had led him to the same program Doc was a part of at the VA. Cookie and Doc always had a lot to talk about.

Doc walked back downtown after washing down his food with a hot cup of coffee. Sometimes, a passerby would feel sorry for him and give him a buck or two. But most looked the other way when he passed by, as if he was invisible. Once in a great while, a particularly sensitive person would give him five or ten dollars. Though many "street people" he knew tried to get enough gifts of money to buy a bottle of cheap wine for the night, or buy cigarettes, Doc did not smoke and usually did not drink. He used these meager gifts for personal needs like hot coffee and a breakfast roll in the morning. One time, he saved up enough to get a discontinued, marked down backpack and a foam pad at Walmart.

Doc had more education than the average homeless person. He had obtained a two-year certificate from a community college before joining the Navy to see the world. Although lower than average education was usual, he had met homeless people with master's degrees and once, a homeless man with a doctorate. They were not dumb, just thrown off the path. Typically, they just had been unable to cope with several back-to-back tragedies in life, and had no support from family, church, or others. This was often followed by abuse of drugs or alcohol, and a loss of hope that things would ever get better. Doc sighed as he remembered that was his story.

Intrigued by medical shows on TV as a kid, Doc dreamed of growing up to be a doctor. But his immaturity in the first couple of years of college had ended his dream to be a doctor. He found an easier option for realizing his dream in signing up to be a corpsman in the Navy. His nickname, Doc, came from its common use as a nickname for corpsmen. Other veteran homeless people started calling him Doc and the name stuck. When homeless people heard his nickname, they thought they could ask him about health problems they faced. He often tried to help and found some self-gratification in it.

Some evenings, as Doc walked around or hung out with a group of homeless people, he would help them out by checking for infection in a wound, feet that were either painful or grown numb, and more. Foot problems are common with homeless people who usually do not take proper care of their feet, and often do not have good shoes. Helping them gave Doc a small sense of purpose in life, something he rarely felt doing anything else.

Doc liked to keep up on the street news, and often did this by hanging out with the talkers, though he knew the stories were most often only partially true. After some time of trying to survive on the streets, many homeless people hone lying and hiding truth to refined skills, having learned these are helpful for getting what they feel they need or want. This evening, Doc did not want to be around other people.

*******

Doc strolled over to the Sweet Tooth Bakery on the corner of two of Bristol, Virginia's busier streets. He hoped it was Grace's evening to work because she would usually give him a cup of almost hot coffee—and maybe a day old sweet roll without cost. Grace was a plump, early 30's brunette with a winning smile. She had dropped out of college in her twenties, had a short, failed marriage with no children and felt out of place in life. She had met the owners of the Sweet Tooth Bakery at First Christian Church who gave her a job and a caring family in the staff at the Sweet Tooth Bakery. Doc had provided Grace with some medical advice once, and ever since she had considered him a special friend. Doc gratefully noticed Grace was there when he entered the front door.

"Hi, Grace. It's getting cold out there tonight. I'll be right back," he said as he shuffled toward the back to the bathroom.

When he came back up front, Grace commented, "Well, it may be cold, but people are not coming in for something hot tonight. I think they are shopping on State Street instead. I would too, but I have to work. Here's your usual."

She handed him a large cup of coffee and a malformed apple fritter. The fritter would have been sold deeply discounted as an "oops". Doc asked how Grace had been feeling and took a couple of minutes for small talk, but avoided any conversation about church. Another customer came in, so Doc used that as an excuse to move to a chair near the gas fireplace. He settled in with his treats and a newspaper someone had left behind.

Around 10:30 p.m., Doc yawned and decided it was time to leave the bakery and head to his place for the night. He preferred going to his place later to lessen the possibility of someone discovering it. He headed up Piedmont to State Street. He made his way slowly east on State Street to Sixth Street, and then right one block. He passed a couple of people leaving a bar, but as usual, they did not notice him. Few people look homeless people in the eyes, and few homeless people look others in the eye unless they want something. Homeless people were, on the whole, invisible citizens of their communities.

Doc took his time, even though the cold made him long to warm up in the bedroll that awaited him. He wanted to be invisible at this time of night so no one would find his place. The heavy clouds that covered the moon helped.

Only a couple cars remained in "his" parking lot. The parking lot had spaces for about fifty cars with a U-shaped drive opening onto Shelby Street. It was surrounded on three sides by aged brick buildings. Doors into the buildings opened off the parking lot, including one for a restaurant on State Street. Usually the doors were not often used except for employees coming to or going from work. Feeling all was clear, he moved quickly toward the corner of the lot where the back of a store and an office building met. His somewhat hidden place was formed by two walls of the buildings, and a third low wall that long ago had been built to hide either an air conditioning unit or garbage cans. Doc had constructed a makeshift roof of three boards and a piece of plastic discarded by a local furniture store. It may have looked like trash thrown into the corner to the casual observer, but it was his secret place. He looked around cautiously. Finally satisfied no one was watching, he crawled in.

The bedroll had been given to him by the rescue shelter. Gray-haired ladies from a Sunday school class of a local church had lovingly crafted and donated a number of bedrolls that usually contained a pair of knit gloves and a knit hat inside. They made the bedrolls by sewing two blankets together on one edge so they could function like a sleeping bag. The rescue shelter distributed them to homeless people who would not or could not stay at the shelter, as was Doc's case.

Doc stretched out into his bedroll. The bedroll was on top of the foam pad he had bought. He wondered why God had treated him so badly when God's people at the church and shelter were so caring for him.

*******

Doc knew that sleep would be slow in coming in spite of the tiredness that had descended upon him like the dark after sunset. Doc had grown accustomed to the uncomfortable accommodations, but not the coughing that started from the dry throat he experienced whenever he laid down, keeping him awake. He hated the cough, but had not determined its cause. He hated even more the haunting thoughts from long ago that relentlessly assailed his mind, and stopped only when sleep snuck up on him.

Just as he was near sleep, Doc heard angry voices approaching, growing louder by the moment. Curious about the combatants in the war of words he was overhearing, he slowly raised himself up and peeked across the parking lot. He saw a blond-haired woman in a waitress uniform, and a taller, slender, blond-headed man dressed in black standing face to face. The man shoved the woman against the wall, slapped her, and walked rapidly away, yelling to her, "Do what you have to do, or I will settle it for you." The man moved quickly to the street where he got into a fancy, dark-colored car and sped off leaving the woman with her head in her hands and crying.

That car. He remembered he had seen one like it before, parked on the street near the parking lot a week ago when he had strolled by on his way to his secret place. He had walked by the car to see if he could identify who was sitting in it. It had a parking sticker for the local college, a staff parking sticker. He had tried to glimpse the man inside with his peripheral vision so as not to appear to be looking directly at him. The man had looked away, but had blond hair. Doc had the impression he might be a young man. He had continued on his way down the sidewalk and rounded the corner, but turned when he heard the car's door open. He saw a blond-headed girl hop in on the passenger side. The door closed and the engine roared to life before the car took off down the street.

His attention went back to the woman the young man had just shoved and slapped. She wadded up what looked like a piece of paper and threw it against the wall. He watched as she walked to the restaurant's back door. He saw her face that appeared even at some distance to be attractive and young. She stood and cried for a minute before wiping away her tears and walking through the door. Doc lowered himself back into his space and got back into his bedroll.

Sleep did not come. Doc's mind was wide awake as an inner debate raged: *What was that all about? It isn't any of my business. Did I see the girl throw something down when he turned to leave? Don't get involved. It can only lead to trouble. I'll go look for what she threw down when the restaurant lights are out, or in the morning. You are foolish to do anything. Go to sleep!* At long last, he obeyed that last thought.

# Chapter 2

*Jan knew her life had become complicated, but the
unexpected interference with her plans was nothing
short of a disaster.*


Brad Jones was the dish washer at the Borderline Restaurant.
That was the only job he could get after dropping out of the eleventh grade a year earlier. He was finishing up the evening's pots
and pans when he heard the back door slam shut and saw Jan
walk briskly to the women's restroom. She walked through the
restroom door and would have slammed it shut as well, if not for
the attached door closer.

Brad liked Jan, an attractive blue-eyed, blond-headed student
at the local college. She had a teasing personality. Brad thought
Jan wore her restaurant uniform very well due to her trim, fit body
that caused sensual thoughts to rise within him. Brad was concerned that Jan seemed to be upset. He thought he would try to
console her when she returned from the restroom.

Jan Meredith cried a cascade of tears. As hard as she tried,
she could not stop. Her thoughts were like a tangled cord that
could not be unraveled. Nothing in her life was going right. Jan
knew her life had become complicated, but the unexpected interference with her plans was nothing short of a disaster. She had
reached out to the guy she thought could help her, but he had
argued with her behind the restaurant and had been unbelievably
ugly about the whole affair—even violent. She gently rubbed her
cheek that still stung from the slap.

Jan's thoughts moved back in time. Getting into college had been the best thing to happen to her in life. But it had proven difficult to manage her complicated life. She was an excellent student when able to focus on learning. However, focus was difficult to find as she juggled the demands of school, work, and an unplanned love relationship with someone special. She could not let go of any of these consumers of time and energy. She had to get her degree to get the chance she needed to forever break free from the rut her family seemed locked into, having lived for generations in coal country. She had to get good grades to keep her scholarships. She had to work to help with tuition and earn some spending money. Still, her work time in the evenings interfered with her study time. Then she met a special person, and their relationship had become intimate quickly. He was on staff at the college. She could not lose him.

Now this! An unplanned pregnancy.

Her thoughts continued to race. A week ago she used two pregnancy tests from the local drugstore and they were both positive. She was sure her secret lover was the father. But then she remembered that there had been one other occasion when she had needed more crystal, but did not have the money. She had to have it and her source would not let her pay later. He suggested something she could do for him in exchange for giving her enough crystal to last until she could get money to buy more. She had to have the meth to keep going, so she had given in. It was an experience Jan had tried to forget—and almost had—until now. Surely it could not be him after just one time.

She needed to talk to someone and could only think of her meth source, Ace, as one who would keep the matter confidential. He was not the nicest guy, but he always seemed to be confident and knew what to do. She felt like she would explode if she did not talk with someone.

Ace's real name, Franklin P. Jaimison, was never used when dealing with his drug trade. He had moved to Bristol from New Orleans, where he had grown up in his family's illegal drug trade. When the police got too interested in him involving the overdose of one of his customers there, Ace had moved to Bristol. It was just a place on the map, though he knew the name from the racetrack in Bristol. It did not take him long to build the drug trade that gave him a healthy bank account. He stayed fit, was just short of six feet tall, and sported a head of blond hair. Ace had never married, and kept any relationships with women to an occasional sleepover. Otherwise, he was all business.

Jan remembered her phone conversation with Ace just before leaving home for work. When he answered his cell phone, Jan blurted out, "This is Jan. I have a problem and I need to talk with you about it . . . and I need you to be quiet about it."

"Hey, Jan. You know I keep everything between us confidential. You need some stuff?"

"No, it's not that. I'm pregnant . . . and I don't know what to do! This baby will ruin my life. I can't have a baby now and keep up with school, work, and other things."

She was so loud, he had to pull the phone away from his ear. "So, call me? I'm not a pregnancy counseling service. Wait . . . you're not trying to say it's my baby, are you?

After a slight pause she said, "I do not think it was you."

"Have you been with someone else in the last few weeks? That baby isn't mine. Get that through your head. I will see you out back at closing tonight. Don't worry, I'll help you take care of this." He abruptly ended the call.

*******

Jan's memory went back again to finding out she was pregnant. She remembered the shock of the positive reading on the pregnancy test just a few days before. She had awakened with the feeling that she had a stomach virus, though she had nothing in her stomach but bile which is all that came out as she vomited into the toilet. Her roommate, Megan Stewart, had already gone to class. Jan did not go to class that morning, and she missed a couple more classes that week due to her sickness in the morning. She was usually better by the time she had to go to work, but the smell of food made her nauseous.

Jan had gone to the campus clinic hoping to get an antibiotic for her problem. The nurse wanted to give her a pregnancy test, but Jan claimed she had done nothing that would make that necessary. However, after she left, Jan stopped by a local drugstore to pick up a couple pregnancy tests. She almost fainted when they both showed positive results, and without thinking, blurted out, "No! This can't be. This will ruin everything!" Then realizing what she said, she had looked around and was glad to see her roommate was not there.

Her thoughts had run wild as she tried to think how she could tell Richard, her lover, who she believed to be the father. She thought of getting an abortion before anyone found out she was pregnant. Then she remembered her mother's strong stand against abortion, claiming it to be an egregious sin. She also recalled a video she had watched showing the heartbeat of a fetus only three to four weeks old. She decided no on abortion, but had to figure out something else.

********

A lingering sting in her cheek brought her back to the present. She rehearsed what had happened when Ace arrived out back that night, he had walked up to her and gripped her arms tightly until she told him he was hurting her. He eased up some and asked, "How do you know you're pregnant?"

"I've been sick at my stomach for a few days. I did two pregnancy tests, and they both came out positive. I am pregnant!" Even though it was dark, she had looked around and tried to see if anyone might have overheard her.

"Does anybody else know about this?"

"No, I called you first."

"Good," he said. He handed her a piece of paper. "Here is information on the clinic that does abortions. You need to go there and arrange for an abortion. Don't tell anyone. I will loan you the money. That will take care of everything."

"I don't know. I was brought up to believe an abortion is—"

"—It's too late for that stuff," he said, cutting her off. "Now, you just need to do what I say and go get this done, the sooner the better. No thinking about it, just do it!"

She began to cry. "Don't be so mean. It's my life and my baby. I have to have some time. It's my decision."

He shoved her up against the wall and said with a gruff, threatening voice, "It is not just your decision. Get this thing done." He slapped her and started walking away at a fast pace before yelling over his shoulder, "Do what I told you or I'll settle it for you!"

She had angrily wadded up the paper and thrown it against the wall like a baseball. After crying outside for a moment, she had wiped the tears from her face, walked into the restaurant through the back door and walked straight for the women's restroom thinking it was the only private place for her to get herself together.

Brad's voice called through the door, "Jan, are you OK? Can I help?" and brought her back to the present. The last thing she needed right now was to get Brad involved. She yelled back through the door, "No, I'm OK. I'll be out in a minute."

Jan finally stopped crying, washed her face, and began feeling somewhat together. She came out of the restroom, brushed off Brad, got her things, and left for her apartment near campus.

*******

Jan walked up hill the five blocks toward her apartment, Jan recalled how it had all happened. She had been a good student at first. And she had quickly found a part-time job waitressing at the Borderline Restaurant on State Street in Bristol. Several guys had hit on Jan, as she was attractive and had a teasing personality that enticed them. Still, Jan did not really have time for dating, so consciously did not develop any meaningful relationships. But then one evening at the restaurant she waited on a man she recognized as a professor at her college, and a woman with him. She had no classes with him, but other students had commented that he was a flirt and to watch out for him—and he was married. Jan assumed the woman with him was his wife.

"My name is Jan and I will be waiting on you this evening. Would you like a drink before dinner?"

"I'm ready to order, but it will be another couple minutes for her," he said. "Hey, haven't I seen you on campus, Jan? Are you a student?"

"Yes, I'm in my second year. Aren't you a professor there?"

"Why, yes. I am Dr. Richard Brantley. I haven't had you in a class, have I? Surely not. I would have remembered someone so attractive."

Jan glanced at his wife. She quickly met Jan's eye, smirked, and then looked back down at her menu.

"I'll be back in just a minute," Jan said as she walked to the next table. *He is a flirt*, she thought to herself, *but a handsome one. Probably has money too. I wonder why he stays with her.* Her thoughts were interrupted by a lady at another table, asking for more water.

In character, Dr. Brantley teased more with Jan and ended up suggesting she come see him if there was anything he could ever do for her. Jan felt swept up by the attractive man of means who gave her attention.

Though she had been too busy the next day, Jan found a reason to visit Dr. Brantley's office a couple days later. He was there. That visit began a new adventure for Jan, no matter how unrealistic it was. The professor picked her up after work one evening to go for a drink. He waited for her in his car, parked on the street behind the restaurant.

The drink led to another, and then to a forward statement from the professor that surprised Jan. "I really like you, Jan," he had said. "You are different, more grown-up than most people your age. Let's go somewhere to get to know each other better. I have a place in mind. You'll like it." She had felt helpless to resist. This began a chain of rendezvous that led Jan to begin dreaming of being Mrs. Richard Brantley. The professor's endearing words for her, and his complaints about his wife encouraged Jan's dream.

The day came at a most inconvenient time. Before a rendezvous with Richard, she realized she had run out of birth control pills. She did not have time to get more because Richard was minutes away from picking her up. She decided she was in a safe zone in her cycle and paid it no mind. She then had a couple more liaisons with Richard before she was able to get the pills. She thought about telling Richard so he could take her to get the pills, but she did not want to upset him. She was sure she could not get pregnant. Then it happened!

Jan vacillated between frustration and excitement. She was frustrated that her life had spun out of control due to her behavior, but especially that she was pregnant by a married man. (Her mom would be so distraught if she knew!) She had moments of excitement, during which she dreamed of sharing love with a successful, handsome professor. She hoped against hope that the pregnancy would cause him to leave his wife for a life with her and his child. She did not know what to do next. She did know she needed to hide the pregnancy until she figured it out.

A fresh breeze sent a chill through Jan as she continued walking on the sidewalk to her apartment. She heard a car coming up from behind her on her left. She heard tires screech as the car came to an abrupt stop right next to her. She turned toward the car and stepped back at the same time. Jan was surprised when she saw who was driving the car.

# Chapter 3

*Gunny pulled up to the scene of what seemed to be a suicide, but he knew from experience not to assume anything, but to deal with facts.*

On Friday morning, Doc jerked awake, wondering if he had slept too long to go look for that something for which he had tried to convince himself he had no business looking. Curiosity got the best of him. He typically liked to be gone from his place before dawn anyway. It was still dark when he slipped out of his relatively warm place to face a harsh chill as he walked across the parking lot.

At first, he did not see anything. But just as he was about to turn back, he saw a wad of paper shaking in the breeze. He picked it up and straightened it out. It was an e-mail from a medical clinic. The only name on the "send to" line was "Ace." It included a suggested appointment date and time "to discuss pregnancy termination." He began to understand what the argument might have been about. He folded the paper and stuck it in a pocket.

*******

Detective Richard "Gunny" Hawkins plunked down at his desk chair in the Bristol Tennessee Police Department. Taking a gulp of the tall, dark roast coffee he picked up from the drive through on Volunteer Parkway, he picked two files out of the stack of cases he intended to work this Friday morning. He liked the bold coffee and felt he especially needed it this morning to keep his eyes open after watching a late football game the night before.

Gunny gained his crime solving abilities in the military police with the Marine Corps. Except for a tour of duty as staff sergeant with a platoon in Iraq, he had served in the military police.

Gunny had not been with the Bristol police long when the chief noticed his experience and tactics had improved the crime solving stats for the department. He was promoted to detective when a popular detective for many years had retired. The chief's decision was a little controversial at first. But Gunny's personality and abilities soon overcame the controversy. He was not quite forty years old and married, with a teenage daughter. Gunny looked a little like Mr. Clean with a buzz haircut.

His cell phone rang. It was a patrolman, Danny Harris, so he pressed the answer button. "What's up, Danny?"

"Good morning, Gunny. We were following up on an anonymous tip this morning and found a body under the Anderson Street overpass. We called the coroner and figure you need to come take a look."

"Sure. I just got in, so will head over there in a couple minutes. What do you know?"

"She's a young pretty girl, maybe eighteen to twenty. There is no ID. We are looking for a discarded purse or wallet in case she was robbed. There is a nearly empty bottle of wine nearby, and some torn, empty packets that look like they could have contained crack or crystal. That's about it so far."

"Right. Check around the area to see if anyone in the businesses over there, or the apartment house above it saw anything. A couple homeless people usually sleep in that area. See if you can find any of them."

"OK, Gunny. It's a shame. Looks to me like a suicide. She was an attractive girl. I wonder what caused her to do it?"

"We'll see. I'll be there in ten minutes," Gunny said just before ending the call. He pulled on his jacket, grabbed his coffee, and headed for the door.

Gunny pulled up to the crime scene that was already marked off with yellow tape. He knew suicide rates were up, especially in the younger and older age groups. He had learned from experience not to assume anything, but to deal with facts. This had been drilled into him by his instructors in the Corps.

He got out of his car and looked around, taking inventory: a couple small storage buildings, a heating and air business, and overgrown vacant lots—all on 2nd Street. Between there and Pennsylvania Avenue were a store, a vacant lot, a two-story apartment building, and further away, the back side of a retail strip center. The residents in the apartment building needed to be questioned, as they were most likely there when it all went down.

Patrolman Harris walked up. "Gunny, we have had no luck with any of the businesses nearby. We found where some homeless people have been hanging out, probably sleeping, but no one was there. The coroner just got here and will start his evaluation of the body if you want to take a look before he starts."

"Thanks, Danny. Get some guys over to that apartment building to see if any residents saw or heard anything."

"We are already there, Gunny." Harris started by calling for one of the other patrolmen to check out a trash barrel someone had located under the overpass about fifty yards away from the body.

Gunny approached the body as the coroner took pictures and checked her temperature to determine the time of death (TOD). Gunny had worked with Dr. Gerald Guttmann long enough to feel comfortable calling him Jerry. The young woman laid on her back. Her blond hair was sticky with the vomit next to her face. He thought it looked as if she had been turned on her back after she died. She wore a waitress uniform. She wreaked of alcohol and vomit. Her blue eyes were open, but there was no sparkle of life in them. The look registered with him as panic.

"What do you think, Jerry?" Gunny asked.

"I think it's too damn cold to be out here checking on a dead body."

Gunny thought Jerry must not be too uncomfortable because he usually described and complained about his inconveniences using a string of expletives.

"Guess you want to know TOD. I estimate she died between 12:30 and 1:00 this morning. The empty drug packets and empty wine bottle found near here suggest she intended to take her life by overdosing, but I cannot verify that yet. Pulmonary cyanosis, evidenced by bluing under her fingernails is consistent with drug overdoses and cardiac failure. There are some markings on her neck I want to check more thoroughly when I get her to the morgue."

Harris said she was attractive and he was right. She did not appear to be a homeless woman. Her clothing suggested she worked for a restaurant. Jerry muttered to himself, "I wonder why a pretty girl like her would be over here at that time of night?" Though a small restaurant was less than a block away, it only served breakfast and lunch. It was likely she would not be at work there in the evening.

Gunny walked over to Danny Harris and asked, "Any luck finding a purse or wallet?"

"Yeah, we just found a purse and wallet in that rusty barrel over by the overpass support column." Another patrolman was just handing it over to Harris. Gunny already had his gloves on, and noticed the other officers had followed procedure by using them as well. Harris handed the purse and wallet to Gunny.

"Let's check it out," Gunny said as he took the items from Harris.

They both walked to the car so Gunny could dump the contents out on a large plastic bag he had placed on the hood of his car. They began carefully going through the contents. There was little of value there, but some Kleenex, lipstick, and hair bands.

"Not much for a lady's purse!" said Gunny. "If there was anything more, it's pretty much gone now. No cell phone. Did she have one on her?"

"No, she had nothing but a dirty tissue."

"Looks like someone ripped her off, either while killing her or after she died," he said as he opened the wallet.

"Nothing. No driver's license, credit cards, or money. This has been cleaned out."

He looked closer and explored each pocket carefully.

"Aha!" he said as he dug out a thick piece of paper stuffed deep into a credit card pocket.

"Looks like a health care card for Covenant College. Maybe she was a student." The name was hard to read due to a crease right where the name was printed.

"Looks like Janice Meredith. There is a middle initial I can't quite make out."

"Looks like she could be a student," Harris agreed. "But she is wearing a waitress uniform. I don't think of students at Covenant working at restaurants."

As he wrote the information down in his notepad, Gunny handed the bagged purse and wallet back to Harris, saying, "Well, I'm going to the college to see what I can find out. Let's see what prints we can get off that wine bottle and those drug packets. I want to know what was in those packets."

He was glad to leave as he saw members of the media forming around the perimeter. He hated having to answer or put off questions from reporters. As he got into his car, he noticed the body being loaded into an ambulance to be transported to the morgue. *I wonder what Jerry will find out about those marks on her neck?* he wondered. He saw a few reporters pointing at him and knew he had to make a fast getaway. He started the car, slammed it in gear, stepped on the gas, and headed to the administration building of Covenant College.

# Chapter 4

*"I've found a couple of things you need to know about this poor girl," the coroner began. "I examined the neck discoloration and believe there is evidence she was grabbed around the throat by a strong hand."*

Gunny parked on the street in front of the administration building of Covenant College about nine o'clock in the morning. Upon entry, a receptionist greeted him. He introduced himself, showed his badge, and explained that he needed to talk with someone who could help him identify a possible current student, based on her college health care card. She used the intercom to call one of the registrars who promptly came out to meet Gunny.

He showed his badge and introduced himself as Detective Hawkins. She introduced herself as Janet Graham, and took him back to her office.

Showing the health care card to the registrar, Gunny asked, "Is Janice A. Meredith a current student at the college?"

Mrs. Graham sat down and turned to her computer. In a moment she said, "Yes, Janice is a sophomore. I hope she's not in any trouble."

"I'm afraid she may be. A body was found under an overpass this morning and the only ID we have is this card, found in a discarded wallet in the area. Here is a picture of the girl that was found. If you have a picture of Janice, does she look like the girl on this card?"

Mrs. Graham looked at the picture and frowned as if smelling a very foul odor. She turned back to the computer and turned the screen toward the detective, a look of shock and horror on her face.

"I am very sorry," empathized Gunny. "It looks like Janice Meredith is our victim. Did she live on campus?"

Looking again to her computer, the registrar said, "No, Janice lived in an apartment near the campus. Looks like she had another student living with her there. I will give you the address."

"Is there a next of kin in your information?"

"Yes, Janice listed her mother, Evelyn H. Meredith, in Lebanon, Virginia. I will give you her address and phone number."

'Does Janice list a cell phone number? We did not find one with her."

"Yes."

In a moment, she handed him a note with the address, cell phone number, and contact information for the Janice's mother.

"How did my little girl die?"

"We are just starting our investigation and there are more questions than answers at this point," he said as he picked up one of her cards and handed her his own card. "Please let me know if you think of anything that might help us."

As soon as Gunny walked out of the office, Mrs. Graham picked up her phone to let others know what she had just learned.

*******

It was just a few blocks to the apartment, but it gave Gunny time enough to call dispatch to get someone to call the Lebanon police to notify the mother of her daughter's death. He gave dispatch the name and address where he was headed.

The apartment was on Moore Street. It was not in one of the best addresses in town, but it was close to the college. It was a green two-story wood building he had visited before on drug case invisigations. He found the apartment upstairs and knocked on the door. No one answered. He knocked again, and there was still no response. After waiting a minute, he turned away and started downstairs, nearly bumping into a young lady who was walking up. She hesitated and then asked, "Can I help you?"

Gunny looked her over and answered, "I'm looking for Megan. Do you know her?" He held out his badge for her to see.

"I'm Megan. What do you want? Is something wrong?"

"I am afraid so. Can we go in and talk about it?"

"Sure." She had already pulled out her keys, and moved quickly to unlock the door. Gunny walked into a room strewn with stuff that reminded him of his daughter's room.

They sat at the kitchenette table. Gunny held up the picture of Janice Meredith on his phone and asked, "Is this your roommate?"

"Yes, I think so, but that person looks . . . well . . . she looks dead . . . oh, my God!"

"We found this girl under an overpass this morning and the only ID we found nearby was a health care card in an otherwise empty wallet. The name on the card is Janice Meredith. If this person in the picture is your roommate, then I am sorry to tell you . . . she is dead."

Megan just sat there staring at Gunny, then at the picture. Tears began to course their way down her cheeks. She said between sobs, "I …I can't … I just can't believe its Jan. Are you sure?

He gave Megan a few moments to recover before continuing. She got up for a glass of water, looked out the window over the sink and returned to her seat at the table.

Gunny said gently, "I am sorry to tell you about this. Do you think you can answer a few questions?"

Megan looked at Gunny with reddened eyes and asked, "What happened?"

"That's what we are trying to find out." offered Gunny, "When did you last see Jan?"

"It's been a while. Jan is usually asleep when I get up, and I am asleep when she gets home from work . . . or whatever."

"What do you mean by, 'whatever'?"

Megan thought for a moment then recounted, "Well, I was awake on night thinking about a big test I was faced with the next day. Jan came in late at night and I noticed it was about 2:30. I don't think Jan knew that I was awake. This was not the first time. I think it happens a couple times each week. And I am sure it is not due to working late because the restaurant closes at 10:00 at night."

Gunny asked, "So, Jan did work at a restaurant?"

"Yes, her family did not have a lot of money, so she worked at Borderline Restaurant to get some spending money. Jan was a good student, but had so much going on that it was hard for her to keep up. She worked three evenings each week, and sometimes on the weekend."

Gunny took notes. Megan talked readily in all directions, so Gunny had to periodically ask focusing questions to get her back on point. Megan knew a lot about Jan's earlier life, but not nearly as much about current personal life. It seemed they both managed busy schedules and had not spent sufficient time together to get into deeper areas of one another's lives.

Megan noted, "Jan tended to be hyperactive at times, especially in the last couple weeks. I think that Jan had been sick, lately—I even found some vomit on the floor next to the toilet just a few days ago and had to clean it up myself. Otherwise, Jan is a decent roommate, who makes pretty good grades in school. I can't think of any reason why Jan might have taken her own life or why someone would want to hurt her."

Megan paused and Gunny asked, "Have you met any of Jan's boyfriends or family?"

Megan looked at the picture of Jan on the table and teared up again as she said, "No, I should have. But we did not socialize together and we just never talked much except one time about her family troubles growing up in Lebanon."

Gunny expressed his regret over the loss of her friend. He got her contact information and thanked Megan for her help. He left his card with her and asked her to call him if she thought of anything else that might help.

********

It was past noon when Gunny got back into his car and he was thinking about lunch. His phone toned noting a new text message. It was from Jerry, the coroner, asking him to stop by the morgue.

Gunny grabbed a fast food sandwich and a cup of coffee. He swallowed the sandwich in chunks and washed it down with gulps of coffee. *No wonder I have indigestion so often,* he thought. He blamed his habit on the Marine Corps. They never allowed sufficient time to eat meals.

Within a few minutes, he had pulled into the morgue's parking lot. He walked to the entrance while gazing at the three story brick building that housed the Coroner's office and the morgue in the basement. The Coroner's office and morgue had its own entrance down a short stairway just inside the main entrance. Gunny stepped lively down the steps and entered noting an aroma of disinfectant.

Gunny winked at the receptionist and continued to the morgue door. Stepping into the lab, Gunny made an abrupt inquiry of the man dressed in a red-stained lab coat and leaning over a female body with an excised stomach: "What do you have, Jerry?"

"Good, you're here. I found a couple things you need to know about this poor girl," the coroner began. "I examined the neck discoloration and believe there is evidence she was grabbed around the throat by a strong hand. Whoever grabbed her neck probably did not mean to kill her that way, but he was strong enough to damage the cartilage that makes up much of the larynx. That did not kill her, but probably made her think she was dying. I think the real cause of death is going to be overdose of a yet-to-be identified drug that caused cardiac failure. She had a birth defect in her heart that made it intolerant to extreme trauma. The toxicology will be a while in coming. You know it goes to the TBI and they are usually backed up. I still have to finish the examination."

Gunny turned to the door saying, "OK, guess I'll wait for that re—"

Jerry interjected, "That's not the biggest news. Your girl was pregnant—had a two-week-old fetus. Guess you have a suicide and a murder . . . or two murders on your hands."

"That explains the late nights her roommate told me about. Wonder who the father is. The neck trauma points to murder rather than suicide."

"You may be right."

"Thanks, Jerry. Let me know when the tox report comes back," Gunny said, as if the coroner needed reminding. He was not the brightest coroner Gunny worked with, but he did the job.

"Always do," Jerry responded as he turned back to the body.

*******

Gunny planned to stop by the restaurant later to talk with the manager. He thought through his findings thus far as he drove back to the office, *Jan could have gotten drugs from one of them, from one of several known drug dealers on Moore Street, or from someone on campus. All were places known to have certain drugs readily available. Crystal meth flows like water these days.* His thoughts continued, *Meth is still relatively easy to make in home labs, in spite of the efforts of lawmakers and law enforcement to limit availability of the ingredients. My top two priorities are to find out who fathered Jan's baby, and who supplied her with the drugs. This case is definitely getting more complicated.*

# Chapter 5

*The unspoken questions in their conversations were whether a homeless person had something to do with the girl's death, or knew something about it. No one wanted to talk about that.*

Doc waited for the local bagel café to open at 7 a.m., Friday. He had just enough pocket money to buy a coffee and a jalapeno cheddar bagel with cream cheese, for which he had developed a hankering lately. When the door opened, he walked in, got his coffee and bagel, and sat down in one of the comfortable overstuffed chairs. Just as he sat down, he saw Jake walk by the front window. Doc hoped Jake had not seen him. Jake had a knack for showing up when Doc had something, and always wanting some of whatever it was. Doc wanted just a few moments of peace.

Jake reminded Doc of a pet dog he had one time that always wanted some of anything he was eating. The dog could be a pest, disturbing the moment, but he was just being a dog. Doc put up with the less desirable dog behaviors to get the good behaviors that made him man's best friend. Jake was not a dog, and though he had his less desirable behaviors, Doc felt compassion for him.

Jake spotted Doc in his last glance through the window. To Doc's dismay, Jake turned around, walked through the front door of the café, and right over to where Doc sat, ending his hope for peace.

"Hey, Doc! What you got there? I sure could use a bite or two this cold morning."

Reluctantly, Doc broke off a bite and handed it to Jake. "Here you go . . . but you are on your own for coffee."

"Well, I'll just go get me a cup—a large one. I found some money last night and I can get my own today. I might just get a bagel, too," Jake said over his shoulder as he headed for the counter.

He returned shortly with a sugar cinnamon bagel and a large coffee, and sat in the chair across from Doc. Jake rarely had much money so Doc wondered where his newfound fortune had come from. He knew not to ask too many questions, though. Besides, Jake was known to say more than he should say.

Jake pulled a small wad of bills out of his pocket, flashed them at Doc and bragged, "I found this early this morning. I've been sleeping over by the railroad tracks and found this when I was walking here."

"I think I would keep quiet about this and keep the money hidden. There's plenty of guys would like to take it from you," warned Doc.

Jake quickly stuck the money back into his pocket, got up, and headed for the door, saying with a bite of bagel in his mouth, "You're right about that. See you later."

As Doc left the café, he glanced at the newspaper headlines through the dispenser's window. He rarely bought a newspaper, thinking they were overpriced and undersized these days—not a good deal given his meager funds. The front page got his attention: YOUNG WOMAN FOUND DEAD UNDER OVERPASS. He pulled out fifty cents and bought a paper, muttering about it costing too much.

The article reported that a policeman on routine patrol had found an unidentified young woman dead under the Anderson Street overpass. No cause of death was mentioned, but the article did say an autopsy would be performed. The victim's name was withheld "pending notification of next of kin." An anonymous source stated she was a student at Covenant College, was found dressed in a waitress uniform, and that it was possible she had overdosed on drugs. There was not much more to the article. *Another waste of fifty cents*, thought Doc. He would read other news and the sports page, and save the paper for other uses.

Everywhere he went that day, the talk on the street was about the dead girl and the location under the overpass near the railroad tracks. That area was frequented by homeless people who even slept there when they could. Paranoia began to grow by the end of the day among the homeless community. They suspected the police would begin looking for them to find out who might have been under the overpass the night the woman died. No one wanted to admit to being there or to give up another homeless person they thought might be there. The unspoken questions in their conversations were whether a homeless person had something to do with the girl's death, or knew something about it. No one wanted to talk about that.

Doc could not get out of his mind the scene he had observed the night before, and the story about the dead waitress.

*******

Brad Jones had tried three times to no avail to call his dealer for crystal. He figured his man might be out of touch for a while and decided to just go later to the place near the college where he had gotten it before. As he walked to town, a homeless man told him about the police finding a dead woman under the overpass. He was not sure whether to believe the man or not. The homeless man offered Brad a phone he could get cheap. He had seen the guy around, but did not know his name. He did not want or need the phone. The guy scooted on down the sidewalk, muttering to himself. Brad headed downtown.

*******

Dr. Brantley frequently came into the office on Saturday mornings. He received the newspaper at his office so the college would pay for the subscription. As he picked it up just outside his office door, he glanced at the headlines on the way to his desk, and the main one caught his attention. He sat down to read more. The article did not have much detail, but said the young woman whose body was found was a waitress, and her death might have been due to an overdose. A chill shot through him as he recalled his encounter with Jan the night before.

Another professor stuck his head in the door offering unwanted words: "Morning, Tony. I see you saw the paper. Word around here is that she was a student here." When he did not respond, the professor continued briskly down the hall. A feeling of anxiety rose up in Dr. Brantley. The article did not mention a name, but he feared it was about Jan, and it might lead back to him. He could not have that. He had always been very discreet and careful to avoid any overt connection with his girls. He made a mental note to check the news later to try and get the identity of the victim.

# Chapter 6

*We ran the prints and found they belong to a Jake B. Worley, who is in the system for a couple of misde-meanors. He has a history of mental illness.*

Janice Meredith's death had Gunny in the office on Saturday morning. His phone rang and his phone ID indicated it was the morgue. He picked it up and answered, "You working on Saturday too? What do you have for me, Jerry?"

Jerry cleared his throat loudly on the other end and said, "The Lebanon police found Evelyn Meredith, Janice Meredith's mother, and she is here at the morgue now. Mrs. Meredith identified her daughter. As expected, Mrs. Meredith is pretty upset. Said she was a good girl and did not do drugs, as far as she knew. I told her about the baby and she about fainted. She could not believe that Jan was pregnant, especially that Jan had not told her about it. Mrs. Meredith said that Jan had been brought up to know better.

Gunny asked, "Is Mrs. Meredith still there?"

"Yeah, she was pretty distraught so I put her in my office and she is trying to pull herself together."

"Can you put her on the phone? I just have a couple questions, and then she can go home."

"Hold on. I'll go get her."

A woman spoke into the phone with a sad, breaking voice, "This is Mrs. Meredith."

"Hello, Mrs. Meredith. I am very sorry for your loss. I am Detective Hawkins. I want to assure you we will do everything we can to find out how this happened to your daughter. I would like to ask you a couple questions, and then we can let you go home. Is that OK?"

"Yes . . . I guess so. I just can't believe my baby is gone."

"I know, Mrs. Meredith. This will not take long. Do you know of anyone Jan might have been seeing in the past few weeks—romantically?"

His query was met with silence

"Mrs. Meredith, did you hear me?" Gunny pressed.

"Yes . . . I'm sorry . . . I am having trouble thinking clearly . . . . I know she said—more than once, when I asked about boyfriends—that she did not have time for that right now."

"OK, ma'am. Just one more question. Did Jan indicate that she had seen a doctor anytime recently?"

"No, sir. She did say a couple of days ago that she was feeling sick at her stomach and planned to go to the health clinic on campus. I have not talked to her since then . . . " Mrs. Meredith said, trailing off before crying again.

"That's all, ma'am. What is your phone number and address? I may need to contact you again with just a few more questions." It took a moment, but Gunny got the information.

"Mrs. Meredith, do you have a ride back to Lebanon?" he asked.

"Yes, a friend brought me here and she will drive me back."

"Good. You may want to talk with your church pastor when you get home."

"I probably should do that. Thank you. Please find out what happened to my baby!"

"I will, ma'am," and with that he ended the call.

*******

Gunny took a gulp of coffee, made a mental note to check with the health clinic on the college campus on Monday, leaned back in his chair and remembered he still needed to talk with people at the Borderline Restaurant. He finished his coffee, drove to State Street and found a parking space a block from the restaurant.

As Gunny entered the Borderline Restaurant he recalled the couple times he had eaten there with some of the other guys on the force. Gunny was greeted by a waiter who motioned to a nearby table.

"Oh, no thank you," Gunny said as he flashed his badge. "I just need to see the manager."

The waiter looked at Gunny quizzically and responded, "OK, just wait there and I'll see if he is in." The waiter walked to the back and into what Gunny thought was the kitchen.

After a couple minutes, a slight man in his early thirties with a pale complexion walked into the room and moved in Gunny's direction. He looked Gunny in the eyes and said confidently, "I am Conrad Manning, Assistant Manager. Can I help you?"

Gunny showed him his badge and asked, "Is there somewhere we can talk?"

Conrad glanced toward the kitchen and then back at Gunny. "Yes . . . it's a little crowded, but we can sit in my office."

"That's fine," Gunny replied as he followed Conrad toward the kitchen.

The office was off a small hallway that connected the kitchen with a supply room. Conrad was right. With stacks of boxed supplies on the floor, there was just enough room left for two chairs and a small desk. Conrad sat in the chair behind the desk, and Gunny sat down in the chair beside the desk as he pulled out a pen and notepad.

Conrad spoke first, "What can I do for you, detective?"

"Do you have an employee named Janice Meredith?"

"Yeah, Jan. She is a waitress here and often works weekends. She did not show up for her shift today. Is anything wrong?"

Gunny was not surprised that Conrad did not know about Jan. The newspaper did not have Jan's name at the time of publishing. "I am sorry to tell you the reason she did not show up is that she was found dead beneath the new underpass yesterday morning."

Conrad looked genuinely shocked at the news. After allowing a long silence for Conrad to absorb the bad news, Gunny asked him to tell what he knew about Jan.

Conrad stumbled for words at first, but then began, "Jan was a student who needed work to help with school expenses. She seemed pleasant and had worked at a restaurant somewhere else. So I hired her to work weekends and some nights. She's worked here for more than a year. She is . . . was a good worker."

Conrad paused and seemed to search for words before continuing. "Jan seemed a little hyperactive lately. She would walk in the kitchen and dining area too fast at times, spilling soups and drinks. I think she dropped dishes on the floor a couple times recently. I just thought she was under some stress at school and warned her to slow down."

"Do you know anything about the friends she hung out with?"

Conrad thought a moment and answered, "She got along with most of the staff, but did not have close friends here. I guess the one who tried hardest to be her friend was a kitchen helper named Brad. Yeah, he seemed to have taken great interest in her."

Gunny's thoughts turned to Brad. "Is Brad here now?"

"Yes, he is. Do you want to talk with him?"

"Yes, I would."

Conrad got up and on the way out the door said, "I'll get him and you can talk in here."

A couple minutes later, a young man, about five feet eight inches tall, with dark brown, ungroomed hair, gingerly entered the room. He was still wearing his dishwashing apron. Gunny was impressed at his paleness and missing teeth. It made Gunny think he might be a meth user.

Conrad introduced Brad to Gunny and dismissed himself, leaving the two alone in the office. Gunny showed Brad his badge and spoke first. "What's your name, son?"

Brad looked at Gunny with a hardness in his eyes. Gunny recognized the look as one used by people who had previously crossed with authorities. "I'm Brad, and I haven't done anything wrong," he said.

"I'm not here about you, Brad . . . did some dishwashing myself in the Marines. I thought you might like a break and could answer some questions for me about Janice Meredith."

Brad just stared at Gunny for a few moments before saying, "I'm not sure who Janice Meredith is, but there is a Jan who works here."

"Yeah, that's who I am talking about. I understand you liked her. What can you tell me about her?"

Brad looked out the door of the office and then asked, "Why do you want to know about her?"

"Did you hear about a young woman found dead under the overpass?"

"Yeah, someone told me about it this morning."

"That was Jan," Gunny said as he looked in Brad's face to get his reaction. He caught a slight emotion for a split second before Brad looked down.

"She was just at work Thursday night, but did not come in today."

"Tell me what you know about Thursday night," Gunny said as Brad looked out the door again before facing him.

"It was a normal night until closing cleanup," Brad began. "Jan walked out the back door of the restaurant. Then I heard voices get loud, like Jan was arguing with someone. She came in all upset and crying, you know. I was going to check on her, but she went straight to the bathroom. Last I saw of Jan, she left with her things and didn't talk to no one."

"Brad, do you know who she was talking with out back that night?"

"No, I don't know who it was. I was washing pots and pans, and the noise was too loud to hear clearly, you know."

"Any idea where Jan went?"

"Not really. Jan usually walked to work and back home, you know."

Gunny could not be sure, but he thought the repeated use of "you know" might indicate growing anxiety over the conversation. He thought he should probe a little deeper into their relationship, so he continued with questions.

"Did you like Jan? I mean did you like her a lot?"

It looked to Gunny as if Brad was looking into the distance, thinking about something. Perhaps picturing Jan.

"She was a real looker," Brad said. "You know what I mean?" He did not give Gunny time to respond to the question. "She had pretty blond hair, blue eyes, and . . ." He stopped and looked at Gunny before continuing. "Yeah, I liked her a lot. When she wasn't too tired, she would tease me. I think she liked me too."

"Was she seeing anyone else?" Gunny probed.

Brad sat up straight and showed a little anger when he said, "I think she was, but I couldn't figure out who it was."

Gunny changed the subject. "Restaurants usually have one or more employees who use drugs. What's it like here?"

Brad shifted in his seat and quickly said, "I don't know of any here."

"Are you sure Jan did not use drugs?"

Brad shifted in the chair again and quickly responded, "One time, she said she was having trouble keeping up and might need something to help her, you know. But I didn't know anything about her using drugs. Hey, I've told you what I know and I need to get back to my job."

Gunny thought for a moment. He felt that Brad knew more than he was saying, but felt it was not wise to push more now. He could talk with him more another day.

Gunny put his pen and notepad away, looked into Brad's eyes and said, "Thanks, Brad, for talking with me. I'm sorry for the loss of your friend. Can you give me a phone number and address where I can reach you?"

Brad was hesitant but said, "Yeah, I don't have a phone, but my address is 334 Moore Street, Apartment 10."

Gunny knew the address was in an area where there were a number of older single family, three-story homes that had been converted to very small apartments. The area was also a hotbed for illegal drugs. Gunny thought Brad was holding back on a phone number because a restaurant employee needs some way to be contacted when the manager wants him to work.

Gunny handed his card to Brad, saying, "Please call me if you think of anything else."

Brad quickly left the office, and Gunny heard pots and pans being knocked about at the dishwashing sink.

Gunny walked out of the office and through a door off the kitchen that he thought led out the back of the restaurant. He looked around the parking lot. There was nothing unusual except a corner area where two buildings joined at an angle with a third short wall, forming a small alcove that looked like someone had been sleeping there. He had found some boards and plastic there, and a used paper coffee cup. He made a mental note to check on it one night. Homeless people are known to sleep in corners where they are out of the way, invisible to others.

Gunny went back inside, found the manager, Conrad, and thanked him. He did not ask the manager about drug use in his restaurant. He had tried that before and found managers became very defensive of their staff and restaurant when asked this. Gunny gave the manager his card and asked him to call if he thought of anything that might be helpful.

*******

Leaving the restaurant, Gunny was walking back to his car when his cell phone rang. Gunny swiped the face of the phone and answered, "Gunny here. What you got?" The phone information indicated it was a tech at the crime lab. A stilted female voice stated, "In regard to the Janice Meredith case, we've got prints on the wine bottle, the purse, and the wallet. Jan Meredith's prints are on all three. There are smudges on the bottle that suggest there could have been other prints, but they had been wiped off—probably before the victim held it. The purse and wallet had prints in addition to the victim's. We ran the prints and found they belong to a Jake B. Worley. He is in our system with a couple misdemeanors. I e-mailed you his name and last known address."

"Thanks for the information. I know you are busy, so I really appreciated getting back to me so promptly," said Gunny wanting to keep a good relationship with someone who provided essential information for his detective work.

"That's what we are here for. Let us know if you need anything else." The tech hung up without waiting for Gunny to respond.

Gunny checked his email on his phone and was familiar with the address. It was to one of a few individually rented rooms on the second floor above a bar on State Street. Gunny walked to the bar and talked to the bartender. He recalled that Jake had been evicted a couple months before for not paying his rent. He had no forwarding address and suggested Gunny check at the homeless shelter, or the library.

Gunny knew that the library functioned as a daytime shelter for some of the homeless, especially when it was very hot or cold. He walked two blocks to the library to find a homeless man who usually gave him good information about the homeless community.

Gunny was crossing the street to the library when he saw the man exiting from the library. The man was surprised when Gunny called to him, "Hey, Cookie! Wait up for me."

Cookie winced and at first, looked as if he was about to run away, but thought again and waited for the detective to cross the street. As he neared, Cookie moved behind a parked car and said, "What you want? I've got to get back to the shelter kitchen. I'm cooking tonight."

"It'll just take a minute, Cookie. What's the word on the street about this girl that was found dead under the overpass?"

"Man, why do you always have to ask me about those things. I don't know an more than what's in the newspaper."

"Come on, Cookie. There's got to be talk about it. Just let me know what you"ve heard."

"There's just a lot of talk about finding her under the overpass. They are afraid the cops will hassle them because some homeless people go through that area. Um . . . I've got to get back to the shelter to start on supper. Anything else you need?"

"Yeah, what do you know about anyone who might have been in that area when the girl died?"

"I don't know anything about that, but . . . anyone who might have been there is not going to broadcast it."

"Right, that's why I am asking you. I know somebody had to be sleeping there that night. Who do you know that frequents that area?"

"I've got to go, man. I don't have any names for you, but maybe I'll listen more carefully and see what I can find out."

"Yeah? OK, well, one more question, where can I find a Jake Worley?"

"Jake?" Cookie acted as if in thought as he weighed whether or not to give Jake up or not. Jake was a hassle to Cookie so he gave him up, "Oh yeah, um, I saw Jake a little while ago. He was bragging that he had come into some money—even had his own cigarette lighter. I think he was headed to the store down at State and Volunteer. Um . . . if that's all . . . I've really got to go. Can we do this more privately next time? It's not good for my reputation to be seen with you too much."

"Sure, Cookie. Don't want to hurt your reputation. That's all I needed. See you next time." Cookie had already started down the sidewalk in the direction of the shelter before he finished.

*******

Gunny walked back to his car and drove to the store Cookie had mentioned. As he pulled up, he noticed three street people sitting together on the curb to the rear of the building. He parked on the other side of the store, got out, and walked around to the back to talk with the men he had seen.

He walked up to the men, flashed his badge, and said, "Afternoon, guys, I'm looking for someone. Do you know where I can find Jake Worley?"

Two of the men reacted by starting to turn to the guy on the left end, but caught themselves. The man on the end started looking for a way to leave. Moving toward him, Gunny asked, "Are you Jake Worley?"

The man shook his head up and down gingerly. "I haven't done anything. Why do you want me?"

Gunny moved in closer, blocking the man's only way of escape. "You guys get lost." he told the other two men,

The two men took off quickly. Gunny looked back at the third man and spoke strongly. "Get up! Are you Jake Worley?"

The man did not move fast enough, so Gunny grabbed him by the arm, lifted him to his feet, and asked, "What's your name?"

"Yeah, I'm Jake. What do you want with me?"

Gunny turned Jake around, pulled his arms behind him, and handcuffed him, all in one practiced, continuous movement. He took Jake to his car, read him his rights, and had him lean on the car.

"You are being detained for questioning in regard to a robbery. I am taking you back to the station for questioning, but first I am going to search you. Do you have anything in your pockets that is sharp or might hurt me?"

Jake did not answer right away, but finally said, "No."

Gunny did a body search. He found little on Jake, just some materials to make cigarettes, a cigarette lighter, and $29.

After searching Jake, Gunny put him in the back seat of the car. Before closing the door, he noted that Jake was shaking. "Don't worry," Gunny told the frightened homeless man. "I'm just going to ask you some questions. If you have done nothing wrong, you will be OK."

Jake looked away and mumbled, "I need to go home. Just let me go home."

Gunny felt a tinge of sorrow for Jake, but that disappeared when he thought of Janice Meredith. "Can't let you go, Jake. Just relax and we'll take a short ride."

Back at the police station, Gunny had Jake put in a room used for questioning suspects. It was a bare room except for a small table and two chairs. He left Jake sitting in one of the chairs to cook a while as he returned to his desk to review the facts.

These were the facts he knew: Janice Meredith was the name of the victim. She was a student at Covenant College. She was also a part-time waitress at the Borderline Restaurant on State Street. He did not have the autopsy results yet, but there were no obvious signs she had been shot or stabbed, but Jerry had found trauma to her throat. She was pregnant. There was little at the scene but an empty purse and wallet, an empty wine bottle, and some scuffing that looked like there had been a struggle. A homeless man had taken money from her wallet. It was very unlikely he was the father of the child victim. This had all occurred during the night after she had gotten off from work, but some distance from the path she would have taken from work to her apartment. She had argued with someone behind the restaurant that night.

Gunny now needed to find out what Jake knew and had done the night the victim had died. To his eye, Gunny believed Jake was mentally challenged, but did not appear to be violent.

When Gunny entered the interrogation room, Jake met him with, "I am really thirsty. Can I get a drink?"

"I'll get you a cup of water," Gunny said.

Just as he left the room, Jake mumbled, "Wish I had something stronger right now."

After returning with the water, Gunny sat down across from Jake.

"Don't I get a phone call . . . or an attorney or something?"

"Yeah," said Gunny, "and if you cannot afford an attorney, you will be appointed one at your hearing in a couple of days. Remember, you are not under arrest. I just need to ask you some questions. You do not have to say anything. But I am going to ask you some questions to try to clear up just what you were doing Thursday night under the overpass where a young woman died. Is that okay with you?"

"Well, I can't afford no attorney—and I may or may not answer your questions. I haven't done nothing except take a little money from a wallet somebody throwed into the trash barrel."

Gunny took out his notepad and pen. He knew the questioning would be recorded, but liked to take his own notes, too. "OK, let's start from the beginning. Tell me about your Thursday evening."

Jake thought about the question before answering, "Thursday evening? I was just walking around town talking to some other people on the street. I needed a cigarette and a light, and they don't always give me one. I walked over to the Salvation Army to get supper. When I finished supper, I left. I don't need to stay there. I mean, I don't like staying there. I walked back downtown. A lady gave me a dollar. No one else gave me anything. I went into a store to get warm. They told me to leave because I made people nervous. (I get mad when they say that!) Two men escorted me out. I walked around. I tried to go to sleep behind a dumpster, but a cop caught me and made me leave. Sometimes I sleep under some bushes near the overpass, so I headed over there."

"About what time did you get to the overpass?" Gunny asked.

"I don't really know. It was later. Maybe sometime around midnight."

"Now get to the part where you found the body. Tell me everything you did, saw, or heard when you went to the overpass."

"I was just walking to my place when I saw someone lying on the ground. I thought she was just passed out from drinking. I could smell the wine and there was an empty wine bottle nearby."

"How did you know the body was a woman?"

"I saw blond hair . . . like a girl's hair. When I turned her over on her back, I knew for sure."

"Did you pick up the wine bottle?" Gunny asked.

"Well, yeah. I don't get it often, so I checked to see if any wine was still in the bottle, and there wasn't any."

Gunny knew there had not seemed to be sexual assault on the victim, but he had to ask. "Did you touch the woman? I mean . . . did you touch her on her female places?"

"No, sir, I did not," Jake shot back. "But, I did check her pockets."

"Is that when you robbed her?"

Jake seemed to be becoming progressively aggravated when he shot back, "I ain't robbed nobody!"

"Then where did you get this money?"

"I found it — finders keepers!" Jake yelled at Gunny,

"You found it on a dead woman under the overpass, didn't you?"

"Well, I was over there and found a wallet in the trash barrel," Jake responded, slightly agitated, "but I didn't kill nobody. She was not near where I found the wallet . . . and I thought she was just passed out."

Gunny was not sure how far to press Jake. He thought he could push a little more without Jake throwing a tantrum.

"Jake, did you kill that woman to get her wallet?"

Jake was clearly angry when he spit his words out. "No way! I did not kill nobody, and I found the wallet in the trash. I told you that and you shouldn't ask me anymore!"

Gunny thought he had reached the limit for now. He used his calm voice. "Now, settle down, Jake. I've just got to be sure. I'm going to step out for a few minutes. You calm down and drink some of your water. I'll be back in a few minutes and we can finish this up."

Gunny could hear Jake mumbling as he exited the room. It sounded like he was saying, "I need a smoke. I need out of here. I . . . I . . ."

Gunny looked at the notes he had taken. He thought that Jake's explanation made some sense. Jake had confirmed his proximity to the location within timeframe, so this made him a prime suspect. He had stolen the girl's money, assuming it was her purse he found in the barrel. And he had tampered with evidence and failed to render assistance to the young woman, even if he had not killed her. But then again, no one would expect a homeless drunk to help someone.

Gunny took a few sips of old coffee that had been left in the pot too long. He left his cup on his desk and headed back to ask Jake another line of questions.

"Jake, can you answer a couple more questions, and then we will be through for tonight?"

Jake was still showing some agitation and squirmed in his seat, but he responded, "I guess so. Just don't say I killed anybody 'cause I didn't."

Gunny asked, "Are there other guys who sometimes sleep in the overpass area?"

"Oh yeah, there are a couple other guys that do, sometimes."

"What are their names?"

"Uh, I can't remember them."

Gunny felt Jake was holding back something, "Well, you let me know if you remember any of their names. You are in deep trouble, buddy, and maybe the people who sleep there know something that could help you."

Jake squirmed and pleaded, "I think I'm wet. I need to get to a bathroom right away to go . . . or I'm going to get real wet."

Gunny called to the officer standing just outside the room and instructed him to take Jake to the restroom, and then return him directly to the room.

When Jake returned, Gunny explained, "You are going to be our guest until your hearing in a couple days. You are being charged with robbery, and you are a person of interest in the death of Janice Meredith, the young lady you saw on the ground under the overpass."

Jake was suddenly pounding on the table in front of him and yelling, "I can't go to jail. I don't like it there. They are mean to me. I can't go there ..."

In time, Jake settled down and the officer that had been outside the door took Jake off to book him. Gunny wanted to go home. So did Jake. Home was a mental state of security for Jake more than a place. Gunny grabbed his jacket and headed for the door feeling like there were too many loose ends on this case and that made him really uncomfortable. Jake was processed and put in a holding cell waiting for transport to the Sullivan County Jail that served as the jail for Bristol, Tennessee as well as the county.

# Chapter 7

*She wrapped her arms around him in a hug and continued, "I need you to get well."*

Gunny was jarred awake just past 3 a.m., Sunday morning. He was lying diagonally across the bed in his Bristol home with the covers thrown off, but he was not there. He was in a land far away. Gunny jumped quickly to kneel beside the bed for cover while grabbing the Smith & Wesson he kept in the bedside table. He was wet with sweat. His anxiety was at peak, and he wondered where the other guys were. The gun in his hand gave him a little comfort.

Then it began to come to him. This was his home in Bristol. He was far away from Iraq, and years from that deadly operation that went wrong and left him wounded in body and soul. Remembering his wife, Gunny noticed she was not in bed or anywhere in the room.

He could not shake the rush from the adrenaline that pulsed though his body. The very real nightmare he just experienced was vivid and confusing. The times and places were all wrong. The girl's body he had seen Friday morning in Bristol was being carried away by Iraqi hostiles. Every time he tried to rescue her, something bad happened. First he was wounded, then one of his men got killed, and finally, he awoke abruptly after a great big explosion.

Gunny put his gun away and went to the bathroom. After refreshing himself, he went out to the living room to look for his wife. She was on the couch, wide awake, and looking at him with apprehension.

"Oh, honey," Gunny blurted out, "it happened again, didn't it?"

"Rick, you were a wild man. I had to get out of bed before you clobbered me. What were you dreaming about?"

He told her what he could remember, still shaking from the adrenaline.

"You have got to go back to the VA and get help again. I can't live with the uncertainty that you might do harm to me at night without realizing it. I am going to sleep in the extra bedroom until you get some help."

"I don't blame you. The last thing I want to do is to hurt you."

"But you can't seem to control that, so you must get some help again."

When Gunny left active duty, he had shown symptoms of PTSD (posttraumatic stress disorder). He would occasionally have a nightmare in some way related to the time when they were on a mission to rescue a hostage and one of their helicopters was downed and two men were killed. He felt distant in his relationships, including with his wife, Karen.

At that time he found some relief in a VA program which combined outpatient psychological counseling and medication (a prescription for Zoloft). In fact, it seemed to help and he felt much better. But the counseling trips took time and the prescription was expensive for him, so he dropped out of the program.

Karen got up and approached him. "Rick, I love you. I know you have been through a lot that many of us could not handle as well as you do. I really appreciate your willingness to get some help again. We will pray about this and ask God to help you in the right time to be healed of it. In the meantime, it's important to get the help that's available." She wrapped her arms around him in a hug and continued, "I need you to get well."

Gunny was confused and struggled to get his thoughts together. He let go of the hug. He thought he had gotten better, but he had acted out again. It scared his wife and she had a right to be scared. Gunny knew he was a trained killing machine, so it scared him, too, to think he could possibly hurt the love of his life. He still shook. He sat down in a chair in the living room.

After several minutes of thoughtful silence, Gunny knew what he needed to do and say. "OK, you are right. I thought I was better, but this case with the dead student has triggered bad feelings in me. I'll call the VA Monday to get back in the outpatient program."

# Chapter 8

*Embarrassment rose up in Doc, and he could feel the
red show up in his face again as he apologized, "I am
so sorry. I did not know."*

December in Bristol is typically wet and cold—not cold enough to
snow, but enough to make a homeless person miserable. It was
late in the day on Monday in mid-December and the Christmas
lights reflected brightly off the wet streets and sidewalks. There
was a special event downtown, so the shops there were open late
and the merchants served hot drinks and cookies to draw potential
customers in.

Some street people took advantage of the free hot drinks
and cookies, but Doc was not in the mood. The prospect that the
girl found dead was the same one he had heard arguing with a
man weighed on his mind. He wondered about the note from the
abortion clinic. He reached into his pocket and found it still there,
wadded up.

The newspaper had not said anything about her being pregnant.
What should he do about the information he knew? If he went to
the police there would be trouble, and he wanted to avoid that if at
all possible. It could be the dead girl and the girl he saw behind the
restaurant were two different people. He wanted to believe that, yet
something nagged at him that they were one and the same.

The finality of death always brought back the thoughts of that
tragic day years ago, yet feeling like yesterday, when Doc came
face to face with death's finality. *Don't go there, Paul*, he thought
to himself. *You know when you do you cannot come back, and*

*you just dig the hole deeper and deeper until you cry out with the bottle to escape your pain, your unanswered questions, and your bitterness. Get your thoughts on something or someone else.* He made himself think about seeing Cookie and getting a hot meal at the shelter. *That's better. You might make it this time—you must make it. Stay away from that stinking thinking.*

Doc made his way up the hill to the shelter for supper, thinking he might stay for chapel. Maybe it would improve his mood. Doc waited for the kitchen to open, sitting on a set of wooden steps that needed repair. He saw the women without children from the women's shelter come to the kitchen for food trays they would take back to the two-story house where they lived. They could remain there for months while trying to get stable enough emotionally and economically to live independently again.

One of the women caught his attention. She looked more together than most, not burdened, and she interacted with the other women with a bearing of confidence. He thought she must be the evening housemother. There was something about her. It was not her attractive appearance that caused him to fix his attention on her. It was the way she carried herself, and the joy that was evident on her face. (He would learn later that she was a volunteer who led an evening Bible study, and she had come a little early to have supper with the women from the shelter.)

Doc had not paid too close attention to women for years. It made him think of the close relationship he had once enjoyed with his wife, and this caused his emotions to well up again. He knew that would lead to other troubles, and he did not want to go there. So he looked away and made himself think of the hot cup of coffee and the food he would soon consume.

Cookie came over to the table where Doc was playing with his food, and sat down with his own cup of coffee. Looking down at his cup, Cookie noted, "Haven't seen you for a couple of days. You alright, Doc?"

"Yeah. I've been thinking about that girl that was found dead. I wonder what happened to her. By the way, I saw a new face with the women. Is there a new housemother?"

"No, she's just a volunteer who teaches them ladies and was here early. She's a looker isn't she? Nice, too. Everybody kind of likes her. She seems to always look on the sunny side of life and treats everybody the same. Probably one of those Christians who grew up in a perfect family but doesn't know how life really is for most of us. Still, I like her, and it is good to have her around."

Cookie took a sip of coffee, glanced at the lady and then back at Doc, "Oh, did you hear they picked up Jake and took him to jail? The two guys with him at the time said they thought they heard the officer say something about a robbery."

"No, I hadn't heard. Jake isn't the swiftest of mind. He did mention to me about having some money now. I told him to be quiet about that or he would lose it."

"I heard from someone else that he was under the overpass where that girl was found. You know, I wonder where he got that money."

"Well, he might have found some money, but I can't see Jake involved in that girl's death."

"Me either. Guess I'd better get back to the kitchen to supervise cleanup. Got a couple new ones and they're pretty lazy still. I'll get 'em in shape."

"See you, Cookie." Doc finished his coffee and went outside with some of the other men to wait for chapel to start. The chatter he overheard was all about Jake and the dead girl under the overpass.

One of the men observed, "I didn't see anything about the girl, but I slept over that way that night and a car woke me up. I glanced that way and saw an expensive black car burn rubber leaving. I think someone in that car did it, and Jake just came along later to scrounge up what he could find." Doc did not know the man talking by name. He made a note of his dark curly hair and that he might be in his early thirties. Someone announced it was time for chapel. The men staying at the shelter were required to go to chapel, so they all headed that way.

A five-piece music group led chapel that evening: keyboard, drums, two guitars, and a bass. Most of the service was music, with only a brief devotional about "Emmanuel." Doc did not hear much of the devotion because his attention was on someone else in the room—the volunteer he had noticed before dinner was there with the women from their shelter. He guessed her age to be in the upper twenties or lower thirties. She had penetrating blue eyes and blond hair. *Probably dyed blond*, Doc thought to himself. She was average build, not too skinny and not overweight. Doc suddenly realized he was staring at her, so he looked away to avoid getting caught. He thought he was foolish for thinking about her so much. He tried to think about why she was so attractive to him. He had seen more beautiful women.

When the service ended, Doc moved to the back door to leave and head back downtown. He looked up and saw Cookie headed toward him with the lady. Doc looked around for another route away from them, but the other men pressed around him and he was stuck. Cookie yelled out, "Hey Doc, wait a minute. I want you to meet someone."

Doc felt like a bashful adolescent when they were introduced. He knew it too, and turned a shade of red as he spoke to her. He thought, *what was her name? Oh yeah, Cookie said, "Angel."*

She was talking to him now, "Cookie says you are called 'Doc' because you were once a corpsman with the Marines in Iraq. My husband was a marine and did a tour in Afghanistan. To be truthful, I asked him to introduce us because I have a pain in my right hip that sometimes hurts a lot, and even runs down my leg. He said you might know what to do, because you help a lot of the homeless around here with minor medical problems."

"I don't know how much I really help them," Doc replied with a false humility. He knew he had been helpful to more than he would have chosen because his reputation had spread around the streets of Bristol. He continued, "I am no doctor, but it sounds like you have a problem with your sciatic nerve. Have you been doing something to stress your back or hip?"

"Well, in the last couple weeks, I have raked a lot of leaves, climbed a ladder to get the leaves out of my gutters, and shoveled mulch. It started about two weeks ago, but I had to finish the work, and it just got worse."

Doc wondered why she was doing those hard tasks when she had a marine to do them. "I think you have irritated the sciatic nerve that runs from your lower back down your leg," he said. "It is probably irritated at your back, where the nerve emerges, and the pain refers down to your hip and leg. What have you taken for it?"

"Just some generic Tylenol when it really hurts."

"I suggest you take it easy on your back and leg. Get that marine husband of yours to do the heavy work, and you take it easy for a while. Alternate applying heat and cold packs to your lower back and hip. Start with four ibuprofen when you go home, and then take two in the morning, two mid-afternoon, and two in the evening. You need to break up the irritation of the nerve and get those muscles to relax. Take some more ibuprofen the next day. Don't stop just because you feel a little better. Maybe you can stop the third day if it is really improved, but sciatica takes time to get better. If that doesn't work, you probably need a stronger muscle relaxer and you will have to get that from a doctor."

"Wow, you sound like a doctor. Will I get a bill for this?"

"Yeah, a cup of coffee sometime will do."

"I'll try what you advise, but I am afraid my marine was killed in Afghanistan, and I have to do my own work."

Embarrassment rose up in Doc, and he could feel the red burn in his face again as he apologized, "I am so sorry. I had no idea."

"Of course you didn't. It's OK. I am grateful for the advice. Are you staying here?"

For some reason, Doc felt a twinge of embarrassment when he said, "No, I am out on the street for now. I usually eat here and sometimes stay for chapel."

"Well, maybe I will see you here, then. I like to cook and might make some chocolate chip cookies to share with you for your medical advice, but only if it works," she teased and laughed.

"I will be sure to come back around for those," Doc said, laughing with her. He remembered that he had not laughed in a long time. He watched her as she moved to gather the ladies and return to the women's shelter. Then he headed back toward downtown with a warm feeling all over that he had not felt in a long time.

# Chapter 9

*Then the e-mail came. He did not recognize the sender.*
*He glanced through one time, and then went back to*
*read it more closely. It was devastating.*

Monday had been consumed with other police business and Gunny did not get anything done on Jan Meredith's case. Tuesday, late in the morning, Jerry called Gunny with the tox report. "I pressed the TBI (Tennessee Bureau of Investigation)for a fast report on the girl's tox screen. This girl had a very high level of methamphet-amine in her blood, along with a high level of alcohol. That alone might not have killed her, but she had a congenital heart problem, a weak valve in her heart. The rapid heartbeat from the meth, com-pounded by the rapid ingestion of alcohol, tore the valve. The baby was affected by the meth and alcohol as well, but died when the mother could no longer provide life support."

"Are you saying that meth with alcohol doesn't usually cause death?"

"That's right. It can, but not usually. She most likely died because of the drugs combined with her weak heart valve."

"It is difficult to determine for sure," Jerry added, "but my edu-cated guess is someone forced her to take meth and drink a bottle of wine with it. It seems like homicide versus suicide, but I cannot be sure there was an intent to kill. Nevertheless, *re ipsa loquitur.*" Gunny remembered the legal term meant, "the thing speaks for itself." He felt Jerry was saying, intent or not, the girl was dead and she might still be alive if someone had not forced her to take an ultimately lethal combination of meth and alcohol.

As they talked, Gunny agreed with Jerry's deduction. Three factors caused them to lean toward homicide. The neck bruising and appearance of a struggle at the scene indicated someone else was involved in her death. The fact that if the baby was a major problem, she could have gotten an abortion without taking her own life made suicide for that reason less likely.

"One more thing, Gunny," said Jerry. "I found some skin cells under her fingernails. You know our DNA studies are done by the TBI and they are still way behind. So, it will be a while before I get results on that and the baby's DNA."

Gunny remembered that the TBI in Knoxville conducted a lot of the lab work for the police in upper east Tennessee, and that there were complaints about how far behind they were. Some staff had been added, but they were still slow in putting out results.

"Yeah, I am aware of lab study delays. Thanks for the report, Jerry. Please send me a copy of the autopsy when it is ready."

"You got it, buddy. Got to go."

Gunny had fingerprints and motive on Jake, but it was too big a stretch to believe he would kill a pregnant woman over a few bucks. He could not believe that Jake could be the father of the baby. Though he could not yet count Jake out, in the back of his mind he thought the father of the baby had to be found. That person would have a stronger motive.

*******

Dr. Richard Brantley was one of many people in Bristol who had read the latest report on the dead student found under the overpass. His thoughts were many and varied, but mostly about how he could protect himself. He was upset by the report that her baby had died with her, and that her death was now being considered a homicide instead of the rumored suicide. Homicide meant more investigation. And as hard as he had worked to be sure no one knew about his little affair with Jan, he still feared it would lead back to him.

He thought back to their times together and how he would regularly ask her about her birth control. She always assured him she was "safe." He might not have asked every time, but she had even asked for money to buy the pills. Surely the baby was not his. Surely she had another partner he did not know about.

Still, he could not take a chance, so he began to think about what he could do to be sure that nothing led back to him. He could not afford to lose his job, but especially not his gravy train wife. Richard Brantley was sure his wife would leave him and take her fortune with her if she discovered he was having affairs with students. He wondered if he was naïve to think that she did not know—or at least, suspect—his infidelity.

He had his black Mercedes cleaned inside and out. He had disposed of the throwaway cell phone he had used with Jan. It was in the kitchen dumpster at the college, and he was sure no one would try looking through that. Any money he had given her was cash. They were careful not to have personal conversations on campus. He would let her off before dawn at least a block away from her apartment when they rendezvoused. What more could he have done or could he do? He did not think about a condemning DNA connection with the baby, but that seemed a remote threat. He began to feel a little more secure. He finally decided he would only show normal concern for a student of his college who had died tragically, and then he would move on with his life.

Then the e-mail came. He did not recognize the sender. He glanced through one time, and then went back to read it more closely. It was devastating. It read:

Dr. Brantley,

I know about your trysts with Jan Meredith. Now that her death is front-page news, I am thinking the police might like to know about them too.

I am a reasonable person and might be persuaded to keep my knowledge to myself should my net assets significantly improve—by let's say about $100,000.

Should you agree, just send back a reply that says "our secret." I will then tell you how to get the money to me.

> Do not try to trace this e-mail. This account will no lon-
> ger exist after you reply, or should you not reply within
> 24 hours. In that case, the police will get the next e-mail
> . . . with my proof.

Dr. Brantley saved the e-mail on a zip drive where he kept his most personal information, and erased it from his e-mail. He had to think a little before responding.

He checked his secret personal investment account that he had grown over the years by having a set amount withdrawn from his pay to invest in it. The amount that was direct deposited in the checking account his wife saw did not indicate that an amount had been deducted already (though his wife did sometimes complain that he was not paid sufficiently). The balance had grown to $253,476. It would take a few days to get the $100,000, but it might be the best investment he could make, given the circumstances.

Dr. Brantley pored over memories of his trysts with Jan and tried to figure who might have seen them. He thought, *what was the evidence—a picture, maybe? Would the blackmailer then want more? How could he limit the payment to a one-time thing?*

Though he realized the blackmail could go on and on, what could he do? He would lose more if he was found out by his wife . . . or the police.

Within twenty-four hours, Dr. Brantley responded back with, "our secret." He also added, "This I will do, but there will be no more payments because I can establish my alibi for the night she was killed." He actually could not because he had seen Jan that night, but the blackmailer probably did not know that.

He then received instructions on how to move the money to an account in the Bahamas, and he processed the transaction.

# Chapter 10

*The DA's case against Jake was building. His finger-prints were found on the wine bottle at the scene. Jake admitted to seeing the dead girl around the time of her death, and to taking money from the wallet.*

Gunny started his Wednesday morning the usual way with strong coffee. He needed it after staying up late to watch an old Western on TV. He did not stay in the office long. He remembered he needed to talk with the nurse at the college clinic.

Gunny's coffee was still hot when he picked up the travel mug and headed outside to his car. It took about ten minutes to get to Covenant College. He had seen the clinic before and pulled into a parking space reserved for clinic patients. He walked up to the front door and entered. A receptionist looked up at him from a book she was reading. He showed his badge to her and said, "I am Detective Hawkins from the Bristol Police. May I speak to the nurse?"

The receptionist looked Gunny over and then said, "Please be seated. I will see if she's available."

Gunny was a ruggedly good-looking man. He was used to ladies looking him over. He thought the receptionist was likely a student working part-time for financial assistance.

In a few minutes, a young woman left through the waiting area, followed by the nurse. Even though just one other person waited, a young woman, the receptionist identified Gunny to the nurse, and then she stepped over to him.

She spoke very businesslike, "I am Mrs. Jacobs. I understand you want to speak with me. What is this about?"

"It would probably be better if we spoke in private," Gunny suggested. "I do not think it will take long."

Nurse Jacobs motioned for him to follow her like she would a student patient. They stepped into the clinic area, and then into a small office where the nurse sat behind the desk while Gunny took a seat across from her.

"Thank you for speaking with me," he said. "Have you heard about the college student who was found dead last Friday morning?"

Nurse Jacobs shook her head and responded, "Yes, what a shame. What happened to her?"

"That is what we are trying to find out. Janice Meredith was her name, and she was a student here. She was also pregnant. Her roommate suggested she might have come to the clinic in the past couple weeks. Do you remember her?"

"Jan Meredith, Jan Meredith . . ." Nurse Jacobs said softly, over and over, as she tried to remember. "Oh, yes. It was two weeks ago. She complained of an upset stomach. It seemed a classic case of morning sickness to me, but she strongly denied that and abruptly left. I figured I would see her again for pregnancy. I can't believe she is dead now."

"So, she did not admit to being pregnant and did not reveal the father of the baby."

"Not at all. She said nothing else and abruptly left the clinic."

"Thank you for your time." Gunny got up and turned to leave the small office. He turned back to the nurse who was now standing, "I wish she had confided in you. Maybe she would be alive today."

"I talk with more students who have surprise pregnancies than I would like to admit." With that she moved to the door, indicating the discussion was over.

Gunny left the clinic, smiling at the admiring receptionist on the way out.

*******

The DA's case against Jake was building. His fingerprints were found on the wine bottle at the scene. Jake admitted to seeing the dead girl around the time of her death, and to taking money from the wallet. He was usually broke, yet suddenly had money on him. In fact, the day after the murder he had bragged to other homeless people about finding the money. There was opportunity and motive. The DA just needed the skin cell DNA from under the victim's fingernails to match Jake's DNA. Then he would have his slam dunk.

The newspaper published an article on the homeless problem in Bristol. Bristol's homeless population was comparable to most small cities, and a lot less problematic compared to the large cities. But the article quoted downtown merchants who were concerned about the negative effects of homeless people wondering around downtown. The writer tried to be accurate, but it was obvious it was meant to sell newspapers, and it did get peoples' attention.

Doc was especially bothered by the treatment of Jake. People jumped on the train, presuming the homeless man was guilty. Yet to Doc, it was not logical. Jake could be obnoxious, but he did not have it in him to commit murder. And where would he get the kind of money it would take to get the amount of crystal they said was in her system? The DA claimed it was already in Janice Meredith's purse, and he just used it, and that he probably had the wine with him. Doc believed Jake was incapable of subduing a woman while forcing her to take meth, and then making her drink a bottle of wine. He believed Jake probably had taken the money from her wallet after she was dead, but that did not merit a murder conviction.

It also bothered Doc that he had witnessed something that might take the heat off Jake and motivate the police to search for the man with the expensive dark car. He struggled over going to the police. He had given them trouble when he was drunk, and he felt sure they would find some way to implicate him. Why did he have to see that argument in the parking lot?

He felt God had been against him ever since his tragic loss several years ago. And now God was picking on him again. Doc was losing sleep over these issues.

The only good thing would be if he could see Angel again and spend some time talking with her. One morning at the Sweet Tooth Bakery, he looked up from his coffee and sweet roll and saw Angel walk in the door. He watched her stand in the line for orders to get her sweet treat and a cup of coffee. After paying, she glanced around the room for a seat and caught him staring at her. Doc felt himself blush, and gave her a nod. She approached him. "Room for one more?" she asked.

"Sure, have a seat," he found himself saying with a bit of excitement.

Doc watched her sit down and arrange her treats on the table. He thought he was acting like a kid in puppy love. He brushed aside the feeling and said, "I'm glad to see you again. I noticed you favored your right leg a little. How is your leg doing?"

She looked up from her muffin with a winning smile, "You did a good job. It is much better. It's not completely well yet, but I can function so much better. Thanks!"

Doc smiled back and said, "It was my privilege to help someone who does so much to help others."

Angel looked at the order line while she chewed a bite of her muffin and washed it down with a swallow of coffee. She looked back at Doc and spoke, "Cookie called you Doc. I assume that is your street name. Do you mind telling me your given name?" Angel asked this knowing that street people normally do not want to give their actual names because somebody might be able to use it to find out more about them than they wanted known. Angel took the risk because she really wanted to know more about him.

Doc looked at her, thinking to himself that she probably knew better than to ask a street person about his given name. He liked her and made the decision to trust her with his name. The only time in years he had heard his given name was when he was admitted to a health care facility, or did business with the VA. "I do not use my given name just as most street people do not," he answered. "However, I feel I can trust you with it. My name is Paul Walker."

Angel smiled at him and said, "That is a good name. I like it and I will be careful with it. May I call you Paul instead of Doc when we are not around other street people?"

"I suppose so. But I might not always know you are referring to me," Doc said with a reserved laugh.

Angel laughed with him. "I will take that chance." After a minute, she continued. "My husband served in Iraq in Fallujah. He was killed by an IED there during the Surge. Where did you serve?"

Doc (now "Paul" to Angel), looked away and grunted before answering. "I was in in Iraq at a field hospital."

Angel noticed that was a subject he did not want to talk about, so she chose not to pry. "For a couple of years after my husband was killed," she began, "I could not talk about it without breaking down. Caleb, my husband, was all to me. He was handsome in a rugged way, so confident, and yet tender toward me. He was gone a lot with the military, but I knew he loved me and felt secure with him."

Angel paused to relish her memories. Paul would glance at her but not hold his gaze, as if embarrassed to hear such personal details.

"I was helped with counseling," she continued. "And I spent time helping others the Lord used me to help heal. I am still emotional about it, but can now talk about it without becoming a wet noodle. I'm sorry . . . here I am spilling my problems to you and you don't know me very well."

Doc knew he was supposed to respond to her last statement, but did not know right off what to say. He did feel uncomfortable, and actually a little jealous of Caleb. He couldn't tell her that.

Angel rescued him by continuing to talk. "My pastor was very helpful with this. His brother had been severely wounded in Afghanistan—a head wound—and he had not been able to work, physically (or mentally), since then. My pastor had to work through his feelings about that loss. His journey has helped me on my journey." She paused and they both sat silently for a couple minutes.

Doc was moved by Angel's openness with him. He liked this woman, and was developing a comfort level with her.

He spoke next. "I am so sorry for your loss. I know it has been difficult. I too suffered a major loss that was devastating. I wish I could say that I have handled it as well as you have."

Angel shifted in her chair and said softly, "Oh, Paul, I do not want to give you the impression that I have handled this all so well. I really struggled, and I still have my down days over my loss. I think I just received mercy and grace to help me make it this far." She paused a moment and continued. "I am so sorry that you have suffered a major loss. I have to leave soon, but if you are willing, I would like to hear more about your loss."

Paul (Doc) looked down at that point and shook his head back and forth. He said, "I know the counselors at the VA have told me that I should talk with them about it, but it hurts so much, and it just leads to me thinking about and sometimes doing bad things. Thank you for sharing, but don't count on me to do the same."

Angel let it go, thinking another time might change things. She told him she was at least thankful that he was now in heaven, and no longer had to deal with the ugliness of this world. She said that her work at school and volunteer work at church and the shelter kept her busy and her mind set on good things. She looked at her phone and said, "I've got to leave to go to a planned meeting at church. Would you be willing to meet again here at the bakery?"

Doc thought for a moment. He enjoyed her presence, even though she had ventured into an area he intended to avoid. He nodded his head, silently indicating yes.

"Okay then. How about this upcoming Saturday morning, back here again?"

Doc gave her a big smile and said almost too fast, "I'll be here."

Angel got up to leave, but then looked back at Paul and said, "Please think about sharing more of your life story with me." She did not wait for his response, but strode for the door and was gone.

Doc sat there in thought. His initial reluctance to share was outweighed by his sense of fairness, now that she had shared deeper feelings with him. His growing respect and genuine enjoyment of being around Angel were further motivation. He wanted to meet with her again. He had learned her given name, Ann Keaton, but he thought "Angel" fit her best.

# Chapter 11

*Jake had been indicted for Janice Meredith's death. Doc's thoughts brought more frustration. "This cannot be right. I was sure the police would find Jake had stolen some things, but he was no murderer."*

It was Thursday morning and Gunny was feeling frustrated that he had not identified the source of the meth that had contributed to Janice Meredith's demise. In his mind he reviewed Jan's contacts. Though he had never understood it fully, in his experience, family members are often a source of drugs—and mothers are just as likely as siblings to provide them. He could only imagine that misery loves company. Mothers wanted to help their kids, and if their troubled children found escape or relief from the pains of life in drugs, they would provide them. It didn't make sense to him, but he was a rational thinker, so he found it hard to understand what he considered irrational thinking.

Gunny did not think family was the source of Jan's drugs. Her college roommate showed no evidence of using drugs. Gunny knew that restaurant waiters and cooks are a possible source of drugs. Restaurant work could be demanding when volume was up, customers were critical, and managers were demanding. Hours could be long and late. The pay did not match the stress, especially when tips were down. He decided to swing by the restaurant to talk with Brad again.

*******

Later that day, Gunny walked the couple blocks to State Street and walked into the Borderline Restaurant. He moved like he belonged there to the kitchen and saw Brad cleaning pots and pans. "You got a minute to talk, Brad?" he said, startling Brad.

Brad said, "Well, I have to get these ready for the cooks, but I can take a couple minutes," he said as he grabbed a towel to dry off his arms and hands. They walked outside to the parking lot behind the restaurant.

"Brad, I am trying to figure out the source Jan used to get her drugs. It seems to me that her work here was a likely place for her to get them. Did you ever talk drugs with her?"

Brad shifted his weight nervously, and looked away for a moment. Gunny sensed his discomfort with the question. Brad looked back and said firmly, "You think she took drugs?"

"Yeah, she had meth in her blood. I want to know who she got it from."

"I knew a cook who used to work here, and he did some crack, but I don't hear about or see any drugs being passed around or sold here now." He paused and looked at Gunny to see if his firm statement was enough to end the conversation.

Gunny just stared at him.

Visibly uncomfortable, Brad added, "I think it is more likely she had a source on campus. I'd check that out."

Gunny kept staring at him.

"There was a rumor," Brad said after a long pause, "that she was seeing one of the professors on campus. I don't know who it was, but he might have helped her get meth."

Gunny sensed Brad felt he had said too much, and was trying to deflect the detective from him or the restaurant. It was time for confrontation.

Calmly and confidently, Gunny said, "Brad, I don't believe you." He let Brad squirm in that for a minute.

"Do you use meth, Brad?"

Brad became especially jittery, rubbed his left arm with his right hand, and looked around nervously, as if concerned someone was watching. Then he looked down at the pavement and mumbled, "I may have smoked some pot, but I don't do drugs!"

It sounded too much like he was trying to convince Gunny that he was not guilty, when he really was.

"Then you won't mind taking a drug test to prove it?"

Brad looked around and rubbed his other arm. "I don't have to do that, do I?"

"No, not until I get a court order for it. If you are clean, why not prove it? But if you are not, things will go better for you if you tell me what you know. I am not after you for taking a drug. I want to know the source of drugs Jan used."

Brad remembered his conversation with Jan and how he introduced her to her source. Brad feared that guy more than the police, so he responded again trying to sound convincing, "Sorry, I can't help you! You will just have to get that court order and it will be a waste of your time!"

Gunny was unconvinced. "I think you're holding back on me. I will be back. If you cared anything for Jan, you should be helping me nail the murderer."

"Don't you already have the guy?"

"We have a suspect, but I am not yet fully convinced that he did it." Gunny heard himself say it, but he had not told anyone else but his wife that he had doubts that Jake was guilty of murder. He felt that Jake would have had trouble forcing Jan to swallow the meth with the wine. He was a rascal and mentally challenged, but Gunny was not convinced he was a murderer. The DA did not question it, and felt the evidence was enough to get a conviction.

"Who does that rumor say she was seeing on campus?"

"I don't know. Nobody gave a name."

Gunny walked off after a few parting words: "You are hiding something . . . and I'll be back. You better be ready to tell me the truth."

Brad broke a dish while rinsing off plates for the dish sanitizer. He wondered whether to warn Ace or leave it alone. He decided to try calling him later.

Gunny headed back to the station thinking he needed to check out the rumor Brad had exposed.

*******

Thursday evening, Doc was thinking about his upcoming meeting with Angel. He was having mixed feelings after his time of sharing with Angel on Saturday. The rest of the day he had felt excited over spending time with her, and over her interest in his life. He wished Saturday would come quickly. At the same time, an old feeling of heaviness and guilt tried to move in on him. He knew if he did not get a grip on his feelings, the heaviness would overtake him and he would seek relief in a place where he did not need to go. He knew it rose like a vapor from a swamp of rehashing the loss of his wife and son.

Last Saturday night had been a toss and turn night. Doc had feared the investigation into the girl's murder would likely bring more attention to the parking lot where his overlooked place would be found. He had gathered his stuff and moved to a new location he had previously noted would be almost as good as the parking lot place. The move to an unfamiliar place joined with the feelings that were trying to overrun his sanity kept him from sleep.

Last Sunday had been no better. In fact, no night during the week had been restful. The mix of uplifting and depressing feelings doing war in his soul were exacerbated by talk among the street people that Jake had been indicted for Janice Meredith's death. Doc's thoughts brought more frustration. *This cannot be right. I was sure the police would find Jake had stolen some things, but he was no murderer.* He did not feel like dealing with the question of whether he should come forward with what he had seen and the e-mail he had kept for some reason.

*Was it enough to help Jake? What would I lose by doing so? I gave the police a hard time the last time they took me in for being drunk in public, and they might discount anything I have to say. They might refuse to hear me out, or worse . . . they might suspect me.*

He could not concentrate enough to make a decision, so he tried to keep himself busy by talking with other street people. It didn't work. They kept talking about poor Jake.

One woman's account stuck out in the chatter. She had been trying to sleep in Cumberland Park the night of the murder, and recalled, "Around midnight, I heard a car stop near where I was trying to sleep. I heard a car door open. I sat up just long enough to see a blond-headed girl with a small backpack get into an expensive black car that moved on down the street." That fit with what Doc had seen.

One of the men offered Doc a drink out of his wine bottle. Doc looked at the bottle and wanted it. Wine had given him some relief from his internal battle before, but only for a while . . . until something intervened to cause him to wake up to reality again. He had suffered a lot from his binges, and he knew if he took that bottle he would head down that path again.

"No thanks, bro," he said with difficulty, and stepped off toward the shelter.

*******

That evening Doc was eating his supper at the shelter when Cookie came up to him and offered an observation: "Doc, you seem agitated about something. What's up?"

"Go supervise your kitchen help, Cookie. I'm in no mood to talk about things, and you can't help anyway." Then, as if he had not just told Cookie to mind his own business, Doc asked, "Is there somewhere we can talk privately for just a few minutes?"

"Sure, no one is in the chapel now." Doc was not hungry anyway, so he threw the food left on his plate into the trash. "Thanks, Doc. That's a surefire way to tick off the cook, throwing his food away."

"I'm just not hungry tonight, Cookie. I know you do a good job with what you have. Let's go to the chapel. "

They entered the chapel and Cookie turned on some lights. They pulled a couple chairs around to face each other and sat down.

"Okay, Doc, what do you want to talk about?"

"I'm not sure this is a good idea, but I need to talk with someone, and I know you will keep it quiet."

"What, are you in love with Angel? Most of us have figured there was a growing thing going on between you two."

"No, and there is nothing going on but a little counseling. So, just don't go there!" Doc said with a hint of anger in his voice.

"Okay. It's not that big a deal. So, cool down. What's up?"

Doc looked into Cookie's eyes, wondering if he should say anything to him. It had been his experience that most street people have trouble keeping secrets, and when they tell someone else, it is often not exactly what they had been told. He decided to tell him.

"I trust you Cookie, but I need you to agree not to repeat to anyone what I am about to tell you."

"I'm pretty good about keeping my tongue quiet when I need to. What's such a big deal?"

"The other night, from a distance, I saw that girl that was killed having an argument with a guy out back of the restaurant where she worked. It was the night she was killed. I saw the car he got into. Another time, it had a parking sticker on it. If I were to tell the police about it, do you think it might help get Jake off?" Doc conveniently left off the part about the e-mail he had found.

"Wow, I see why you need to be careful with this. If you tell the cops, why would they believe you? They would probably discount you as a homeless friend of Jake's, and think you are just lying to try to help him. They believe everything we say is a lie anyway." He paused a moment before adding, "Besides, they would probably begin to suspect your involvement in the murder."

"I know. That's why I haven't said anything. But they have indicted Jake and I am worried they might determine he did it when you and I know he couldn't do something like murder that girl."

"Yeah, you're right. But you need to be real careful about this. No, if you do decide to talk with some cop, see a detective who goes by 'Gunny.' He is pretty levelheaded when it comes to us street people. I would never tell him that, but he's really okay."

Doc had immediate regrets, thinking, *I wish I had said nothing to Cookie. He knows a cop well enough to think he's levelheaded? Is he in that cop's pocket? Would he repeat to him what I share?*

"Don't you say anything to that cop! I've got to think about this and I'm not ready to do anything."

"Hey, I don't really like the guy that much, and I don't give him anything I don't have to. Chill out, Doc."

"Thanks, Cookie. I just need some time. Do you know if Angel is here tonight?"

"Nothing to it, eh?"

Doc glared at him with daggers in his eyes, causing Cookie to drop his kidding and simply answer, "Haven't seen her today."

# Chapter 12

*Brad delayed answering for a moment and tried to think of how to answer the question, but the delay was long enough that Ace did not believe him when he answered . . .*

Gunny rose early on Friday morning, got his coffee, and headed for Megan Stewart's apartment. If he could catch her before class, he might find out more about the rumor of Jan's involvement with a professor. He knocked on the door but there was no answer. He was just about to knock again when a sleepy voice called through the door, "Who is it? What do you want?"

"Megan, its detective Hawkins. Can I talk with you a few minutes?"

"Detective Hawkins? Oh, yeah. Just give me a few minutes to get dressed."

"Okay, I can wait."

Gunny pulled his phone out and took a look at his schedule for the day. He looked up his unread e-mails and read a couple, then put the others in the trash. He was just about to go to his games file when the door opened.

He stepped in and offered an apology for coming so early, adding, "I hoped to catch you before classes and remembered you often left early in the morning."

"Well, usually that would be true, but I had a late group study session last night and was sleeping in. What do you want?"

"In my investigation into Jan's death, someone mentioned a rumor that she had been seeing a staff member of the college. Do you remember anything that might suggest this was true?"

Megan responded like most others he had talked with lately. "I thought you already had the case wrapped up. Why do you need to know anything about that?"

Gunny responded with silence and waited for her to answer his question.

"I had dismissed it as unimportant, but Jan came in late," said Megan. "I mean, like early in the morning, after I had gone to bed. I was not sleeping that well, worrying about a test that morning. I heard her say to herself, 'I can't wait until Tony divorces his wife.' It was confusing to me, but I thought it was personal to her, so I forgot about it."

"You sure she said, 'Tony'?"

"Yes, I'm sure she said, 'Tony.' "

"Anything else?"

"That's it. She really was not here very often. We had little time to get to know each other."

"Any idea if there is a Tony on campus?"

"There is a student named, 'Tony.' I don't know of any staff members by that name."

"Thanks for your time," Gunny said, moving to the door. "Sorry again about waking you up. I hope you can get a nap now," he continued apologetically.

*******

The next stop for Gunny was the college administration building to talk again with Mrs. Graham. He reintroduced himself and said he needed a list of the full names of students and professors. She went to her computer and typed in some instructions before disappearing down the hall and returning with the lists.

"Thanks. You are really efficient."

"Anything we can do to help put away Jan's killer," she said. "I thought you had him. Why do you need these lists?"

"Just wrapping up some loose ends. Thanks."

With that, Gunny exited the building and headed for the office, but stopped for a fresh cup of coffee first. Gunny reached his office and immediately looked over the list of professors. There was one possibility on the list: Anthony Thomas Brantley, PhD, Professor of English Literature. He felt like he was chasing a rabbit, but could not leave a ravel unresolved. He was trying to decide what to do next when the phone rang.

"Gunny here."

"Detective," said Brad Jones on the other end. "I'm not saying that I do any drugs . . . but I thought about Jan and feel you need to know something. Jan asked me where she could get something to help her have more stamina for the long hours she was keeping. I had heard about this guy from some of the other guys around town. I gave her his name, Ace, and a phone number one of the other guys gave me. I do not know if she used it or not."

"Okay, Brad. That's good. What's the number?"

"I tried the phone number the other day and he did not answer. It was forwarded to another guy."

"What's the phone number?"

"Just a moment."

Gunny thought Brad had just given away that he did have a phone after all and the number was on his contacts list. He probably dialed it frequently.

Brad gave Gunny the number and asked, "Does that make me good with you?"

"I don't know about 'good,' but I will not pursue you for your drug connections or use. I am homicide. Thanks for calling with the info." Then the line went dead.

*******

Gunny leaned back in his chair and took a gulp of coffee that was already cooling off. He hated loose ends, and now he had two of them: a professor named Tony and a drug dealer called "Ace." He was unclear what to do next. The DA made a case that seemed pretty sure to get a conviction. Yet Gunny felt there were too many loose ends a good defense attorney could pounce on to give the jury enough doubt to decide against a conviction. In Gunny's thinking, the case was not so strong.

The professor had met Jan late at night. It would take some home time away, but he felt he needed to tail the professor a few nights to see if he had moved on to another student. It was Tuesday. He would start a stake out the next night.

And what about Ace? He would talk with the guys in narcotics to see if they knew anything about a dealer going by "Ace." He picked up the phone and called a detective that handled drug cases. It was late on Friday afternoon and Gunny wasn't sure he would get through.

A man's voice came through the phone, "Art here. What you need?"

"Art, this is Gunny. I need some help with information about a drug dealer selling to the college kids. Do you have anything on someone with a nickname 'Ace'?"

Art had to gather his thoughts to answer Gunny, but finally said, "Are you clairvoyant? I was just reviewing notes from an arrest we made. We know that the kid got his drugs from a dealer near the campus, but he did not know any names. He gave us a general description—said he was Caucasian and had a good tan. He was maybe six feet tall and trim. He felt he was in his thirties. We tried to get more info on the dealer, but his trail seems to have grown cold lately. That's all I've got . . . . Oh, yeah, he was dealing in pot, crack, and crystal. Do you think he is the source of the vic's meth?"

"Well, I don't know. I'm just tying up some loose ends, and I would like to ID her source. That guy might have been the one, and if his trail has grown cold, it may be he is feeling the heat and laying low somewhere."

"Could be. I'll let you know if anything else turns up. Talk with you later."

Gunny hung up thinking that Brad might still know more than he had let on, and then thought about how he could get it out of him.

********

Brad finally got a call back from Ace, late in the evening. He was out of town. "Hey, Ace, where you been?" Brad knew as soon as he asked the question that it was the wrong thing to say.

"It's none of your business what I do or where I am. What's up?"

"A cop came to see me and wanted information about Jan. He wanted to know who sold the drugs to her. But I told him I didn't know. He wanted to drug test me, but I said he would have to get a court order to do it. I thought you would like to know that."

"Good. You didn't give him any info about me…like my name?"

Brad delayed answering for a moment and tried to think of how to answer the question, but the delay was long enough that Ace did not believe him when he answered, "No—no. You know I wouldn't do that. I think he might try again, though."

"Yeah, he might. Brad, I think you need a vacation. I've got a cousin in New Orleans. He likes having guests to entertain. How about a vacation in New Orleans until this passes over?"

"That sounds great. But I don't have the money to afford something like that."

"Don't worry about money. I'll get you there and he'll keep you up after you are there. Get your stuff together. Don't warn your employer or tell anyone else. I'll meet you at the bus station about six in the morning. Be ready to get on the morning bus. I'll get you a ticket to New Orleans."

"Wow, thanks, Ace. I'll be there. I think…" He heard the phone go dead and thought Ace must have been in a hurry. Brad went to his rented room and packed his backpack as full as he could. He did not sleep well that night, so had no trouble getting to the bus station.

When the station opened, Ace drove up, bought the ticket, and saw Brad off on the morning bus that would eventually get him to New Orleans. Ace had called his cousin and arranged for him to meet Brad at the bus station . . . and a few other things.

Brad arrived at the station after a tiring ride in the bus, which stopped in many small towns. He got into Ace's cousin's car.

No one in Bristol heard from Brad again.

*******

Ace had a busy drug business in Bristol. He sold most of his drugs around the Covenant College part of town. He had moved to Bristol from New Orleans, where he had grown up in his family's drug trade. When the police got too interested in him involving the overdose of one of his customers there, Ace had moved to Bristol. It was just a place on the map, though he knew the name from the racetrack in Bristol. It did not take him long to build the drug trade that gave him a healthy bank account.

He stayed fit, was just short of six feet tall, and sported a head of blond hair. Ace had never married, and kept any relationships with women to one or two night stands. Otherwise, he was all business.

Ace liked Jan, and she was a regular customer for crystal. He was not happy about her death. He had told his drug source that he needed to lay low for a while during the investigation of the college girl's murder. He told him that she had bought drugs from him. He reassured the source there was no problem. He just thought it best that he be unavailable for questioning should the police start looking for her source of drugs. Ace told his source that another guy handled his business for brief times on other occasion when he had taken time off. Besides, he had worked hard and needed to enjoy some of his earnings.

Ace decided to take a month off. He decided to drive on Saturday to New Orleans to stay with a cousin of his. He always had fun with his cousin. He had left a message on his phone for callers to call the guy he had left in charge. He never answered the phone while away . . . at least not that phone. He used a different phone for personal calls.

Each day he checked the Bristol headlines online. When it became clear that the police were set on Jake, one of the street people, as the murderer, Ace felt he might risk returning to his business in Bristol. After all, he did not want anyone to move in on it.

*******

Dr. Brantley's testosterone was at peak again, and he had identified another student who kept coming to his mind. He wondered if enough time had passed to go there again. He still felt anxiety over Jan's death. Nothing had come his way from it. His efforts to stay below the radar seemed to have worked. They had evidence on a homeless man that was sufficient for an indictment. He guessed the homeless man would be found guilty and he would be free from a problem.

He did not want to wait for the jury to make its decision to enjoy another affair. He decided he was safe enough to approach the student that kept coming to his mind.

# Chapter 13

*An odd feeling struck Doc. He did not want her to back off. He was afraid that if she did, he might never get away from the abyss of bitterness and despair he had fallen into again and again.*

Saturday could not come fast enough for Doc, and yet, in another way, it came too fast. Doc planned to keep the conversation on a surface level.

He made it to the Sweet Tooth a few minutes before the 9 a.m. time they had set. He hoped he had enough money to buy both their orders that morning. He sat down, took a deep breath, and realized he was more keyed up than he wanted to be. He knew he was more attracted to Angel than he had been to any woman since the loss of his wife. But in reality, he thought it all might just be a futile exercise that would end up nowhere. He feared he might end up acting like a fool.

Doc always tried to maintain a reasonable level of personal hygiene—it was his training. He wore clean clothes by getting Cookie to wash them at the shelter when Doc wasn't staying there. He even got deodorant, a toothbrush, and toothpaste from the shelter.

He thought about what Angel might want to hear from him. He would say as little as possible about his history, and try to focus the conversation on her again.

Doc glanced to the entrance and there she was, coming in the door, thanking the gentleman that held it open for her. He stood and walked over to where she was now looking for him. Their eyes met. Those sparkling blue eyes disarmed him. She had a smile that was contagious. Doc said something in greeting, but he was sure he fumbled it somehow. Why was he so anxious?

They ordered. She would not let him pay—she even wanted to pay for his apple fritter and cup of coffee. They settled on Dutch treat. They moved upstairs to the corner of the loft where two over-stuffed chairs and a lit lamp on a square table between the chairs made for a warm, cozy appearance. Doc liked the fact that it was away from the crowd.

Doc started the conversation. "So, how is your Bible study with the women in the shelter going?"

She finished her bite of chocolate covered doughnut and said, "Oh, it is going alright. I have seven ladies in the group now. We are studying the book, *Bad Girls of the Bible*."

"Bad girls? Why bad girls? I would think you would study the good girls of the Bible."

"Well, the bad girls became good girls, so they had history best described as bad girls—just like many of the women coming through the shelter. In fact, I guess it's true of most of us. A couple of the women are really into it, a couple are doing the work even though they are not sure about it, and the rest are just there because they have to be."

"I guess you are in good company. If I recall my Sunday school lessons, Jesus's followers all ran off on him when the going got tough. One even betrayed him. So, a couple who are really into it is pretty good."

"I never thought of it that way before. Maybe you're right," she said before deciding to pursue the Sunday school comment. "So, where did you go to Sunday school?"

Doc realized he had slipped up and opened the door to talk about his past. He could not think of how to back out on the question, so he jumped in, "Oh, I grew up in Richmond and we sometimes went to the Community Baptist Church there. Mom and dad didn't go to church a lot, but the church sent a van by for my sister and me. So, I got a pretty good dose of Sunday school. How about you?"

"Well, yeah, I grew up around here, and we went regularly to Calvary Baptist Church. I went to Sunday school a lot, too. I'm afraid it didn't really take until later."

"Me too. Not sure if it ever really took. There are times when I really don't like God . . . and I think He has plenty of reason not to like me too."

That statement made Angel even surer that she wanted to find out more about this man, "You mentioned a loss you experienced a few years ago. Is that when you became homeless? Can you tell me about it?" she asked, sticking the last piece of doughnut in her mouth.

He wished he had a big bite of apple fritter to do the same, but it was gone. He looked away from her probing eyes and said, "I really don't like to talk about it. It changed my life for the worse. When I start thinking on it, I get really down. It is the trigger for my drinking episodes. So, I try to keep it out of my thoughts." He thought this would keep her from pursuing it further, but no such luck.

"Based on what I have learned about dealing with hard times, it does more good to talk about it with the right person than to keep it pushed down, only to come spewing up when we least want it. You know that I have been through a gut-wrenching disappointment in life when I lost my husband. I wanted so much to just go around blaming others and God about my loss, but a friend at church would not let me go. In time, I began to see things better. If you will talk with me, I think I can be helpful."

Doc was surprised at how strongly he reacted. "I don't really want or need someone to feel sorry for me and rescue me. I've been through VA programs twice and they have done all they can." He got up to leave and took several steps toward the exit. He stopped, looked at the door and thought, *now I've done it. She probably won't want to be around me at all now.*

Angel was not totally surprised at Doc's reaction, but it was stronger than she would have expected. She looked after him, hoping he would rethink and come back to her. She was trying to decide whether to go after him or just let him go. All she did was to take the last sip of her coffee.

Doc just stared at the front door. An odd feeling struck him. He did not want her to back off. He was afraid that if she did, he might never get away from the abyss of bitterness and despair he had fallen into again and again. Doc turned around, walked back toward Angel, and sat down again.

"Perhaps you are right," he found himself saying. "If you still want to hear, I will tell you a little of what happened."

Angel wanted to hear, but she realized she had moved too quickly with him and said, "Paul, I am interested in your story, not because I feel sorry for you, but because I think I can relate to the loss you have suffered. You are free to wait until another time or never tell me, but I do care and want to hear."

Doc looked into those blue eyes and he felt his heart pounding. What he saw were eyes filled with beauty and compassion. He wasn't sure that if he tried to speak, anything would come out. His care for her motivated him to try anyway.

Doc began, "I married the most wonderful woman in the world. Her name was Angela, and she was a schoolteacher. I had enlisted in the Navy and was stationed at the hospital in Norfolk. She lived in Norfolk and was finishing her master's degree in education at Virginia Commonwealth University (VCU) in Richmond. Her church came to carol at the hospital around Christmas. I saw her and fell in love at first sight. I found her church and attended there, mainly in the hope of seeing her. And I did! About three months later, we were married. A year later, we had Stephen. A year after that I went to Iraq with the Marines."

He explained that he was a Navy corpsman—it was like being a medic. Since the Marines did not have their own corpsmen, some of the Navy corpsman were assigned to Marine units, as he was. He spent a year in Iraq and mostly worked at a health facility in the green zone. He told her about leaving the Navy after four years of service, and returning to Richmond.

"We moved to Hartford, Connecticut, for jobs. It was easy for me to become an EMT with all the training and experience I had as a corpsman."

Angel could tell by the brightness in his eyes that he loved his wife, son, and working in emergency medicine. Then the light went away like a light switch had been turned off.

"One day, I stayed on past the end of my shift to work accidents. It was icy cold and there were many accidents. I called Angela to pick Stephen up from school. It was my turn to do so, but I had to work late."

"Later, I got a call from another EMT. He said I needed to get to I-84, mile marker 40, right away. That was all he said. But the sound of his voice was urgent, and I had finished the accident I was working. I had just heard of a bad accident on I-84. When I got there…"

He paused to catch his breath, but he could not keep his chest from jerking . . . or the tears from coming. He felt suddenly embarrassed to cry in front of Angel. He looked around, but no one else seemed to be watching.

"I am sorry . . . I can't help it. Maybe I should stop there."

Angel had been mesmerized by the account. She spoke encouragingly, "Oh, no, you can't leave me hanging like that. Take a moment, but please finish telling me."

After a brief pause to wipe tears from his face with his sleeve, Doc continued, "It was bad. I could hardly recognize the car. They had to get Angela and Stephen out using the Jaws of Life. Angela . . . was killed instantly. Stephen . . . still had a heartbeat when they got him out . . . but he had a broken neck and . . . died at the scene."

His tears flowed again. He felt awful, but the tears seemed to give him some relief from his surging emotions. Angel looked at him with the face of compassion. She reached into her purse, took out a pack of tissues and handed it to him.

Doc pulled out a tissue and wiped his eyes before continuing, "Everything I loved in life was gone and I was helpless to do anything about it. The one who could have stopped it chose not to, was helpless himself, or was busy somewhere else. I felt like Job, but there was no hope of having my fortune restored . . . no hope."

There was silence, except for Doc clearing his nose. Angel reached over to gently, but firmly place her hand on his arm. The warmth of her touch felt good.

Angel spoke pleadingly, "Didn't you have someone—a brother, sister, church friends, your fellow EMTs—to help with your grief?"

"They tried. My sister lived in California then, and called once with condolences. I had not attended church enough to develop any friends. The pastor came by and did the funerals. He visited once after that, and then I did not go back. So I lost contact with the church. The one EMT I knew best would take me for a drink at a bar, saying it would help me forget my problems. He had too many of his own to help me. "

Doc thought about stopping at that point. But Angel's eyes did not seem to show sorrow for him as much as interest in him. She had noticed the pause and spoke up encouragingly, "Paul, I am caught by your story. Please tell me more."

"I tried drowning my grief in the bottle," he continued. "You know what happens. I started missing work and eventually lost my job. I was already having trouble keeping up with payments on a two-income mortgage. I lost the house. I also owed a lot on credit cards, felt overwhelmed, and just ran. I came here, went to several other cities, and eventually came back here . . . I have been on a drinking binge three times, and each time ended up being arrested and referred to the veteran's alcoholism program. It hasn't worked yet. When I talk about this in the program, they give me medicines to keep me from thinking about it. I feel this terrible guilt for not being there to pick up my son from school. I developed this terrible feeling of anger toward a God that took two innocent lives before their time!"

He realized he was speaking with increasing anger, and fell silent. Angel kept her thoughts silent. After a couple minutes that seemed like an eternity to him, Doc spoke again, quietly.

"That's why I don't like talking about it. I get angry . . . then I feel despair and hopelessness—not a good place to be."

Angel had not removed her hand from his arm.

"I understand," she said gently. "Maybe I have asked too much from you. Are you going to be able to process your feelings without getting…?"

He looked her in the eyes and finished her sentence, "Drunk? I think so. It actually seems better speaking these things with someone who has been there. I have been shoving these feelings down every day—more than once a day. I feel a little relief getting it out and not being judged about my feelings . . . or being told Twelve Steps will fix it all."

"You have some very deep questions without answers," Angel said softly. "Not all my questions have been answered either. But I have found a way to cope with living—even to find joy in life again. That is not to say I do not have my own down days."

"You? I've not seen that in you."

"No, I usually hide my down days at home when I can. There are fewer of them now. Would you like to talk about this more? How about next week? Maybe some of my journey will be helpful for you."

He thought for a moment and responded, "It's so hard for me to share these things . . . but it would probably be good for me . . . I'm not sure I like hanging my feelings out in front of the world to see, though," he said, glancing around.

"Maybe we can find somewhere more private," she suggested.

With that, Angel stood. Doc stood as well. She approached him to begin a hug and paused just short of it. He realized she was silently asking permission. He put out his arms and they hugged briefly. With her hands on his shoulders she said, "I will probably see you at the shelter during the week and we can make plans then. I have to get to my group now." Then she turned and was gone.

# Chapter 14

*"I saw something on the ground by the bridge pillar. I thought maybe the guy in the car threw out a bag of trash, so I went over to check it out. That's when I saw her lying on the ground."*

Kim Epperson, Jake's court appointed defense attorney, met him for the first time at the hearing for setting a trial date. It was Monday morning, a cold, dreary day in Bristol. Jake had been brought into the courtroom in his jail garb. When Kim entered the courtroom, the prosecutor, the Sullivan County District Attorney (DA), was already there and talking to different courtroom staff members. He kept impatiently looking at the time on his phone. Kim shook hands with the prosecutor and sat down in the chair to the right of Jake. She looked over at him and announced that she had been appointed to represent him as his attorney.

The judge entered the room after the bailiff announced, "All rise." The judge seated himself behind the bench and talked to his assistant for a few moments before looking over a file. Then he stated the case and the purpose of the session to set a trial date in the case of the State of Tennessee versus Jake P. Worley in the death of Janice A. Meredith.

The DA wanted to set a date within a month. Kim argued that four weeks was insufficient for her to prepare an adequate defense because the Tennessee Bureau of Investigation's (TBI) lab operations were running behind, and she needed the time to get some key lab test results. The judge set the date for two months later.

******

Kim returned to her office and began reading the case file for Jake Worley. She set up a meeting in jail with Jake for Monday.

Kim was an experienced attorney who worked for a large law firm for two years after passing the bar exam. But she found herself unable to continue putting up with the sexist climate of the firm. It was not easy to start up business as a solo attorney, but it had been worth it to her to be free.

One of the less attractive strategies for helping achieve a minimum required level of income was to contract with the county to provide public defender services for lower income defendants. This was her third case, and she had surprised herself in that she was feeling a sense of personal satisfaction in helping the poor.

Kim thought to herself that justice was not so swift anymore, yet she was grateful for having some time to get things together for the trial.

*******

Kim was slow on Monday afternoon, so she had arranged to meet with Jake. They met in a room reserved for attorney/client meetings. She was taken aback when Jake slumped down in the chair across the table from her. His left eye was swollen, and he had bruises on his arms. She had read in his file that Jake had a diagnosis of schizophrenia, but it was not severe and manageable with medication. She made a note to talk with the jailers to see if he was getting his meds, and to address the bruises. Jake did not look at her.

"Jake, I am Kimberly Epperson, your court appointed defense attorney."

Jake looked up at her and then looked away, mumbling, "Yeah."

Kim remained standing. He noticed she was about his height, with a stern face and brown hair. She was not beautiful, but something about her was attractive. He did not like having a woman attorney, but realized he could not do anything about it, and he kind of liked her at first sight. He hoped she could help set things straight for him.

"Jake, how did you get those bruises? What happened to your eye?" She did not remember that people with mental illness often do not handle multiple questions well.

He looked down at his arms and grunted, "Uh, I don't know. I've had them before. Some people don't like me."

"Are you eating okay?"

"Yeah. There could be more food though."

She knew it was difficult to sleep well in jail, but she was trying to establish enough relationship with Jake to ask other questions. She knew she needed to get past the schizophrenic's usual paranoia. So she asked, "Are you able to sleep?"

"Not much."

"Is there anything you need?"

"You got cigarettes? I need a cigarette and they don't like me asking for them."

She assumed he meant that he had been asking the other prisoners. Her experience had taught her to bring a pack of cigarettes for clients, even though the Sullivan County jail did not allow smoking. She pulled out the pack and handed it to him, expecting they would be absconded either by the jailers or other prisoners. However, the gesture served her purpose in that Jake was now in her pocket.

Eventually she asked, "Do you know what you have been charged with?"

"Yeah."

"Tell me what you think you are charged with."

"They think I hurt that girl they found under the bridge. But I didn't. I took some money from her—that's all."

"Okay, that's what I'm here for, to get your side of the story about what happened that night. Can you tell me about it?"

"I already told the police. I don't like thinking about it."

"I know, but I'm here to help you and I need to hear all that you know. Can you help me with that?"

"Okay. I'm thirsty. Can I have some water?"

Kim's patience was being tested, but she asked the guard outside the door to get him a Coke, and gave him money for it.

"Can you tell me about that night, Jake? Start before you went to where the girl was found."

He started with going to the library in the afternoon for warmth. He knew a slightly hidden corner there where he could grab a nap. After his nap, he left the library to look for enough butts to make a good cigarette. He then hung around some guys for a while, and then went to the Salvation Army for supper.

Jake hesitated, then continued, "Oh yeah, a couple guys at supper challenged me to go to a store and rip off something. They said they would give me some cigarettes if I did. So, I went there and the guy who works there ran me off, but not before I ripped off some crackers the guy didn't know I had. I just walked around town looking for those guys to show them what I took so I could get some cigarettes. I couldn't find them. So, I ate the crackers."

"Did you know that what you did was shoplifting, and that is against the law?"

"I did not think about that. I know a bunch of guys who do it. It's like a game. I just wanted some free cigarettes."

"Well, it is against the law. I would not mention that part to any-one else. What happened next?"

"I walked around trying to find cigarette butts. After smoking a cigarette I had made from the butts, some lady gave me a couple bucks to get something hot to drink. I got a cup of coffee and walked around some more. Later that night, I got sleepy and laid down out of the wind by the back door of a store. I had just fallen asleep when a policeman drove by, stopped, and told me to get away from there and find a shelter. I didn't think I could stay at the shelter again. I wore out my welcome last time. That's when I started walking to the bridge. I knew the cops wouldn't bother me there."

The guard brought in a can of Coke for Jake. After he opened the can and chugged half of it, Kim asked, "Do you know what time you got to the bridge?"

"No, ma'am. It was past midnight, I think. It was dark because it was cloudy. I heard a car drive away from under the bridge.

I wondered if they threw something out I could use, so I walked over there."

"Did you see the car?"

"Not well. All I could tell was that it was dark-colored and not too little."

"Then what?"

"I saw something on the ground by the bridge pillar. I thought maybe the guy in the car threw out a bag of trash, so I went over to check it out. That's when I saw her lying on the ground. I looked around to see if anybody was looking and didn't see anyone. I moved a little closer. She wasn't moving. I saw a purse nearby and I went over to it. I looked through it for cigarettes."

"Did you find any?"

"No, but I found several little things like lip balm and some other stuff. Oh yeah, there was a small wallet and a cell phone."

"Did you think these things belonged to the person lying there? Did you think it was OK to take them?"

"Um, I was excited about those things and just thought she wouldn't miss them."

"How did you know she was a she?"

"Her long blond hair was showing, and when I turned her over, I noticed she looked like a girl."

"Why did you turn her over?"

"I couldn't tell if she was passed out or, well . . . maybe dead."

"Were you looking for jewelry?"

"Um, I did look around, but I did not find anything but some earrings she was wearing. Her face was covered with vomit and dirt. She smelled bad, so I just left the earrings. I saw a wine bottle near there and checked it, but it was empty."

"What did you do with the purse?"

"I was pretty sure she was dead . . . and I was getting nervous about things at that time. So I took what I needed from the purse and wallet, and threw them into a trash barrel a few feet away."

"Did you see any drugs in the purse, wallet, or anywhere around her?"

"Well, there were some open packets that probably had had crack or crystal in them at one time, but they were empty. I did not see anything else."

"What did you do with the cell phone? Did you tell the police about it? There was no mention of it in the file."

"Oh, I forgot about it. It was a cheap phone, and no one wanted to buy it. I threw it away." He did not mention to her the other phone, an iPhone he had taken and sold on the street for ten bucks.

"What did you do next?"

"I went back downtown. I didn't get any sleep that night. I was too excited about having some money."

"Did you tell anybody other than the police about the things you just told me?"

"Not really. I told some friends about the things I found."

She paused to look at her notes and then continued. "Are there any other homeless people who regularly sleep under that bridge?"

"I'm not sure. I don't usually sleep there. I think a guy called 'Chicago' sleeps there some."

"Chicago! Why Chicago?"

"I think he came here from Chicago, and he talks a lot about Chicago."

Kim thought to herself that this might be an interesting case to learn from since she knew little about the homeless population in Bristol, or anywhere else. She told Jake that it would be a tough defense, but that she believed him. He did some wrong things that he would need to confess, but she did believe that he had not killed the girl. She told him the trial would start in a couple months. She verified he did not have money for bail, and said he would be a guest of the state until the trial. She called the guard, told Jake to "hang in there," and left.

On the way back to her office, Kim made note that there was no mention of the cell phone on the victim or of anyone named Chicago. She knew the detective on the case and thought she would have a chat with him to see if it had been looked into and just not recorded in the file.

*******

Gunny thought that Professor Brantley would not leave for a secret meeting from his house. It would more likely be from his office on campus where he had identified the window of Brantley's office. About 8 p.m. on Monday, he drove to the campus and found the light on in the office. This was the third night Gunny had checked, and the light had been out the other two nights. He pulled into a parking space on the road where he could watch for the light to go out. The location also gave him a good view of the door used by professors to come and go to their cars. He had already identified Brantley's car from state records. It was a two-year-old black Cadillac with a parking sticker for the staff lot at the college.

The coffee in his thermos was fresh and hot. Gunny looked at the snacks he kept in stock for such times and decided coffee was all he wanted at the moment. A thought struck his mind that intrigued him. It was a question: *The description of Dr. Brantley and Ace are very similar. Could they be the same person?*

The light in the window went out about 9 p.m., and Gunny watched the professor leave the building and get into his car. He then drove away, taking a route Gunny figured would lead to his house in the expensive country club area of Bristol, Tennessee, and it did. He parked a couple houses away and waited to be sure Dr. Brantley would not sneak out later. At midnight, Gunny headed home.

The same pattern repeated for a week until Gunny finally decided he did not have time to keep up the stakeout. After all, he was just chasing a rumor.

*******

New Year's Day was a day of sumptuous food, fellowship with family, and TV watching—parades in the morning, football all afternoon and evening. This was the tradition of the Hawkins household. Angel had prepared a less voluminous, but equally sumptuous meal for guests at her house. Her guests included a couple ladies from the shelter, a friend of hers from church, and Doc. Dr. Brantley and his wife did their traditional thing of traveling to Raleigh, North Carolina, for New Year's dinner with Mrs. Brantley's parents and her two brother's families. Among other favorite recipes, they served the traditional ham and black-eyed peas for good luck in the year ahead. The police labs, courts, and Covenant College were all closed for the holiday. The jail was staffed with a skeleton crew 24/7 on Thursday, New Year's Day, through Sunday. Nothing got done on the case from Thursday through Sunday except Doc kept worrying about what he should do, Jake took a couple more beatings and Mrs. Meredith grieved over the loss of her daughter.

# Chapter 15

It all came crashing in on Doc about midweek. He had not slept well for several days. He felt as if a huge weight was pulling down on him like an anchor tugging on a boat that wanted to get away. He could not take a deep breath. His mind would not stop jumping from one cloud to another. His mind turned in on him like a cat chasing its tail. The thought haunted him that things would have been different if he had not worked over that fateful afternoon in Hartford, and instead had gone to pick up his son. Like others living in the bondage of guilt, he was not rational in his thinking.

Doc was bothered that he had feelings for another woman, and scolded himself for it, feeling like a traitor to his dead wife. He felt like a traitor for withholding information that might help Jake, and was torn up inside about it, though he tried to reassure himself that he did not owe Jake anything and that the judicial system would eventually work it all out. He was miserably cold from the falling mixture of rain and sleet. That morning he had awakened to wretched sinus drainage that tasted like something dead was in his mouth. His cough had gotten worse, especially when he tried to go to sleep.

Doc was worn out physically and emotionally. He had no defense when the thought came to him that he had found relief from these times when it seemed God had turned against him by turning to anesthesia in a bottle. He forced himself to cast off that idea at first, and felt proud for doing so. That did not last long, and the thought invaded again.

Another street person sitting near him offered him a drink from his bottle of wine. Doc surprised himself by quickly grabbing the bottle. He justified it as something he needed, and as a reward for putting off getting drunk for so long. Besides, one or two swigs of wine would be all he needed, and then he would resist after that. The first swig of wine did not soothe his sore throat like the second swig soothed his feelings. The third was the best, and he began to feel a warmth flow over and through him, as if meeting an old friend again.

After giving the almost empty bottle back, Doc checked his pouch for money. He had enough to get a bottle of cheap wine—maybe two. He knew a store where he could get low priced wine that did not taste so good, but had the same alcohol content. No questions would be asked there. He started walking in the direction of the store.

The argument within started all over again, *why would I want to start drinking again. I know I will go on a binge. I know the terrible feeling he had when he suffered withdrawal from his last binge.* Then he countered that thought with another argument, *I need a break from the unfair burdens building up on me. Besides, No one really cares, especially God. Maybe I'll get arrested and be out of this miserable weather. I can't handle the condemnation I'm feeling. I deserve to die. I need out. Why not do it with something that makes me feel better on the way?* The argument raged on while he walked in the direction of the store. His thinking was all about himself. He had a brief thought about Angel that just contributed to his guilt in caring for her. His thoughts did not include the reality that a drinking binge right now could cost Jake his life.

That evening, Doc snuggled into his sleeping place with two bottles of the cheapest wine he could get. It had taken most of his money. Another homeless man coming out of the store expressed surprise that he was going inside. But Doc was set on doing the deed. He emptied the two bottles within three hours and fell asleep.

*******

Doc woke up late the next morning. He felt sick, gagging once, but only some bile came up. He begged on the street for enough money to go get another couple bottles. He stayed drunk, drinking in numbness, caught in a passed-out time warp, staggering around town when he awoke enough to notice he was out of wine. He could not break the cycle and did not really want to break it.

Friday afternoon, Doc came out of his hole to beg for money. He staggered up to a lady on the sidewalk that had just come out of a retail store. He tripped, lost his balance and fell against her. The lady screamed, "Get away from me!" She was more shocked than afraid. Instead of getting away, Doc moved toward her to apologize, but the words did not come out right.

A nearby storekeeper who had stepped out on the sidewalk in front of his business pulled out his cell phone and called the police. At the same time he moved toward Doc and yelled at him, "Get away from here, you drunk."

Doc turned to the storekeeper and tried to yell an obscenity at him, but his tongue was not working right. It was as if his tongue and mind had a short circuit between them. He turned back to the lady, but she had moved on down the sidewalk.

The storekeeper was still angrily shouting at Doc: "You're not wanted here. Why don't you just go off in the woods and kill yourself! I don't know why the police let you linger around here, anyway. They ought to take you to the interstate and send you somewhere else. Why does that shelter let you drunks come down here anyway?"

Doc was too inebriated to stay up with the man's rapid-fire words, so he just gave up and started across the street, when a police car pulled up. Two officers got out, immediately determined Doc's condition, arrested him, and took him away to the jail in Blountville, Tennessee.

There were not many places to detox from alcohol or drugs in the Bristol area if you did not have good insurance or plenty of money. So detox frequently occurred in the jails. Even the hospitals would not provide detox unless a person was convincingly trying to hurt someone else or commit suicide. The jails did not offer the drugs that the hospitals did to ease the process, so in the jails, drunks would go through alcohol detoxification "cold turkey." Nonprofit organizations in place would have been glad to help, but the cost of professional staffing, medication, and liability insurance was too much for them. It was hard to get donations to help pay for such a facility. So, Doc detoxed in the Sullivan County jail. The judge said he would be there for twenty-nine days for public intoxication.

Doc began to think more clearly again after three days of agonizing detoxification. His joints hurt and he had little appetite. In fact, he was nauseated much of the time. His cough was worse and productive. The only thing he got from the jail to help him was an occasional dose of a generic analgesic.

He began beating himself up over giving in to alcohol again to escape from his inner pain. Doc thought to himself, *I can't face Angel again. She'll probably give up on me. She'd be right to do so. I don't even like myself. What did I have to live for anyway?*

About the sixth day he remembered Jake and worried about whether he could be of any help to him now. He had not been very hopeful that anyone would listen to him anyway, and now he had no hope.

He wondered when the trial would start. He asked around about it. One guy had heard that the DA was pushing for a quick trial and that probably meant that he felt he had all the evidence he needed. Doc was not worried about doing the time in jail. He was more worried about the damage he was certain this binge had caused in several ways.

On Thursday, the seventh day in jail, the jail chaplain came through and stopped at his cell.

"Paul?" Doc had not been called that for a long time except when in court. The guards knew his street name and usually used it. He did not respond at first. He remembered that Angel called him by his name as well.

"Paul Walker?" the chaplain queried again.

"Yeah, that's me." He noticed the name badge. "Richard Hunter. So, you're the chaplain."

"Please, call me Rick. There is a lady in my church who knows you. She asked me to check in on you and asked if she could see you at some time. Her name is Ann. She said you might know her as Angel. Do you want to have a visit from her?"

Doc was shocked. Seeing her after he was out of jail would be embarrassing enough. To see her inside would be too much. "Chaplain, I respect her a lot, but I don't think I can handle seeing her in this jail. She might not ever want to see me again. Just tell her that I'll be done here in a few weeks, and I'll see her when I'm out. That is, if she still wants to see me."

"Well, Paul, I don't think you know Angel very well. She's not the type to pay much attention to the setting. She's more concerned about you, and I think she might be helpful to you. She said you had just begun talking with her about personal things, and felt further conversation would be helpful. Her name, 'Angel,' is not an accident. I would think again about turning her down."

"I'll think about it," Doc responded just trying to get off the subject.

"I'll check back with you tomorrow or the next day, at least. I suggest you seriously think it over. This might be the opportunity for you to get better. By the way, I hold a chapel service here on Sunday morning. You might try to be there," he said as he smiled and moved on to another cell.

"Yeah, sure, chaplain. Thanks. I will sincerely consider it."

Doc had wanted to see Angel. Things had not worked out well, and he knew it was his fault. He did think if anyone would give him a second chance, it would be her. She might be helpful to him. Her faith was amazing, and he realized he needed to catch some of it. She did seem to genuinely care about him—not in a physical way—but as a person. But for her to see him in jail . . . that was too much.

The next day, he told the chaplain to tell Angel he wanted to get with her, but after he was out of jail.

*******

The next Sunday morning, Doc went to chapel. It was a chance to get out of the cell for a while, and he hoped it would encourage him in some way. He believed in God and even felt he might have genuinely become a Christian when he was a boy. After a couple old-time songs, the chaplain began speaking. He did not expect the message to hit him between the eyes like it did.

Chaplain Rick spoke about a prophet, Jonah, who did not want to do what God said to do. He ran from God, so God had to put him through some very hard times to get his attention and humble him. Doc had heard the story as a child, and thought it was just that—a story with a moral to it. But the chaplain explained that God does that with us sometimes. We rebel against what He wants for us, and we go through hard times until we get humble enough to say yes to God and give up our rebellion. Doc thought, *many of these men feel humbled already. So, what is it that God wants from us? After all, I'm the victim here when you (looking up to the ceiling) took my family from me.*

Then the chaplain got personal: "I know you all are going through a hard time, maybe in several ways. Many of you have been humbled by these hard times. I want you to think back to see if there was something you were supposed to do, but had decided not to so you could do your own thing instead. Maybe you were just too proud and needed to be humbled so you could do what God knows is best for you. Maybe you have not done what God knew to be best for you because you are too bitter about things from the past. In any case, if God has put something on your heart and you have rebelled against doing it, then give it up to God. Pray to Him and ask the Lord to forgive you. Then obey Him in that thing, just like Jonah did."

Afterwards, Doc told Chaplain Rick he had given a good message and headed back to his cell. He felt it did not please God when he drank. He thought God should not have allowed the tragic event that he believed led to his drinking. He wanted to quit thinking about it because it usually made him angry at God. This time he was determined not to let go of the truth of the message he had heard.

As he entered his cell, the words "humble" and "proud" rose in his thoughts. Was he proud even though he had been humbled by circumstances? Was he rebellious? He knew he was bitter. Then he remembered that Angel wanted to see him and realized pride might be keeping him from allowing it. She wanted to help and would not look down on him. She had proven that she was sincere, and she had treated him with respect. Maybe it was pride that kept him from seeing her. He would rethink his decision. It did not take long before he decided to let the chaplain know he wanted Angel to meet with him there.

*******

The following Friday, Angel came to the jail to see Doc. She had not done so before, so it was all new to her. She watched how the person ahead of her handled all the questions and requests. She went up to the window and asked to see Paul Walker. The lady behind the window asked her relation to him, and she explained she had counseled with him some and that Chaplain Rick had suggested she see him. The lady checked a list on a pad of paper as she questioned her, and told her to have a seat as someone went to get Paul.

Angel watched the other person in the waiting room—a young woman. Just as she was about to speak to her, the woman got up, looked through a small window in the door to another room, and walked in.

Angel looked through the small window to see what was happening. She saw several reinforced windows with small holes she thought were there to better let the sound through. Small dividers between the windows provided a sense of privacy. The woman went up to a window with a man seated on the other side. He was dressed in jail garb. She watched for Paul to see when he would come.

A couple minutes later, Paul walked into the room and sat down. He looked like death warmed over. She would ignore that and do what she could to be positive in the few minutes she had to talk with him. Angel entered the room and sat down in front of Doc.

"I didn't know I was that threatening, Paul," she said with a smile.

"It's not you," he said, overcome by emotion, his feelings a mix of warmth that she cared enough to come to jail to see him, and embarrassment. "When it all builds up and I am overwhelmed, I've got this habit of hiding. I know it's wrong . . . I just can't seem to stop it."

"I look forward to talking about that later. Right now, we need to look at what you do when you get out of here."

"I guess I will go to the shelter for a few days like I usually do."

"Paul, I have another idea for you to consider. I own a duplex. I live in one side, and right now, the other side is vacant. I want you to come live in the other side for a few weeks, and then we will see from there."

"What? No . . . I couldn't do that. I don't need charity!" Paul was instantly struck by the thought of being proud.

"Don't be silly. We haven't finished our conversation yet, and that would help us do so. Your cough seems worse, and I think a good shelter out of the weather for a while would help that get better. I've prayed about it, and I've talked to the chaplain and my pastor about it. They had a little reservation, but have agreed it might be your opportunity for a new start. Oh, it's not charity, it's ministry. It is what the Lord wants me to do, and you should not fight what God wants."

"Whoa! Slow down. Maybe I don't want that." He had heard himself say ridiculous things before, but he knew this beat all the others. A long silence followed. As the seconds ticked away, thoughts of Jonah being swallowed by a big fish came to Doc's mind.

Angel spoke softly: "Of course, it's up to you. I've been in that cycle you are trapped in, and I know there is a way out. I just want to help you find it. Just come. You can leave if it doesn't work for you. It's furnished, so you can move right in."

"I really appreciate your consideration, and I probably should jump on it, but let me think it over and I will send word to you through the Chaplain Rick."

With that, time was up and Angel stepped out of the room. She felt that she had gained a small victory in that Paul had not rejected the idea outright.

Paul had two more weeks to go before he would be released. He rationalized to himself, *the jail requires someplace for me to go to stay in order to release me. The street is not acceptable. It had been the shelter in the past. To live in a place with a roof, heat and furniture would be something I have not experienced since losing the house.*

He was doubtful about getting out of his cycle, and almost found a type of security in knowing what life had dealt him, even if it included suffering. Many homeless people find a sense of security in a consistent pattern of life, even if it includes suffering. Fear and hopelessness are barriers to achieving a meaningful change in their patterns.

Still, a glimmer of hope inspired him when he remembered Angel's countenance. She had a captivating, sparkly-eyed smile and sense of confidence that attracted him. He thought she might be his way out . . . and the only way to find out was to accept her offer. He feared what might happen if he rejected her, wondering if she would continue to be interested in him.

Two days later on Sunday, Doc notified Chaplain Rick that he would accept Angel's offer. Rick called Angel that afternoon to let her know Doc had accepted her offer. She corrected the Chaplain saying, "His name is Paul." The Chaplain apologized and said he would let the officials know Doc, I mean Paul has a place to go.

# Chapter 16

Dr. Brantley had not yet found a way to approach the student that would be his next "toy" to enjoy. He was trying to come up with a way to meet her when he opened the Monday newspaper and saw a brief article in the "Local" section saying that Jake Worley's trial would start in five weeks. It could not come fast enough for him. He felt no regrets over a bum going to jail for life. To him, a homeless person would not have to worry about shelter and food anymore while in prison. He was ready for everyone to get past the girl's death and forget about it. So far, he had not been drawn into the case and he wanted it to stay that way.

Still, he wondered about the throwaway phone he had given Jan. He had set it up so it would not be traceable back to him. He paid cash for it and wiped it clean of his prints before giving it to her.

He had destroyed the other throwaway phone he had purchased so that Jan could call him. He had smashed it and thrown it away in the college's kitchen dumpster. He had also paid for it with cash and the name for the number was coded. It was highly unlikely it could lead back to him.

He wondered about his encounter with Jan the night she died. It had not gone well. Just a little before midnight, he had driven up to her as she walked from work to her apartment. He thought no one had seen them. Earlier that day, she had called and left him a message that she was pregnant and needed to talk with him. He had not taken the news well.

He wanted her to get an abortion, but she argued with him. He lost his temper and grabbed her arm so hard that she screamed. How could she do this to him? He had wondered if she was pretending to be pregnant to get him to marry her, but now he knew she had really been pregnant.

He thought about his carefulness in checking with her about birth control before each rendezvous. He believed she would not lie to him about something that important. He took a deep breath and told himself to settle down and quit worrying over "what ifs." He assured himself she was no longer a big threat to him. He was sure the DA finding so much evidence pointing to the bum had saved him.

He shifted his thinking back to the new target. Evidently, she did not have to work, so she would be more flexible, but he had not found a safe opportunity to meet her. He did know that her roommate, Janet Summers, was a former student of his. He did not like involving anyone else, yet maybe he could get Janet to introduce them. He decided against that idea. It was too risky. He would have to think of something else.

*******

Kim saw Gunny in the courthouse hallway. They had gone to the same high school and dated a couple times. He answered her call to him with, "Gunny here."

"Hi, Gunny, this is Kim Epperson. We went to school together. You got a minute?"

"Hey, Kim. What's up?"

"I'm the appointed attorney for Jake Worley. I saw you are working that case."

"That's right."

"Would you be up for a cup of coffee at the Sweet Tooth Bakery? I have a couple questions to clarify the police file, you know . . . off the record. I'll buy—no bribe—just a friendly cup of coffee."

Gunny knew he should not agree to her request, but he thought he could find out if she knew anything that he didn't know. So, he answered, "Sure, I can do that. But it will have to be later today."

"How about two o'clock?"

"That works for me. See you then."

*******

Two o'clock came quickly and Gunny walked into Bristol's favorite bakery on time. He did not see Kim at first. Then he heard her voice behind him. "You still like it black?"

"That's right, good memory."

"I'll get the coffees; you find us a seat."

"Okay, I'll look upstairs on the balcony."

Gunny found a table on the balcony where no one else was seated. His thoughts drifted back to high school days. He liked Kim and found her attractive, though he did not think of her as "beautiful." Part of it was her confident personality. He was always attracted to women who were self-confident. He would have to watch out for that in this conversation. He did not mind clarifying some things for her, but he would have to be careful not to be manipulated.

Kim joined him on the balcony, and sat down at the small table Gunny had selected. "We haven't talked much since high school," she started, "but it is interesting that we are in the same business now, somewhat."

"You might say that, but we got here by different paths."

Kim glanced at his left hand and commented, "I see you are married. Any children?"

"Yeah, one daughter. She is a teenager, and at times, a bigger challenge than solving crime in Bristol."

"Right." She thought to herself, *I remember that Rick (Gunny) is challenged by women who can stand on their own but he seems to like the challenge.*

"If I remember right, you were strong willed too." Gunny said, uninterestedly. He was growing uncomfortable with the chitchat, so he cut to the chase: "What is it you want clarified about the file on Worley?"

Kim recognized that Gunny was ready to move on from the personal stuff. She was tempted to go further because she enjoyed putting men off guard. But she did not want to jeopardize her real goal for the meeting. She glanced at her file and began, "In reading the files on the student's case, I did not see anything about a cell phone. It would be highly unusual for a student to not have a cell phone."

"Right. I thought the same. Jake did not say that he saw one. I asked about it and he stuck with his story. We checked the trash barrel and did not find one there or at the scene. That seemed strange to me. I assume that someone else found it, or someone did not want us to know about it." (Kim noticed he had used the defendant's first name, a sign to her that he might feel some compassion for him.)

"My thinking as well," she agreed, choosing not to mention at this point that she knew Jake had thrown it away.

"I also did not find any mention of possible witnesses. Surely there might be another homeless person who sleeps under that bridge. Did you find any?"

"Nothing much there to mention. Jake said he thought someone usually slept there, but could not remember any names. I checked it out one night and found no one there. I asked some guys on the street. They said there might be somebody, but they could not or would not come up with a name."

"Hmm. If I was going to look for someone like that, I would look for someone who goes by the name, 'Chicago.' Just saying, you know."

"Just saying, huh. Sounds like Jake got his memory back. Maybe I will check around for that name."

"Gunny, I think Jake stole from this girl and lied about some things, but I cannot believe he killed her."

"The case is pretty strong. The DA has him at the scene, and he thinks there will be DNA evidence. He has motive in that he stole from her. The coroner found her vomit and wine residue under his fingernails. His prints were on the wine bottle, the purse, and the wallet." He chose not to mention that they should be getting the DNA results on the skin under her fingernails soon. "It's a pretty strong case."

"I know it seems strong, but I can't see her being overpowered by Jake. I do not see him forcing her to drink a bottle of wine or take the meth just to rob her of a few things. I think he happened upon the scene right after she was murdered or was dumped there, and the real murderer is lucking out that Jake showed up at the scene and has been indicted."

"Well, neither of us is the judge or jury. I will give you this—there are a couple loose ends I am trying to tie up."

Kim had accomplished what she wanted to do. She mentioned as she stood to leave, "Well I hope a phone and a potential witness called 'Chicago' will be on your list of 'loose ends.' See you in court." She left the bakery.

Gunny finished his coffee thinking about what Kim had said.

*******

Gunny drove back to the office and found a young, man waiting for him. They went to Gunny's desk and sat down.

"What's your name, son?"

"I'm Jeff. I don't want to get involved, but my friend Brad hasn't been around for a while. I just wanted to pass on something he told me."

"You have a last name?"

"Do I have to give you that?"

"Not right now. What did your friend say?"

"Brad worked at the Borderline Restaurant, where Jan worked. He followed her when she left work the night she was killed. He said he did it because she was so upset that he was concerned for her. He saw a black car pull up beside her. The passenger door opened and she got in."

Gunny's thoughts went immediately to the professor who had a dark car.

"Brad said he was trying to get closer without being seen," Jeff continued, "but they drove off before he reached them. He said the light inside the car when the door was open was enough for him to recognize the guy in the car. He said it was a professor from the college he had seen in the restaurant."

"Did he know the professor's name?"

"No, except he said he thought he heard his wife call him, 'Tony.' "

"Why didn't Brad come tell me this?"

"That's the problem. He told me he had to get out of town and had a bus ticket south. He wouldn't tell me what it was about, or exactly where he was going, but I am worried about him. I can't reach him on his phone."

"Okay, Jeff, now I need your last name and how to reach you."

Jeff reluctantly gave Gunny the contact information he needed.

Gunny stood to leave and assured Jeff that he would look into Brad's whereabouts.

*******

Gunny thought this new information over. It was significant that the professor had picked Jan up a little before the time of her death. The problem was, it was not exactly a smoking gun and it was third party—hearsay.

Gunny went by the bus station and found that a ticket for New Orleans had been sold to a passenger a couple days earlier. Gunny contacted the New Orleans police and asked them to see if they could verify that Brad arrived.

After giving them a description of Brad, he ended the call. He punched in the number for the district attorney's office. "Hi, Beth, is John in?"

"Hi, Gunny. Yes, but he's on the phone. Oh, He just hung up. I'll put you through."

"Gunny," John answered, "what do you have?"

Gunny could sense his impatience. He was an inconvenience to John, an up-and-coming DA Gunny felt was more interested in his career growth than justice. "John, I just wanted to give you a heads up. I'm tying up some loose ends on the Jake Worley case."

"Why spend time on that? The case is a slam dunk and I'm not worried about it."

"I have learned that a college professor picked Jan up when she was walking toward her apartment the night she was murdered. I have also learned that a homeless man might have been sleeping in the area of the murder, and it isn't Jake."

The DA swore over the phone and added, "Gunny, don't mess me up on this!"

"John, these loose ends could be enough for Jake's attorney to give the jury reasonable doubt about Jake. I know his attorney. She's a go-getter. Don't you think it's worth knowing about all this, first?"

"Yeah, I know Kim. She has a reputation. I don't like it, but go ahead and tie up your loose ends. Just don't mess me up!" The DA's phone went dead.

Gunny did not like John's attitude, but had to work with him anyway. He thought that maybe he should just let Kim destroy John's case and it would serve him right and get Jake off. But that was not Gunny's way. He needed to tie the loose ends up and let the truth be what it is.

He thought about trying to find Chicago that evening. No. Gunny thought he had done plenty for a Monday and his daughter was playing in a basketball game that he had promised to attend. He decided to work on finding Chicago the next evening. The loose ends were getting more interesting, and he could not shake his feeling that Jake had not committed murder.

# Chapter 17

*A warning coursed through his mind and emotions,
causing him to question whether he really wanted to
open himself up. He looked at Angel in the kitchen and
got the courage he needed.*

Doc had been in jail twenty-five days. He was sitting on his bunk when he heard a commotion and went over to the cell bars to look out. A stretcher passed by . . . and Jake was on it, covered all over with bleeding cuts and bruises. Doc felt as if he had been stuck in the heart with a dagger, and cried out, "Jake!" He saw Jake open the one eye that was not swollen shut and peer at him. He said nothing as they carried the stretcher away.

One of the guards saw the look of shock in Doc's face and answered Doc's implied question about Jake, "Jake did not get along with the other inmates, and they took it out on him. It's probably a good thing they are taking Jake for medical help. The next beating might do him in."

"Why don't they put him in a cell by himself?" Doc snapped.

"Hey, can't you tell we are kind of crowded here? Besides," the guard said over his shoulder as he walked away, "that is none of your business."

Doc was due to be released in a couple days. He had accepted Angel's offer to live in the other side of her duplex. The jail had a way of putting inmates out one minute before midnight on the twenty-ninth day to keep them a maximum length of time without getting into a thirtieth day. It put an inmate in a different category somehow. He did not understand it all, and it was very inconvenient, but Angel had said she would pick him up and take him to his new place no matter what time it was.

Doc's conscience was pierced by seeing Jake in so much pain. His thoughts drifted back to his grandmother. She would say, "When you are not sure what to do, do what is right for others and what gives you peace inside." He thought about peace, something he had not felt in more than five years. He knew the right thing to do in regard to Jake was to tell the police about what he had seen, and about the e-mail he had recovered from the parking lot behind the restaurant where he had seen the student arguing with the man.

He argued with himself, *It will just come back to hurt me if I go to the police. They will not like that I withheld information. They will want to know what I was doing there at that time of night. They probably will not believe me anyway. They might even suspect me!* The sight of Jake reappeared in his mind, and his grandmother's saying hit him again. She had added, "The Bible says that the truth will set you free." Doc thought that it might set Jake free, but not him. He could not sleep as the argument in his soul continued through the night.

*******

The twenty-ninth day finally arrived for Doc to be released. He was given a few things he had on him when arrested. One of these was his jacket. He felt inside the pocket and the e-mail was still wadded up in the pocket. For some reason the Sullivan County jail let the prisoners there for public drunkenness go just before midnight on the twenty-ninth day of their internment. He was put out just before midnight.

The Chaplain had suggested Angel be there about 11:45 p.m. and she was there waiting for him. He met her with embarrassment, gratitude, and humility. She handed him a cup of fast food coffee, noting that it was decaf in case he wanted to sleep later. She drove them to her duplex. There was little conversation.

He could not get used to the odd feelings he had when he was around Angel. She was pleasing to his eyes, but there was more to it than that. He felt secure with her, like all was or would be well in the world. He did not want the time to come when they would part.

He refused to think he was in love with her. How could he be? He could not let himself love any woman after Angela.

On the way Paul had something he needed to get off his chest, "I saw Jake in the jail. He was in bad shape from being abused by other prisoners. I feel so bad for him. I can't imagine that he killed that woman. Oh, he probably took the money, but he is no killer."

Angel responded, "You are probably right, but the case has built up against him. They did hold his hearing and the judge is holding him without bail while the case is being built for trial."

"Great, they will probably kill him before he can even be tried," Gunny said harshly. He looked over at Angel and said apologetically, "Sorry, I'm not mad at you, I am upset with the system that seems to have one set of rules for the poor and another for the rich. If he was rich, Jake would have been out of jail on bail in a couple of days."

They finally arrived at the duplex. It was located in Bristol, Tennessee, just off Broad Street, not far from Steele Creek Park, away from downtown. He was used to walking a lot, and considered it reasonable to walk the couple miles to town. Unlike the average American, walking is the primary mode of getting around and they accept walking distances most people would scoff about.

Upon entering his side of the duplex, he noted it was sparsely furnished, but more than he required. He thanked her three times before Angel said goodbye saying, I need to sleep because I have a busy morning planned. Would you join me for supper that evening at 5:30?

Doc answered without really thinking. "Yes, that would be great."

With that, she left and he was alone.

There was no TV. That did not faze Doc. He was not used to watching one. He looked in the refrigerator and found some groceries she had put there for him. Most of it was frozen meals and a frozen pizza. That was fine with him. He looked in the kitchen cabinets and found more groceries, plates, glasses, and coffee cups.

Doc took his bag into the bedroom and pulled out fresh underwear. He thought a hot shower would be a healing balm to him, and found it was. After that, he sat down on the couch and noticed a book on the lamp table. It was *The Key to Triumphant Living,* by Jack Taylor. He thought he needed that and set it back down planning to read in it after he got some real sleep.

Doc stretched out on the couch and fell asleep within a couple minutes. In his sleep he kept dreaming about Jake, and saw his beaten face and that swollen shut eye peering at him. He received a message that he needed to help Jake get free of a false charge for murder. In his dream he agreed that he needed to tell the police everything. Then a feeling of relief and peace came over him like the warmth of the shower he had taken before falling asleep.

*******

Doc knocked on Angel's door about 5:30 that evening as she had suggested. Angel invited him in and an aroma met his nose that he had not known for a long time. It was homemade spaghetti with meatballs. Angel served a fresh tossed salad and buttered garlic bread. Salads served in jail or at the shelter usually had several pieces of wilted lettuce you had to pick out, and never smelled or tasted as fresh as Angel's salad. It was a treat for him to sit at a table and eat such a delicious meal, especially in Angel's company.

After supper, they sat in her living room, sipping decaf coffee and chatting about Angel's work and her teaching at the shelter. Doc shared that he planned to start looking for work the next day.

After a few moments of silence, Doc told Angel that he wanted her opinion on something important to him. She nodded in agreement and he shared with her what he had observed in the parking lot the night of the student's death, including the e-mail he had found. He pulled the now folded up sheet of paper out of his shirt pocket and reached to hand it to her. She pulled a tissue out of a nearby box and took the paper, holding it in the tissue.

"Why the tissue," he queried.

"Oh, I guess it's from watching TV detective shows. If this could be evidence, there might be a fingerprint or some DNA on it, and I don't want to mess it up or have my prints on it."

"I didn't even think about that. I guess I have already contaminated it with my prints."

"We can put it in a plastic bag in a minute. So, what do you propose to do with this?"

"That's what I want to get your opinion about. I think it might help get Jake out of the slammer, at least to free him from the murder charge. The man she argued with might have come back later and killed her. I've been reluctant to get involved."

He told her about the dream he had and that in it, he came to realize that to tell about the things he knew was the right thing to do. "But how do I go about it?"

There was silence for a few moments. Doc did not speak because he sensed that Angel was thinking. She began to verbalize her thoughts, "I know a guy at my church. He's a police detective in Bristol. He's a decent guy and would treat you right. He was in the Marines . . . and they call him Gunny. In fact, I think he is working on Jake's case."

"Oh, Gunny! Doc exclaimed. Cookie mentioned a detective by that name. He thought he was a good guy."

"That settles it. I'll take you to the police station tomorrow morning and you can give this to Gunny."

"I don't know. I'm not sure they want to see me at the police station again. I gave them a rough time when they arrested me. Can't you just tell them for me and give them this paper?" Doc knew the answer to his question, but he hoped she would feel sorry for him. She did not agree. Instead she had another idea.

"Okay, I'll call him in the morning and see if he can come by here tomorrow afternoon after I get off work. You can talk with him here. How about that?"

"I guess that's best. I'll be sure to be back from looking for work before he gets here."

Angel refilled their cups and sat down again. "Do you mind if I use your name rather than Doc?"

"I guess that's okay," Doc answered gingerly.

"Paul, it was not a program or a formula that set me free from the overwhelming grief at the loss of my husband. It was another relationship that was even more satisfying than the one I had with my husband."

Doc squirmed and thought that this was not what he expected. He was not sure that he wanted to know about her relationships.

Angel noticed his discomfort and clarified, "I'm not talking about a relationship with people, but with God. To be specific, a relationship with Jesus. I couldn't tell from our last conversation at the Sweet Tooth whether you had a real belief in Jesus, or if it was just a thing you said you had to please your mom or the Sunday school teacher. Do you think you have a real relationship with Jesus?"

He cleared his throat and responded, "You did get me thinking that day. I do remember a time when my grandmother asked me the same question. She explained that I had sinned against God. Well, that was not hard to understand. I was pretty good at sinning. Then she explained there was a penalty due for my sins, and how Jesus took my sins on himself, paying the penalty for me. She told me that's why Jesus had to suffer and die on the cross. He took my punishment for my sin on himself. She said if I prayed and admitted that, Jesus would save me and even give me eternal life. All I had to do was believe Him. I knew if my grandmother believed, I should too."

"I did not pray right away like she suggested. That night, after going to bed, I prayed for Jesus to take my sins away and give me eternal life. I tried to quit sinning after that, like grandma said. It didn't last long. Then bad things happened in my family and I basically forgot all about it. I sometimes wonder if God has it in for me anyway, and I'm just one of those that will never make it."

"Oh, Paul, you are not one that will never make it. No one understands everything about living the Christian life or relating to God when they express faith in God. You may have given up on your relationship with God, but He has not given up on you if your prayer was really from your heart."

"I believe it was from my heart at the time. I just didn't stay with it. And then my family was killed and I felt God did not love them or me. If anything, I felt like I might have lost my relationship with God."

Angel did not have words to use right away and she needed to think about what Paul had just shared from his heart.

Doc realized he had finally put in words what he had feared to say before but really felt. He glanced over at Angel who was looking down at her hands fiddling with the bottom edge of her blouse. He wondered if he had offended her with these hard words. He thought about that and rejected that idea. She was strong and he wanted to hear her response to his honest feelings.

Angle did not disappoint him, "I felt that way too until someone I trusted shared with me that God really does love me and my husband, even on the day he was killed. I like to think that maybe God knows best, and may have saved him from something very hideous that he might have suffered. This life on earth is only temporary duty, and the real life we have is in eternity, knowing God without the fog of sin. God took my husband and your family to a much better situation than this earth could have ever offered. How can I begrudge God for doing that? Any anger with God is out of my own selfish desires and I had to choose to let that go."

"I have never thought of it that way. I'm not sure I buy that now. I'll have to chew on it a while."

There was another pause in their conversation. Angel got up, headed to the kitchen and said, "I need a glass of water. Would you like one too?"

Doc said quietly under his breath, "I could use something stronger than water."

Angel heard a mumbling sound and spoke loudly from the kitchen, "I didn't get that. What did you say?"

Doc was glad she had not heard him and answered, "Yes, I would like some water. My throat is dry."

When they sat back down, the pause continued while they were remembering where the conversation had paused.

Angel remembered and responded, "Paul, I don't think God cut you off. His love is enduring. If anything, your unsatisfied hurt motivated you to blame someone and you have just admitted your blame is aimed at God. That is not all that bad. God can handle our honest feelings even if they are unjustly aimed at Him. In reality a lot of what we suffer hear on earth is the product of sin that entered mankind's lives with Adam's choice to rebel against God. Our only hope to make sense of our hurt and the bitter consequence we experience and see all around us is to get closer to God, to gain a closer relationship with the One who is in control, the One who has the answers."

Angel paused, reached over for Paul's arm and said, "I'm sorry. I got preachy. I can do that without thinking."

Doc was thinking over her sermon to him. It would take him a little time to absorb it. He silently agreed that she knew a lot more than he did about God and His ways. He felt he wanted to spend more time with her because he liked her more and more and so he could learn more about the God he knew so little about.

Doc commented simply, "No need to be sorry. I think I need a sermon."

She took that as a pass to continue, "You get to know God better by reading frequently about Him in the Bible and talking with Him in prayer. It's important to go to a caring church where you will be encouraged in your relationship with God. Why don't you come with me to my church while you are here?"

"Alright, I can do that. Maybe it will help me."

Doc liked being with Angel. Maybe it was that she seemed to really care about him, that she was real with him, or had been through a tragedy in her own life and seemed to be getting a grasp on her thoughts about it. Maybe it was because she was substantially helping him, putting feet to her words. It might be all of that. He just knew that he liked being around her.

After they called it a night, Doc returned to his side of the duplex and went to bed. He spent about a half hour thinking over their conversation and talking with God in prayer. He prayed out loud, "God, I do not know you well, and honestly, I don't like you sometimes. If you are real, I need some help here. Please help me get over my hurt and bitterness over the loss of my family. I am thankful that I met Angel. Is she a real angel? Oh, please help the police find out the truth about that girl's murder. I know Jake is not such a good person compared to what you want, but neither am

I. But he is sort of like an orphan, and I know you like to protect orphans. So, please help Jake."

That felt pretty good. Doc turned on his side and fell asleep, not waking up until early the next morning.

*******

After a cup of coffee and a bagel, Doc walked into town and put in applications at a couple fast food restaurants and convenience stores. They took his applications and gave no indication as to whether they wanted to interview him or not. Angel had said he could put her phone number down since he did not have a phone. Many homeless people have cell phones since the government initiated a program that paid for a small amount of cell phone call time for the homeless person. Doc had one, but then lost it during his last binge.

Doc returned to his place. Angel had left a note on his door to say the detective would be at her place about five o'clock that evening. He felt a sudden reluctance. Doc walked to the refrigerator, pulled out a can of soda, and started working on getting up enough nerve to talk with the detective.

*******

Paul knocked on Angel's door just before five o'clock that evening. The detective was already there and stood up when Paul stepped in the door. Angel introduced them and she tried to encourage Paul. "Paul, this is Detective Richard Hawkins. He goes by 'Gunny.' He is a fine man, Paul, and he will treat you right." She looked at Gunny when she made the last comment as if reminding him to be decent with Doc.

"Gunny, this is Paul Walker, the man I told you might have some important information about that student's case." Gunny reached out his hand to Doc, who was slow to take it.

Doc immediately felt a sense of competition with Gunny when Angel called him a "fine man". He wanted her to think of him that way, but felt unworthy. He got a glance of Gunny's left hand and felt a little better when he saw a ring on his ring finger.

"I'll get us some coffee," Angel offered. She went into the adjacent kitchen that opened to the sitting area where Doc and Gunny sat down at the table across from each other.

Doc looked into Gunny's eyes. He saw a strong, confident man, yet there was a hint of compassion there that let Doc feel a sense of ease with him. "Paul," Gunny began, "Angel says you might have some information that would be helpful to me in my investigation of that student death case. Is that so? Can you tell me about it?"

A warning coursed through his mind and emotions, causing him to question whether he really wanted to open himself up. He looked at Angel in the kitchen and got the courage he needed. He began, "I'm called Doc on the street, but feel free to call me Paul. That is my given name, Paul Walker. I would be homeless except for the kindness of Angel in letting me stay in the duplex apartment next door."

"Oh, yes," Gunny said, "I've heard of you. The guys at the station are not so fond of you, but the street people think of you as a kind of doctor, a medical Robin Hood, helping the poor with their injuries and sicknesses. Don't worry. Angel says you are for real and that's good enough for me."

"I don't know about Robin Hood, but I do try to use my medical training and experience from being a Navy corpsman assigned to the Marines in Iraq, and some time as an EMT in Hartford. I hope I'm not breaking the law with that." He was suddenly self-conscious about the law in Gunny's presence.

Angel spoke up, "Gunny was with the Marines in Iraq."

Gunny grunted. "I'm a Marine. But I am not here for that, Paul, so don't worry," Gunny said reassuringly. "I would say as long as what you do is merely first aid, you don't have to worry. Besides, Marines always take care of their corpsmen."

"Well," Doc began slowly, "I . . . was sleeping in the parking lot behind the Borderline Restaurant. I slept in the corner of the parking lot. One night, I heard a commotion after I had settled in for the night. I peeked out and saw a man arguing with a woman. She was blond and wore a waitress uniform. He shoved her against the wall and yelled something to her. I couldn't make out all he said, but I did hear him say, 'I'll take care of it!' He turned around to leave and yelled back at her. I saw her wad up a paper and throw it down on the pavement. He got into his car parked on the street. It was an expensive, dark-colored car. He drove off in a hurry. She was left standing there, crying, and then stomped back into the restaurant. I noticed then that she was a young lady. I think she was the same girl you found dead the next morning."

"Had you seen the man before?" Gunny queried.

Doc seemed to be thinking and then responded, "Yes and no. I saw his car a couple other times, usually late at night. One time, out of curiosity, I walked down the sidewalk and passed by the car. I think it was a black Cadillac. Oh, and it had a college staff parking lot sticker on the bumper. One thing I know is that the man was not Jake."

"Are you sure the car you saw the man get into that night is the same one you walked by?"

"Um, probably, but I cannot say absolutely for sure. It looked the same."

"What else?" Gunny asked.

Paul continued, "Later, toward morning, I went over to see if that paper was still there." Paul fumbled in his back pocket and pulled out a plastic bag containing the wadded up e-mail. "I found it. I'm sorry. I picked it up and handled it while I read it. Angel let me know to be more careful with it in case it had prints." He handed the plastic bag to Gunny.

"Paul, why didn't you come forward with this before now?" queried Gunny.

Doc thought to himself, *Okay, here it comes. He won't believe me.* He responded, "Well, you see, I cannot believe that Jake killed that girl . . . and I'm afraid he's being railroaded into something he did not do. Oh, I think he stole from that girl after she was dead, but he didn't kill her."

Gunny was silent a moment. Then he looked Paul in the eyes and said, "I am inclined to agree with you about Jake, Paul, but I have not had anything to question his guilt. The evidence that points to him may be enough to convict him. This paper should be helpful. Unfortunately, the chain of evidence is not the best . . . but we can deal with that. Now, you still haven't answered why you waited until now to come forward."

Doc decided to state the truth from his perspective, "I'm a homeless man who has been in jail around here for public drunkenness. I didn't think anyone would believe me or be interested in what I had to say. I also know I wasn't so nice to some of the officers when they arrested me. I thought something else would come along to clear Jake. Now his case is speeding to trial and he could go to jail over something he did not do. So I had no choice."

"I hope we can get prints off this paper," Gunny thought aloud. He had read it as Paul talked. "It looks like someone wanted to get rid of that baby really bad. Anything else, Paul?"

"I think that's all. Anything else would just be hearsay from the street."

"Have you heard of a homeless man that goes by 'Chicago'?"

"Yeah, in fact he was put in jail for being drunk while I was there. He's probably still there."

"Thanks, Paul. That's helpful. All this is. I guess you aren't going anywhere, but I have to tell you not to leave town."

Gunny looked back and forth between Angel and Paul (Doc) and said, "Thank you both. We will see if this additional information will help Jake." Gunny left the two at the door.

Angel looked at Doc with concern. "Are you okay, Paul? You look a little pale."

"Yeah. It was not a real pleasant experience for me. It is not the detective. He's okay. Doing this just took a lot out of me. I'm glad it's done. I'll be okay."

Doc started to step over to his apartment's door when Angel took his hand leading him around to face her. She gave him a hug and said, "I am proud of you for taking this step. I pray it will help Jake."

Doc said, "Me, too. Thanks for encouraging me to do it, and for setting up this meeting. Now, we'll see what happens."

He was embarrassed by the hug but warmed by it at the same time. He felt good about her words. He stepped through his door. Sleep was sweet and deep that night.

# Chapter 18

*"I heard them arguing, and a sound like they were scuffling around. The scuffling sound lasted for quite a while. Finally, it got silent and I heard the car door close and it left."*

After finishing his coffee on Friday morning, Gunny turned in the e-mail in its plastic bag for fingerprint analysis. He knew he had Paul's (Doc's) fingerprints. He was not sure about Dr. Brantley's prints. The lab used a special procedure to get prints off paper, and that would take a while. He looked at his calendar and counted the days. It had been forty-five days since Jan had been killed. It was just under four weeks until Jake's trial started. Gunny winced. He hoped it would be enough time to get the loose ends cleared up.

He picked up the phone and called the sheriff's office in Blount-ville to verify that Chicago was still in jail. He drove the six miles to Blountville and the jail. Charles Smith, also known as Chicago, was brought into the interrogation room.

Gunny looked Chicago over and saw the typical picture of a homeless man who traveled from town to town and stayed as long as he could. Typically, a nomadic homeless person like Chicago would eventually get in trouble with the police, another homeless person, or a group he could not intimidate. He would move on to the next place and go through the same cycle.

It used to be easier for homeless people to go from town to town or state to state. But things had tightened up because of increased security after 9/11, and it was more difficult to get around without having to pay for a bus ticket.

Gunny asked the man, "Are you the man who goes by the street name, 'Chicago'?"

"Yeah. Why do you want me?"

"A student was killed near the overpass in Bristol a few weeks ago. I think you were sleeping there the night she was killed. You might know something that will help us find the killer."

Chicago slumped in the chair and put his hands behind his head, saying loudly, "I may or may not have slept there sometime, but I had nothing to do with that girl's death."

"I did not accuse you of doing anything other than being in the area. Were you?"

"I may or may not have been. What do you want to know?"

"Did you hear or see anything unusual around the time of the murder—around midnight or a little after?"

"Umm, I think I remember hearing a car come up under the bridge one night. I was trying to sleep under a tree with some bushes. I turned over and tried to go back to sleep. I heard them arguing, and a sound like they were scuffling around. The scuffling sound lasted for quite a while. Finally, it got silent and I heard a car door close, and it left."

"What did the car look like?"

"It was an expensive looking, dark-colored car, maybe black. I couldn't see it that well."

"Did you check on the girl?"

"I don't have good eyes. I saw something on the ground and started to get up and check it out, but then I heard someone else come by. I saw Jake come up to whatever was on the ground. I just watched while he messed with whatever it was. Then he went to the trash barrel and threw something in it. I decided I needed to leave the area, which I did."

"Anything unusual about the guy's voice?"

"I didn't notice. He seemed familiar in some way, but I couldn't tell for sure."

"If you remember anything else that might help, please ask for me."

"Yeah, sure. I hope you can get Jake out of jail before they kill him. He doesn't belong here. He's a little slow, if you know what I mean. They like to take it out on him. He may have taken some things that girl no longer needed, but he did not kill her."

Chicago returned to his cell and Gunny returned to his office.

*******

Back at the office, Gunny checked his e-mail and found one waiting for him from the New Orleans police. It notified him that Brad had arrived there on the bus, but they could not find out where he went. He seemed to have disappeared. No one knew who had picked him up at the station.

Gunny wondered about Brad. He did not think Brad was capable of setting up a disappearing act. However, he might have been the victim of someone who wanted to get rid of him. Could the professor do that?

Gunny called the Borderline Restaurant and spoke to the manager. He asked if Dr. Brantley ate at the restaurant regularly. The manager said the professor and his wife often ate there on Sunday nights at about 7:30 p.m. He said they were there three out of four weeks in a given month. Gunny thanked him and then called his wife.

Karen Hawkins, Gunny's wife, was a couple years younger than Gunny, She was five feet, seven inches tall and quite attractive with dark brown hair that matched her big eyes. Her one hundred thirty five pounds generally showed optimism even to a fault. She liked to tease and was fiercely loyal to her family and church.

Karen answered the phone having seen on the readout that it was Gunny calling, "Hey handsome, our daughter is in school and I thought you might want to drop by the house to see me."

Gunny was used to her stunts and ignored her, "Hi, honey. I have an offer for you. I want to observe somebody at the Borderline Restaurant this Sunday night. How about dinner together there about 7:30 p.m.?"

Karen was coy, "I don't know. I would be second to your work and would not have your full attention. What's in it for me?"

He had anticipated this. "You wouldn't have to cook that night . . . and the food is pretty good there. You would be seen in public with the best looking guy in Bristol. Besides, I could use your womanly perspective on this couple."

"You make a good argument. I'll put it on my calendar."

"Thanks, honey. I love you." She reciprocated and they hung up.

He heard someone down the hall ask for Gunny. He looked over the cubicle wall and saw Paul. Gunny called out, "Paul, you're brave to come by this place where all these officers have it in for you." He hoped Doc would take his words for the jest he intended. He liked Paul. There is a brotherhood of soldiers who have been to war. Gunny surmised that Paul must have had some bad luck in his life that had messed him up.

Doc looked at Gunny trying to figure out if he should be concerned or laugh. He finally chose to laugh, and Gunny laughed with him. They sat at Gunny's desk. Gunny asked "To what do I owe the pleasure of this visit?"

"I am worried about Jake," said Doc. "I just wondered if you had heard anything about when he might get out of jail."

"Nothing yet. I'm afraid the wheels of justice turn a lot more slowly than our fore-fathers thought they should. I'll give the DA a call and see what's up."

"Thanks, Gunny. Umm . . . Angel told me a little about your experience in Iraq. She said you had been treated for PTSD."

Gunny was taken back by the comment. He looked at Doc for a few moments and decided to answer him briefly, "She talks too much sometimes. Yes, I had a bad day in Iraq and I've had some trouble with letting it go."

Doc reciprocated, "I had a bad day several years ago too, only it was not in Iraq. It was in Hartford, Connecticut. I lost my wife and son in a bad accident in one day. I couldn't let it go, either. I think maybe I have some PTSD."

There was an awkward moment of silence.

"Maybe we could get together some time to talk about that," Doc offered.

Gunny had never had anyone ask him about this before. He took a sip of coffee and delayed his answer by offering Doc a cup of coffee.

Doc readily accepted. The street had taught him not to turn down something offered freely.

Finally, Gunny answered, "Paul, I'm not one to readily talk about these things. But I have been told that I need to talk about it. So, I think we could do that. I'll check my calendar and get back to you on when we could get together. It might be short notice."

Gunny was really thinking that if he put off setting a date that Doc might forget about it.

"That's fine," said Doc. If you don't want to do this, just let me know. Angel has been a big help, but I think your experience might be helpful also. I'll just wait to hear."

"You got it, Doc . . . I mean, Paul."

Gunny continued, "By the way, have you heard anything on the street about a drug dealer that goes by the name 'Ace'?"

"No, I'm not really into the drug culture in this area. Now I can tell you about alcohol, but not drugs," answered Doc.

Paul got up to leave and said, "I'll look forward to our getting together." He walked out and Gunny stared after him wondering what he had gotten himself into.

Gunny tried to call the DA. Beth, the DA's secretary, told him that John was out until the next morning, so Gunny left a message on John's phone saying that he had significant new information that might cast doubt on Jake's guilt. He thought he might get chewed out for messing up John's case, but the truth was the truth and John would just have to deal with it.

Gunny had done about all he could for now. He would have to wait for the fingerprint report, and for Sunday night to hopefully get the professor's fingerprints.

# Chapter 19

Doc was not getting anywhere with his job hunt. He had heard about a mattress business in Bristol owned by a Gideon. The Gideon ministry was a group of Christian businessmen who majored on getting Bibles, especially little New Testaments, into the hands of students, hospital patients, prisoners, and military personnel. Doc thought a Gideon might be more sympathetic to his needs. After seeing Gunny, he had gone by the mattress store, filled out an application, and left it with the owner's wife since the owner was making a delivery.

The next afternoon, Saturday, Doc was napping when Angel knocked on his door. He opened the door and she said she had a message for him: "Mark, the owner of that mattress store called and asked you to stop by Monday morning to talk with him. That could be good news!"

"Maybe so! You want to come in?"

"I'd like to, but I have to get prepared to teach my class of ladies at the shelter this evening. Are you doing okay on food?"

"So far," Doc said. "I've eaten at the shelter a few times, and I'm not a big breakfast eater. By the way, can you give me a ride to the shelter? I think I'll eat there tonight."

"Okay. I will be leaving about five."

While they traveled to the shelter, Doc told her about going by to see Gunny to find out if Jake had been released. He told her Gunny had not heard back yet from the DA, but that would hopefully not take long.

"Gunny asked if I'd heard of a drug dealer who goes by the name, 'Ace.' I said I didn't know him, but said I would see what I could find out about him."

"Be careful, Paul, those guys don't play around." Angel felt a sense of foreboding about Paul looking for a drug pusher.

"Oh, I can handle myself. That is something I learned from the Marines."

Doc and Angel parted when they parked at the shelter.

*******

Doc had supper and hung around the shelter with a cup of coffee while others finished and moved out of the dining area. Cookie came over and sat down with his cup of coffee. "What's up, Doc?"

"I have news. I talked with your friend, Gunny, and told him what I had seen." He did not tell Cookie about the e-mail.

"He's no friend of mine. I just know he's not bad as cops go."

"He's a pretty good guy. He's a Marine, ya know."

"No, I didn't know. That might make him a little better."

"He said he's looking for a drug dealer called Ace. You know, I don't do drugs so I don't know the pushers here. Do you know anything about Ace?"

"You better leave that to the police. Even if I knew him, I wouldn't tell you. He and his organization are dangerous. They can hurt you. Why do you need to know?"

"I want them to find out who really committed that murder, and Gunny seems to think he needs to talk with Ace. He has been unable to find him."

"There's a reason he can't find him—he doesn't want to be found. I heard from a customer of his that he was out of town for several weeks. When they indicted Jake for that girl's murder, he came back to town. It seems that he didn't want to lose his business. He works the college area especially. You remember that you did not hear this from me . . . and I don't know any more, so don't ask."

"Thanks, Cookie. You're not as bad as they say. Hey, I may get a job at that mattress store on State Street. I talk with the guy tomorrow morning."

"Good luck, my friend . . . and you leave that Ace alone," Cookie said as he got up to return to the kitchen. He looked back at Doc again and with a very serious look, said, "You will get hurt."

"I hear ya."

Neither of them noticed the slight turn of the head of the man sitting at the next table. He had listened to their conversation with great interest.

"Hey, what's that weird smell on you?" Cookie teased smelling what he thought might be cologne. I notice you've been combing your hair more, wearing better clothes that actually go together and smelling better lately. I bet you even brush your teeth. Anybody special you're doing that for?" Cookie knew Doc cared for Angel and he wanted to tease him a little.

"Drop dead, Cookie." Doc got up, took his cup to the kitchen window and left. He heard Cookie still laughing as he walked out the door and headed toward State Street.

*******

Doc walked across State Street onto Moore Street, and headed uphill toward the college. About a block before the college he noticed a dark, expensive car parked along the street. There was someone in the driver's seat. Doc walked by it, heading north. He wanted to turn around and look at the guy when he walked by, but did not dare to be that obvious.

As he walked, Doc thought about Cookie's teasing and it struck him that ever since he had begun living in the duplex, he had done better with his hygiene and keeping himself clean. He shaved every day and was dressing nicer. At the shelter's thrift store, Angel had picked up some name brand clothes in great shape for him. He would not be as invisible as he had been as a homeless man.

Doc turned onto a walkway that led up to the front entrance of a classroom building. Night classes were going on in them. He looked back but could only see the hedge between him and the car. He stepped into the door alcove which was just elevated enough for him to see what was happening on the road below.

After a half hour of watching with nothing happening, Doc observed a guy and girl separately approach the passenger side of the car, speak through the open window. The guy opened the passenger door and got in without closing the door. He got out of the car after a short time and he and the girl walked off. Doc wondered to himself, *was this Ace or a stoolie of his dealing drugs to college students?*.

Doc decided to walk down to the sidewalk and by the car to see if he could get a look at the driver. He stepped out, took the concrete walk down to the sidewalk along the street. He tried to act normal, whatever that was. Doc turned left on the sidewalk in the direction of the parked car. When he approached the car he tried to catch a quick look at the driver in the car, but it was too dark. He went on by the car and headed into town. Doc heard the car engine come to life when he was about one hundred feet past the car, He glanced backward and saw the car pulling away.

Doc got back to the shelter just in time to catch a ride home with Angel. He chose not to tell her about the results of his stakeout.

*******

Monday morning, Doc went to the mattress store and spoke with Mark, who offered him a part-time job helping with deliveries. Doc accepted and liberally thanked Mark. He would start two days later.

Doc walked the three blocks to the police station to see Gunny. It dawned on him that he was no longer anxious about entering that building. Gunny was not in and no one was sure when he would be back. They asked if he needed to leave a message but he said he preferred to talk personally with Gunny. He walked home.

*******

Doc looked up when he was approaching the duplex. Something was wrong. His door was open and Angel's door was slightly ajar. That was unusual. He moved inside carefully and observed that a couple chairs were turned on their sides, and a lamp had been knocked over. He found a note on the bathroom mirror, written with a Sharpie. The note said, "Back off or worse will happen. You know what I mean!"

Doc ran next door and found Angel lying in her bed. She was out. He soaked a washrag with cold water and patted her face with it as he spoke to her over and over trying to rouse her. She began to come around.

"Angel, what happened? Are you hurt?"

"I don't know," she said groggily, "but I have a terrific head-ache." She reached up and felt an egg-shaped knot on her head and saw a small pool of blood on her pillow. She lay still looking around the room with glassy eyes, awake, but not totally there.

"You lie still there," Doc said. "I'll get you some water." He went into the kitchen to get the water and saw her phone on the counter. He took out the business card Gunny had given him and called the number on it.

"Hi, Angel. What do you need?" Gunny answered,

"Gunny, this is Doc. I just got home and found my door and Angel's door open. Angel had been knocked out with a hit to the head. Someone left me a threatening note. I found Angel lying in bed, out cold. Can you come over?"

"Okay, Paul. Just calm down. Are they gone?"

"I think so, but I did not check everywhere yet."

"Alright, just stay put there with Angel and I will be there in about fifteen minutes."

Paul hung up and took a glass of water to Angel. She was more awake and even sitting up a little, holding her head.

"Gunny is coming."

"Good."

"What happened?"

"I heard someone banging around in your apartment. I went to see what was going on and found the door open, so I stepped in. They saw me, grabbed me, and then I felt a terrific pain in my head, and all went black."

"I am so sorry you got hurt when it was meant for me," said Paul. I'm afraid I'm at fault for this. I think I found Ace last night, and thought I had done a good job of not being obvious. Guess I did not do so well. There was a note on my bathroom mirror telling me to back off or they would do worse."

"I said to be careful or you would get hurt. I didn't know it would be me getting hurt! I think you had better leave the detective work up to Gunny."

Gunny arrived with another officer who began checking out both duplexes. Angel and Paul told him what had happened, and about Paul's reconnoiter the evening before. Gunny scolded Paul for doing what he had done with such dangerous people, yet he secretly respected his bravery and desire to help.

Gunny talked Angel into getting evaluated at the emergency room, since her knot was so large. Gunny wouldn't let Angel drive, and Paul did not have a current license, so he drove them all to the ER.

At the ER, Angel was thoroughly checked. The only problems were the nasty cut on her head and a bruise on her arm that probably occurred when she fell after the hit. She required five stitches. The nurse gave Angel a sheet that described what to look for in case of concussion. Gunny had left for a while but returned to get them back to the duplex.

That night Doc did not sleep well. He was angry at the aggressors and angry at himself for bringing harm to Angel.

*******

Gunny walked along Moore Street Monday night, but he did not see a black car or anyone sitting in one that might be selling drugs. He set up a more frequent patrol along Moore Street for a few days, but it seemed Ace had relocated his hookup site.

# Chapter 20

*"I had become angry with the truckers involved, with
the EMTs who didn't save them, and most of all, really
angry with God."*

Karen Hawkins, Gunny's wife, and Angel were friends from church
and talked on the phone a couple times each week. One conversation on Tuesday was about PTSD (posttraumatic stress disorder) and their concerns about how it affected Gunny and Paul.
Karen wanted to get together to talk about it with the men. Like
a counselor, Angel was not so sure about the idea thinking that
people with PTSD often do not want to talk about it. But her friendship with Karen and her belief that there is a spiritual aspect to
overcoming the life effects of PTSD resulted in her agreement to
pursue the idea.

Karen pulled up her calendar on the phone saying, "We can
have dinner at our house and then spend some time talking about
it. I will have to check with Gunny. When would you be available?"

Angel thought about her schedule and also about Paul. She
realized that he was available most evenings, so she gave Karen
a few choices and added, "Let me know when you settle on the
date with Gunny and I will talk with Paul."

Karen talked with Gunny who was reluctant to have the meeting. He felt his condition was private, and he and God and his
doctor needed to work on it. But as usual, Karen prevailed and he
reluctantly agreed. Gunny hoped to get called in that evening to
avoid the meeting. Karen set the date with Angel.

*******

Angel laid low as she recovered from the hit on her head. She did not show signs of a concussion, and was just very sore and felt drained of energy for a couple days. Doc checked in on her when he was not working his new part-time job.

One night, Angel invited Paul over for coffee and some warm, homemade blackberry pie—with a scoop of vanilla ice cream.

"Wow!" Paul exclaimed after taking a bite. "That is too good."

"I picked the blackberries myself. Blackberry pie was a family favorite when I was growing up. I am glad you like it, Paul."

"OK, this is where I ask you . . . what do you want?'"

"Well. There is something I want to ask you to do."

"For you, anything. You make the pie and I will do what you want."

"Wait until you hear what it is. You know about Gunny's PTSD and the situation that he thinks caused it, right?"

"Yeah, he shared it with me. He still has some trouble with it."

"Well, Karen has asked us to come to dinner with them tomorrow evening to talk with him about it. I've had some feelings and reactions from my husband's death that I think are a form of PTSD as well. We have talked about your sudden tragedy and how it left you with a form of PTSD. I think if we all get together and talk about it, we could help each other." Angel thought she heard a little groan from Paul.

Paul set his plate down on the lamp table beside his seat. He looked around like a bird looking for a way out of a cage. Without looking straight at Angel, Paul said, "Angel, I know you really care for Gunny and me, but I think you might be getting into something that should be left alone."

Angel expected this reaction. She knew by now how Paul reacted to situations where he might have to get into his real feelings and deep thoughts. She also realized that after Paul thought through and prayed about doing things he initially did not want to do, he came around later and saw the wisdom in participating, even if uncomfortable. She gave him space to process and sat silently for a couple minutes.

Paul picked up his plate and took a bite. Angel set hers down and said, "Paul, I have found that one of the best therapies for me is getting with others who have suffered similar things, who understand what I am going through. We are able to help each other. Because of the common experience, no one judges anyone else, typical—"

"—Yeah, I know that," Paul interrupted. "I can stand talking about my own situation with you, but I still don't know Gunny that well, and do not know his wife at all. Besides, he probably would prefer not getting into his own problems with us."

"That remains to be seen. He has agreed to the meeting even if he was reluctant. We will just get together and see where the conversation goes. Don't feel pressured to say any more than what you think you should say."

All Doc would say is that he would consider it.

They had prayed together at times for their own needs and the needs of others like Jake, other homeless people, and their church members. It was something Doc was very awkward with at first, but he had grown used to it and even liked it. It helped him get to know Angel better and he liked it when she prayed for him.

They bowed their heads and Paul prayed, "Heavenly Father, here we are again, Doc and Angel. You are our Father, since we have been adopted into your family. Jesus death on the cross paid for our adoption. You want relationship with us, and you made the way for that where there was no way. We want to please you, and you have said that it pleases you for us to come to you in prayer. So here we are."

Angel wiped tears from her eyes. She was moved at how the changes she was seeing in Paul's prayer life indicated he was growing in his spiritual understanding and walk. He was refocusing his life from his own wants to what God wants.

Paul continued, "Lord, I have a question and need your direction: Should we, no, should I meet with Gunny and his wife to talk about the loss of my family? I guess I am hanging out a fleece, like Gideon did. I don't always see your will so clearly. Could you make it clear as a billboard?" He had heard a man in his church pray for that and liked it. When he had asked about it, Angel said it came from one of the more conversational versions of the minor prophet, Habakkuk.

After a moment of silence, Angel picked up the prayer, praying, "Dear Lord, we want to help each other live our lives in a way that pleases you. If we can be helpful to each other by getting together with Gunny and Karen, please make it clear to us. If not, put a red flag in front of us. Thank you for caring enough to help us understand what is right to do. In Jesus's name we pray, amen." They said good night to each other and Doc returned to his side of the duplex. He thought to himself, *I wonder if that red flag is already waving to us since neither Gunny nor I really want to talk about these things.*

Doc got a half sandwich he had leftover and a glass of water for a snack before he got ready for bed. While sitting there Doc may have expected a bright light in the sky, a cryptic phone call, or a tangible sign, but instead something happened that was obviously from God.

"He thought, *Could God answer me immediately— I mean right now*? A feeling had overwhelmed Doc. It was two feelings, actually. One was a deep concern for Gunny, like he might have for a family member. It was quickly followed by a peace that washed away his fears . . . his reluctance. God had given him the answer."

The next morning Doc knocked on Angel's door about eight o'clock. He wanted to catch her before she might leave.

Angel opened the door after a few moments and just as Doc was getting ready to knock again. "Hi, Paul. What's going on?"

Doc gushed forward with words explaining his experience the night before. He finished by saying, "I guess I better meet with ya'll."

With tears still on her cheeks, Angel took Paul's hands in hers and agreed with him. "I believe you are right. Something like that has happened to me before. That is amazing! Praise God for His love for us to meet our needs so sensitively."

Doc was still standing at the doorway and Angel said, "Paul, I would invite you in, but I have a class to teach this morning and I need to go."

"Okay, I'm glad I caught you. Let me know when the time is to get together."

"Right. I'll call Karen today."

Paul turned back to his door and thought to himself when he sat down, *I think God's response affirmed for me that I have a relationship with Him that is real.*

Angel called Karen later in the day and set up for them to meet at Gunny's for dinner.

*******

Angel rang the doorbell at the Hawkins's house about six o'clock on Thursday evening. Karen opened the door and greeted Angel and Doc with her smile.

"Hi , Angel. Welcome to our home…should I call you Paul or Doc?"

Karen led them into the hallway and Doc answered, "Well, Angel likes to call me Paul, so you can do the same."

Karen motioned them to the living room, "Make yourselves comfortable. Gunny is late getting here, as usual. Would you like a glass of apple or orange juice?"

Angel answered first, "I'll take orange, please."

Doc answered, "I guess I'll have apple juice. Thanks."

Karen disappeared into the kitchen and reappeared a couple minutes later with the juices and one for herself. She sat down across from the sofa where Angel and Doc sat.

"Gunny is so busy with his work that he forgets what time it is sometimes," Karen said in trying to make an excuse for Gunny. In fact, Gunny always had work to do, but not that night. He stayed at it longer than usual, hoping for a crisis to come along that needed him, but none came. *I'm a wuss*, he finally told himself. *It's time for me to step up—for Karen's sake at least.* He stacked his folders, locked his drawer, and headed out the door.

Karen had prepared a sumptuous banquet of pork loin steaks covered with a peach sauce and a slice of peach on top of that. She served yams, marinated vegetables, and crescent rolls to fill out the menu. Gunny and Paul ate heartily, forgetting that a rich desert would surely follow such a meal. The dinner conversation was mostly about passing food around the table and about sports for Gunny and Doc. The two ladies talked about a lot that the men did not really hear.

After dinner, they all decided to retire to the closed-in back porch before serving desert. There was a large low coffee table surrounded by four chairs, two wingback chairs across from each other, and two overstuffed chairs across from each other. The ladies took the wingbacks and the men plopped down into the overstuffed chairs.

Neither man was willing to start the conversation, choosing instead to brag about how good the food was and discuss food in general. They both knocked military food.

Next they talked about how the Tennessee Titans had missed the playoffs and what chances the Carolina Panthers had of advancing. The ladies chatted and did not enter into the football conversation.

After ten minutes or so, true to her calling, Angel dove into the serious stuff. "Gunny, you had a very traumatic situation in Iraq that left you with symptoms the VA diagnosed as PTSD. Of course, Karen is affected by Gunny's life. Paul had a very tragic, sudden loss in Hartford, Connecticut, that left him with symptoms I think are consistent with PTSD. I had a traumatic loss when my husband died, and it left me with symptoms I would call PTSD related. Karen and I felt that it might be helpful if we could all get together to talk about it, and hopefully, encourage one another." She paused to let that sink in to their thinking.

Gunny and Doc looked like deer caught in headlights. They were both thinking they liked the football conversation a lot better, and how they could skip this part. Neither vocalized his thoughts.

Angel continued, "So, I will start by sharing what has happened lately that shows I still need to deal with my problem, and what I am doing about it."

Angel glanced around at the others, noting the men were looking out the windows, and Karen was sitting on the edge of her seat, focused on Angel. She knew this would be hard for the men, and felt that if she shared first, it might help open them up a little.

Angel started a brief account of her story. "After my husband's death in Iraq, I suffered a lot from depression. Caleb (her husband) was life to me, and I did the usual: first denial, then anger at the Iraqis who killed him, anger at the military, and finally, anger toward God. I moved on in time to bargain with God to set this right, or to at least take away my ever-present hurt. I am not sure when I fell into depression. It consumed me. I took meds for it, and eventually, I began to accept my loss and to want life to move on. I felt the meds were as much a problem as the depression I had experienced. I was growing in my faith because of my participation in church, especially in a women's Bible study group. I talked with my doctor, and he helped me step down the depression meds. It took a while, but I finally quit taking them altogether." She sighed and paused. The room was silent, except for a cough from Doc.

"Does that mean you don't suffer any depression anymore?" Karen asked.

Angel knew that Karen knew better than that because she had been a go-to person for Angel when she was depressed. Karen always seemed to be up, and in a loving way, helped Angel to start looking up again, mostly by just listening to her and praying for her over the phone.

"I ignored my doctor one time and stopped all the meds too fast," Angel continued. It threw me for a loop. I ended up in the ER. My doctor knew what had happened and convinced me to come off the meds at a slower pace. I did, and it worked. I still have occasional low times, but not what I would call real depression. I have friends like Karen I can talk to at those times, and know they care and will pray for me. Sometimes they intervene by picking me up and going somewhere with me to help me get my outlook back where it needs to be. Sometimes I feel like God does that, too, especially with some of the psalms."

Angel felt that was deep enough for this time and stopped her story there. She looked at Gunny and then Paul, hoping to hand one of them the "baton." They only glanced at her, preferring the view out the windows. "How about you, Gunny?" she said.

"Isn't it time for that coffee and cake?" he said, squirming in his chair.

"Not yet, Gunny," Karen chimed in. "We'll take a break after you share. Tell them what happened recently."

"Oh . . . yeah," Gunny sighed. "I don't know if they really want to know what happens privately here." He looked out the window again and realized that to say nothing would cost him later with Karen. He reluctantly began, "A few days ago I had a dream—more like a nightmare. I was back in Iraq at the time of the action . . ." He paused a moment and then continued. "Let's just say it was a bad time. We suffered losses. Actually, I don't remember a lot about it. I was wounded. I've had trouble getting over it, and I have bad dreams related to it. I am generally better thanks to some help from the VA. But it bothers Karen when I have the dreams."

"Bothers is right! I get scared sometimes," Karen interjected, looking at Angel as she spoke. "I know Gunny would not scare me on purpose, but when he has nightmares like that, he might not realize what he is doing. He said he would go back to the VA for help again. I think he should have stayed with his medication."

Gunny looked down at the laminate floor, his shoulders slumped. He wanted to be anywhere but sitting where he was at the moment. Everyone else remained quiet for what seemed like hours, though it was only a little over a minute. He had said all he intended to say.

However, he felt he needed to defend himself, so he added, "I've got an appointment with the doc at the VA in Johnson City to see if I can go back on my medication. Paul loaned me a book that he says Angel loaned him, and it has been helpful in looking at life and God differently. Maybe it will help."

After silence for another few moments, Karen sniffled and stood up to go to the kitchen. Before she got to the kitchen she came back, sat in the overstuffed chair with Gunny, put her arms around him, and kissed him on the lips. After a few moments, she tried to rise, but it was harder to get out of the chair than it was to get into it. Gunny gave her a gentle push and Karen went to the kitchen for coffee and pineapple upside-down cake.

Gunny blushed. He cleared his throat and started to speak, but his thoughts would not come together. He watched Karen all the way into the kitchen. Angel and Doc glanced at each other. Doc felt flush and looked out the window again.

"It's a good time for coffee and cake," said Angel.

Paul was happy to get up and go to the kitchen for dessert. He hoped something would happen so he would not have to share. It did not happen. They moved back to the porch and sat down with their desserts. A few snowflakes fell outside and the conversation turned to the weather. After the men enjoyed a second helping of pineapple upside-down cake, Angel called them back to the serious stuff.

"Well, I guess its Paul's turn," she said, looking right at him. She thought she saw panic in his eyes.

He swallowed hard and opened his mouth. It shut again and he cleared his throat before speaking. "Okay, I think I can do this. I guess you all know my story, except Karen." Doc looked at Karen and her eager attention encouraged him. "I lost my wife and son five years ago in a terrible auto accident on an interstate in Hartford, Connecticut. I was supposed to pick up my son at school, but I worked over because we had a lot of accidents to handle. My wife Angela...." He stopped, looked down at the floor, and reached up to his face to wipe a tear away. Some seconds later he began again. "My wife picked up my son, Stephen. Like you said, Gunny, it was bad. By the time I arrived at the scene they were already gone. I didn't get a chance to say good-bye." He could not hold back his tears, though at first he tried.

Karen took a cube-shaped box of tissues to him. Doc pulled one out of the box and wiped his cheeks and eyes. He looked at Karen and Gunny and said, "Sorry, I did not want to do this." There was silence for a couple of minutes while Doc settled down.

"As you can see," He continued, "I'm not doing very well at getting over it. I don't think I ever will. The first several days, I could not believe they were really gone. When my boss called for me to come back to work, I got angry with him. Like Angel, I was really angry and eventually turned my anger on God. I kept asking, 'Why would God allow innocent people so special to me to die so tragically before their time?' "

Doc looked right at Angel when he asked that question. She saw anger in his eyes. She met his eyes with compassion and allowed him time to settle down. His eyes began to soften.

"Nobody helped me. I don't blame them. If they had tried, I would have resisted. I just wanted to be left alone with my grief. My work buddies took me to bars after work. That's when I found the hurt inside me could be relieved by the bottle. I lost our house because I could not make the payments. Then my boss called me in and said they could no longer tolerate my absences and 'sloppy' work. He let me go. I became more depressed than angry. I got sick and felt life was hardly worth living. It was on the street that I found others who had suffered major losses, too. The street people seemed to accept my grief and pain. Like me, they were trying to bury something in the bottle or with a drug. Then I met Angel. She was different. Maybe it was . . . I just felt she genuinely cared. She was not judgmental of me. She seemed so confident I could get better. She did not quit when I rebuffed her—and help she did. I am cleaned up, physically. I've been dry for over a month and I am getting back my spiritual life again. That book, *The Key to Triumphant Living,* has been very helpful, and the Bible is on my reading list again."

After a long pause, Angel said, "I think you are doing great. By the way, I don't think any of us will forget, or even want to forget. I know that I don't want to forget Caleb, but I do not want to be so controlled or obsessed with my good and bad memories that I can't live productively in the life God has given me to live. I am grateful for doctors and medicines that help with that. I am also grateful for skilled counselors that help me. And I am very grateful to God who has good in mind for me and has empowered me to heal."

Angel paused before saying, "Uh-oh, I've gotten on my soap box again. Sorry about that! I love you all and want to see us all do better."

Karen went to get coffee and poured the rest into Paul and Gunny's mugs. When she returned, it was to a long, awkward period of silence. Karen thought it was probably best to invite Angel to clean up things in the kitchen with her, so she suggested that. The ladies got up and went to the kitchen.

Gunny and Doc were glad it was over.

Paul cleared his throat and said to Gunny, "You OK?"

"Yeah, how about you?"

"Yeah."

They both relaxed enough to slump down in their chairs, and began to talk about sports and food again. When the kitchen was done and the chitchat was over, Angel and Doc thanked Karen for fixing the delicious meal, and left for home.

There was no conversation in the car on the way back to the duplex. Doc was talked out. Angel worried that she had said too much. When they got back, Angel handed Doc a wrapped up slice of pie Karen had sent for him. Doc wished Angel goodnight, and she smiled in response before they entered their respective sides of the duplex. Once inside, neither went to sleep right away.

Karen picked up a book she had been reading and got into it. Her thoughts occasionally intruded into the book's story with the question, *did we do good or not tonight?*

Gunny watched a TV show. He had been stirred enough that he did not fall asleep in the chair as usual, but only after going to bed and lying there a half hour trying to get his mind to settle down did sleep come.

Minds and memories had been deeply stirred. All slept fitfully with bothersome dreams or thoughts that interfered with sound sleep.

# Chapter 21

*"Oh, crap! I thought this was a slam dunk. I don't like it,
but I guess I am glad we have some time to clear these
things up. Get busy and keep me informed."*


When Gunny came to his office on Friday morning, he reviewed in his mind the new information he had gathered the last few days. He wanted to be ready when John called.

Gunny went back over what he did have: Doc had seen or heard an argument between a man and a woman (Janice) behind the Borderline Restaurant. Doc had given Gunny a piece of paper Doc said the guy had handed to Janice. He also said that Janice had read what was on the paper, had wadded it up and had thrown it down. The paper e-mail message was about a place to get an abortion. The man might have thought he was the father, but clearly did not want that role. Doc thought the man left in a dark colored car. The professor has a dark colored car and had met Janice there before. The e-mail was being processed for fingerprints and might reveal who had argued with Janice that night.

Gunny suspected the professor was having an affair with the girl, and it seemed likely he was the one who pushed her toward an abortion. He clearly had the most to lose. Brad, who was now missing, had seen a man pick up Jan as she walked back to her apartment after work the night of the murder. The timing was shortly before the time of death determined by the coroner.

Brad knew about Janice's drug use and her source of drugs. If the professor saw Brad when he picked up Janice, Brad was in double jeopardy. In any case, Brad went to New Orleans on a bus using a ticket someone else bought for him, and now he was missing. Without Brad's personal testimony, his account would be treated as hearsay. But it could cause doubt with a jury, and that was just what defense attorneys looked for, doubt in a jury.

The drug dealer might want to be invisible in the investigation, but why would he have wanted Janice to have an abortion? He remembered that Doc had said the drug dealer also drove a dark car. He thought about it for a moment and then felt that the professor was clearly the most likely suspect, after Jake.

Gunny had an idea that was a long shot, but might point to which of the dark cars was at the scene. There had been a little rain and not much snow in the past few days. Mud puddles often formed on the road under the overpass. There might be a tire tread still there. He wished he had thought of this earlier. Then a discouraging thought occurred to him, that there might be a myriad of tire tracks there. In any case, he needed to identify the professor's tires, and then see if a tread at the scene of the murder matched.

The phone rang, and as Gunny expected, it was John. John's voice was so loud, Gunny had to hold the phone away from his ear. John spouted his rage: "I told you not to mess my case up, but it seems you are trying to cause me trouble! What's your problem, Gunny? Haven't you got some unsolved cases to work on?"

Gunny moved the phone closer to his ear and responded, "How would you look if you put a homeless man on trial, only for the defense attorney to reveal another person with a better motive and opportunity to murder the girl, and then explain away the evidence against Jake?"

"Why would you say that?"

"There is possible testimony that the victim was having an affair with one of the college professors, and that he was seen picking her up the night of the murder not long before the time of her death. The problem is that the person who saw this, Brad Jones, is now missing, and I got this information from a third party, his friend. It seems Brad got a one-way ticket to New Orleans, and the police there have not been able to find him yet."

"Oh, crap! I thought this was a slam dunk. I don't like it, but I guess I am glad we have some time to clear these things up. Get busy and keep me informed of what you find. I want these loose ends resolved before trial starts." Then the phone clicked off.

Gunny was glad John had finally listened to him, but did not feel too good about John's continued prosecution of Jake, or the tight time window to clear up the loose ends.

*******

Later that day, Gunny drove to the Covenant College campus and found the professor's car. He checked and they were all Michelin tires with the same tread. He took a picture of the tread and noted the information on the tire. Then he called Danny Harris, the patrolman who had helped him at the scene of the murder.

"Danny, this is Gunny."

"Hey, Gunny, what's up?"

"When you processed the crime scene for Jan Meredith's case, were there any fresh tire tracks?"

"I don't remember seeing any, Gunny, but I'll check with those who processed the scene to see what they found."

"Right. It's a long shot, but if I give you a picture of the tread of a tire from a vehicle owned by a potential suspect, could you check what they found to see if it matches any of them?"

"I guess so, but it's been a while, and I thought the DA had the perpetrator already. Are you sure about this? It'll take some time."

"I know it's a hassle, Danny. I'm tying up loose ends. It might save putting an innocent man away for life, or even help us find the true perp."

"OK, you got it. I'll get back to you. Leave a fax of the tread on top of your desk. I'll drop by and get it."

Gunny drove back by the office, moved the picture of the tread to his computer, and printed a copy to leave on his desk.

*******

Gunny heard the major's voice in the room. His office was really a cubicle. Cubicles had been set up in a large room so the detectives would have at least a semblance of privacy. The major's voice carried as he spoke to a couple other detectives at their cubicles. The major was Gunny's boss and head of the detective group.

When the major reached Gunny's cubicle, he said, "Hey, Gunny. I'm glad you are here. I need to chat with you."

Gunny thought to himself, *Uh-oh. A chat means I've done something he doesn't like.*

It was no surprise when the major continued, "I got a call from the DA. He said you are digging into things that are messing up his case on this student's murder. Said he has the perp and it is a strong case. So, what are you doing that has gotten under his skin?"

"Major, he does have evidence that points to a homeless man who was at the murder scene and who has motive, but I think the motive is weak. I am just following up on some loose ends that could be trouble for him if not resolved before the trial begins. I am trying to clean up those loose ends. The trouble is that the more I work on them, the more facts show up that might lead a jury to have doubts about the man who John thinks did it."

"Yeah, well, be sure it's worth it. We need good relations with the DA. Keep me in the loop. Give me a report each week on what you are doing on the case. Don't keep chasing loose ends if they are not significant to the case."

"You got it, Major."

The major walk out of the room and Gunny felt the DA had pulled a cheap trick on him. He knew that happened sometimes—it came with the job. He also knew what he was doing could end up keeping an innocent man from going to prison. He picked up his things and headed home. His thoughts went to the prints from the e-mail that he hoped would come through soon. Then he thought about Paul and said a little prayer for him to stay sober in case he had to testify at the trial.

# Chapter 22

*One thing he knew for sure was that he would fight with all his ability to resist anything close to a relapse. Still, the past nagged at him, and all his ability was not always enough.*

Doc felt good about working again, but there was a level of anxiety beneath the surface he was not sure about. He thought it might relate to going back to work after not working for so long. It might be he had become used to independence, so working for someone else and coming under their authority required an adjustment. It might be due to his concern about Angel and wanting to be there to check on her and encourage her. He definitely was concerned about Jake's welfare, and the delay in getting him out of jail. It also might be all of these thoughts combined.

One thing he knew for sure was that he would fight with all his ability to resist anything close to a relapse. Still, the past nagged at him, and all his ability was not always enough.

Friday after work, Doc knocked on Angel's door. When she opened it she invited him in. Angel said she was over the bump on her head and was getting back into her routine. She asked, "Do you know if Jake has been released from jail?"

Doc shook his head back and forth. "The owner of the store gave me a prepaid phone so he could call me if there was a special delivery, or he needed me. I called Gunny and it seems the DA does not think there is enough evidence pointing to anyone else to justify backing off the case against Jake. Gunny is working on it, but it takes time."

"Well, we just need to pray more about that," Angel suggested.

Doc looked up at Angel and thought silently, *she is a lot more religious than I am, thinking to pray for Jake. I am not doing enough of that.* "That's right, he said. "I need to pray for Jake. I have prayed for you, but forgot to pray for him."

"I pray for you, Paul. I know you have a lot more on your mind— a lot more to give you stress than you have had in a long time. I am praying that God will keep you strong."

"I'm glad you are praying. Sometimes the person with the problem does not recognize what's happening until it's too late and needs others to pray for him."

Doc leaned toward Angel who was sitting in a chair across from him, and said with feeling, "Angel, you are making a real difference in my life. No one has touched me like you have, not since…," he paused and wiped a tear from his left eye, "… since Angela." He hung his head and continued, "I'm sorry. I'm just moved by how you care about someone like me. If I ever believe again that God does love me, it will be because of you."

Angel got up and moved to Paul, taking a seat beside him. She put her hand on his and said, "Paul, you are loved by God. He has never quit loving you. You have just not always seen it. You are worth caring about, and if I can be used by God to touch your life and help you know God's love again, then I am the blessed one."

She squeezed his hand and got up, saying, "How about a cup of decaf?"

Angel had counseled on a volunteer basis long enough to know that these special moments needed to be cherished for what they were, and she needed to be sure it did not move into an inappropriate emotional expression.

They drank their coffee together in silence for a few minutes. Then Angel allowed Doc to give her a loose hug before leaving for his side of the duplex.

Once back in his home, Doc thought about his mixed feelings for Angel. He felt a kind of attraction that was more than physical, but went with the physical. He wanted more of her, and more time with her. He wanted to know her more deeply. At the same time, her sense of loving devotion to God, care for others, and sense of peace and hope appealed to him. He loved her quiet nature that allowed her to accept bad news without getting upset or angry. All of this led him to feelings of reverence toward her that made him ashamed when he began thinking of a sexual relationship with her, and that he had never felt that kind of reverence toward Angela.

********

Gunny had still not received a report on the e-mail fingerprints or tire tracks. When he headed home for the weekend, he felt a sense of anxiety over his inability to make things move faster, and from the seeming lack of progress. His thoughts transitioned to the anticipation of dinner with his "girlfriend", Karen at the Borderline. His thought, *now that's the way to work, a beautiful woman and good food.*

Gunny arrived home and found Karen already dressed for a date. He freshened up and put on a better shirt before they drove to State Street and the Borderline Restaurant. Gunny noted that Karen garnered a few looks when they entered the Borderline Café. A short time after the hostess seated them, in walked Dr. Brantley and a woman wearing too much makeup. She did not appear to be a student, so Gunny assumed she was Mrs. Brantley. The large stones in the two rings on her fingers removed any doubt. Mrs. Brantley showed some extra weight, and her face indicated that unhappiness was a frequent acquaintance in her life.

Gunny's ribeye was prepared just the way he liked it: medium rare and tender. Though he usually ate fast, he took his time eating it. He ate so slowly, Karen noticed and commented. He whispered that he needed to outwait the couple at the table two tables to her left, but warned her not to look.

She glanced anyway and commented that they looked like a nice couple. He smiled at her southern manners.

Gunny ordered dessert, causing Karen to comment again, as he normally did not get dessert. He said again he was trying to out-wait the couple. This was a challenge, as it seemed the professor ate European style, making the meal an all evening experience.

After a third glass of wine, the professor finally paid his bill and got up to leave. When they stepped out the front door, Gunny jumped up and beat the busman to the table. He put on gloves and picked up the water glass. He showed the stunned busman his badge and said he needed to take the glass. Though surprised, the busman simply said, "It's not my glass. Do what you want." Gunny placed the glass in a plastic bag and promptly sealed it.

"Thanks," Gunny said as he walked out of the restaurant. Gunny and Karen headed home.

*******

On Monday morning, Gunny turned in the glass for fingerprints with instructions to send it to the TBI for DNA testing after they were finished. Later that morning, he followed up with Danny Harris about the tire treads, but Danny had no results thanks to a busy weekend with several traffic accidents.

Then Gunny called the tech in the lab about the prints on the e-mail. The lab tech reported nothing yet. She claimed, "We have a backlog built up and paper prints are a special procedure. The way that paper was so wrinkled, we might have trouble getting anything anyway."

Gunny thanked her for their hard work and requested again that she let him know as soon as they got it done.

He thought there might be something else the defense attorney, Kim, mentioned in their meeting at the Sweet Tooth. He took out his notes and perused them. There it was. Jake had taken a throwaway phone, but ended up throwing it away because nobody would buy it. "Why would a college girl have a throwaway phone?" he mumbled to himself. "And why would a college girl not have a smart phone?" He thought on that question and finally concluded that she had used the throwaway to contact the professor. What about the smart phone? Then it came to him. Jake might have found a smart phone too, but had not admitted to it because he sold it.

*******

Gunny headed for the jail in Blountville feeling that he needed to get something done. He felt a little anxiety that was familiar to him from just before going on an op in Iraq. He thought it might be he had enjoyed too much coffee lately. He finally had to admit to himself that he was concerned about missing the boat on proving Jake had not committed murder.

Jake sat down across from Gunny in the interrogation room and just stared at the tabletop. He still had a bandage on his left arm, but seemed to have recovered a bit from the abuse he had suffered from the other prisoners.

"Jake, are you doing better?" Gunny began.

"Yeah, but I'm afraid they'll kill me next time."

"Well, we are trying to prevent a next time," Gunny assured him. "But I need your help to do that. You did not mention the throwaway phone you threw away. Why not?"

"I forgot about it."

"Are you sure you threw it away. "

"Yeah, I threw it away. I threw it away because nobody would buy it. One guy said it did not have enough time left on it."

"Where did you throw it away?"

Jake was growing anxious about this line of questions. He stood up. Gunny told him firmly, "Sit down, Jake." Then he remembered his training to ease up on people who are paranoid and very anxious. Gunny looked at Jake, sighed and spoke more gently, "Jake, I'm trying to help you and I need to tell me these things to help you. Come on and sit down so we can finish this up. You would like that, wouldn't you?"

Jake seemed to be considering what Gunny had said and then settled down, sitting back in his chair.

Gunny said gently again, "Where did you throw the phone away?"

Jake responded, "I was in the library, and I threw it in a trashcan there."

"Okay, did you see anything on the phone—any names or conversations?"

"No, I didn't. I really don't know how to operate those things. But the guy that looked at the phone said it looked like it was for her and her boyfriend, a guy named Tom . . . or Tony maybe."

Gunny took out his notebook and made an entry.

"Jake, I cannot imagine a college kid today who doesn't have one of those special phones that take pictures and get e-mails—a smart phone. Are you sure that girl didn't have a cell phone like that—a second phone?"

"Umm . . . now that I think about it, there might have been another phone. I can't remember for sure."

"Come on, Jake, help me out. You are up for murder and you need to help yourself here. I think there was a smart phone and you sold it . . . didn't you?"

"Yeah, I didn't say anything about it cause I was afraid you-all wouldn't like that I sold it."

"Think back. Who did you sell it to?"

"I'm not sure. I tried to sell it to a guy that works at a restaurant downtown. There was a guy with him who bought it. He wouldn't pay what I wanted, but he paid ten dollars for it."

"Was his name Jeff?"

"He didn't give me a name, but I think the other guy might have called him Joe or maybe Jeff. It think that's it."

"Okay, Jake. You take care and you let me know if there is anything else you remember that you have not already told me. I can't help you if you hide stuff from me."

"Okay, I'll try."

* * * * * * *

Gunny headed for the car, checked his notebook for Jeff's phone number and called him before starting back to the office.

"Yea, who's this?" Jeff answered.

"Hi, Jeff. This is detective Hawkins. Where are you?"

"Umm, I'm at a friend's house. Why?"

Gunny knew that probably meant he was doing drugs with a friend, or at a girl's house. "I want to meet with you, now. Where can I meet with you?"

"I can be at Cumberland Park in ten minutes. What's this about?"

"That's good, but make it twenty and meet me by the bandstand. I tell you more there."

Gunny did not like giving him twenty minutes, but he was too far away. He imagined the phone Jeff used to answer the call was Jan's phone. He did not want to give Jeff too much time to think and possibly hide the phone before the meeting. He stepped on the gas to get there as soon as he could.

Jeff walked up to the bandstand at Cumberland Park just as Gunny pulled up to park on the street. He walked briskly to meet Jeff.

"Hey, Jeff. Thanks for meeting me on short notice. Have you heard from Brad?"

"No. It's like he just disappeared and has forgotten all about us."

"I haven't heard from him, either. Give me your cell phone for a minute."

"What? My cell phone? Why do you need it?" He suddenly grew jittery.

"I need to look at something. You got your phone from a homeless guy, right—for ten dollars?"

Jeff still did not reach to get his phone. He looked around as if he had somewhere else to go. Gunny turned up the heat and spoke firmly, "Get your phone out now, or I will search you and arrest you for interfering in an investigation."

"Okay, okay," he spouted as he reached into his rear pocket and pulled out an iPhone. He reluctantly handed it to Gunny and blurted an excuse for purchasing it: "I thought it would help that guy out—get him some money."

"How generous of you! Ten dollars for a two hundred-dollar phone is real generous." Gunny looked through the phone's call and text history. Jeff had not even cleared it. He saw a number of Jan's calls on it. "Sorry, guy, but this used to belong to the girl who was killed, so it is now evidence and I am taking it with me."

"Will I get it back?"

"Maybe, when this is all over. You may want a more up-to-date phone instead by then, but it will cost you more than ten dollars. Got to go." With that, Gunny turned and headed back to the office to research the phone.

Jeff moved off with his head down; not because he was ashamed, but because he was out a smart phone.

*******

Gunny returned to his office and began checking the phone. The phone contacts included her mother's number, Megan's number, the restaurant, and several others he did not recognize. The first number was identified only as "A." He remembered that the e-mail had also been addressed to "A." He called it and the number was no longer in service.

He continued looking. One listing was identified with only a smiley face, not a name. He assumed that would be the professor. He probably told her not to put him on her personal phone when he gave her the throwaway, but she decided to put it in her contacts and disguise it. The number was not the professor's home or work number, as Gunny had noted these in his notebook. He thought it was probably to another throwaway. He tried the number and was met by a recorded message: *This number is no longer in service.*

The call history had not been cleared in months. Jan had called the listing for A about once a month. He noted that she had called A in the early afternoon the day she died. She had also made a call to the smiley face number that same afternoon.

Gunny checked the Safari searches. There were searches for "pregnancy signs," "effects of meth on pregnancies," "baby names," and "abortion." *This girl considered abortion, but she wanted this baby*, Gunny thought to himself. Other searches were clearly related to schoolwork, and that was it.

He checked pictures. Jan had some silly pictures with friends, and a couple selfies she sent to someone in Richmond, Virginia. It was probably a friend—not much to help there. She had nothing in the Notes app to help him. She was too busy with school, work, drugging, and an illicit love affair to use her phone much. Too many people had handled the phone to get prints, so they would not tell him anything anyway. He put the phone back into an evidence bag and sent it to the TBI to check for any other information like erased messages that they might be able to pull off the phone. Bristol did not have that capability, so the TBI took care of that function.

It was getting dark and Gunny was packing up to head home when a call came in from Danny Harris. "Hey boss, we checked the area over very carefully, and found no matches for the treads you gave us. There were three tread prints not too far from where we found the girl that were clear enough to get a picture. I'll e-mail them to you."

"Thanks, Danny. Good job. I appreciate your work on this. It does not nail the guy, but those other prints might be helpful later. Thanks again."

Gunny felt that he had at least accomplished something to move the case forward. His thoughts shifted to his family and the pork tenderloin his wife was fixing for supper. He loved her cooking, something she had learned from her Mom. With that thought he headed home.

# Chapter 23

Several people took a keen interest in the headline of the Tuesday *Bristol Herald Courier*: "Two Weeks until Start of Homeless Man's Trial." It gave a brief overview of Janice Meredith's death and the case against Jake. The judge had put the case on his docket in February. There was a quote from the DA, John Erickson, who would be prosecuting the case himself. He was optimistic he would convict Jake based on the strong evidence.

Gunny read it with a renewed sense of urgency. The headline reminded Kim that she needed to spend more time on prep for the case. She wondered if Gunny was making any progress in finding the real perpetrator. The professor read it feeling it could not start soon enough. Jan's mother read it with tears. She fought a battle between Biblical teaching on forgiveness and a desire to see the man they thought killed her little girl get death. John read it with satisfaction that the reporter got his quotes right. Cookie and the other men at the shelter read it with regret that Jake was in jeopardy of being convicted and sent away for a long time for something they believed he had not done. Angel thought of Gunny, Paul and Jake. She prayed silently for God to help them. Many read it thinking it was probably just an exercise in justice, and the homeless man would get what he deserved. The mayors of both cities wondered how they could cut back on the homeless population in their cities.

Jake had been returned to a cell with other prisoners. The guard had given the others a stern warning to leave him alone. Still, Jake was more paranoid than ever. Life was out of his control and he felt threatened and extremely anxious. His feelings did not help him.

Most prisoners tried to leave him alone, but some with less self-control did get a lick in on Jake at times. Jake would scream for the jailer, but by the time he got there, all the other prisoners looked as if nothing had happened. Jake feared they would kill him. The jailer hoped the trial would come soon so Jake would be at the trial and not a problem in his jail. However, the jailer was not sure Jake was in any shape to behave at the trial, so he might not be allowed to sit in on it.

*******

Gunny walked to his desk with his morning cup of java. His phone was already ringing. He picked it up just in time, answering, "Gunny here."

"Good morning, Gunny." It was Kim. "I was thinking about a cup of coffee and a sweet roll at the Sweet Tooth about three this afternoon. If you're there, I might sit with you."

Gunny knew she would seek an informal update on the information she had shared with him. Knowing he had to be very careful with any conversations with the public defender (PD), he still wanted to help Jake. So he responded, "I might see you there. I like a cup about that time of day. But you know we can't talk about any active cases."

"I know. It's just two high school friends having coffee at the same table if we happen to be there at the same time. You know, Jake is having a bad time in jail with the other prisoners. I've asked for a separate cell for him."

"I've heard. That's not likely to happen. The jail is overcrowded as it is. The jailers are trying to stop the abuse."

"Good luck with that. See you there." She ended the call.

Two hours later, Gunny walked into the Sweet Toothe Bakery. He looked around and barely saw Kim at a table on the balcony.

Gunny climbed the stairs and sat down at Kim's table in the loft. They did not want to be easily seen. She had his coffee ready and was drinking a chai tea herself.

He told Kim about Chicago, "Your lead about Chicago has paid off, but it hasn't yet been enough to get Jake off the hook."

"Couldn't he verify that Jake didn't kill her?" She queried.

"Not exactly. It casts some doubt, but it wasn't enough." Gunny explained.

Gunny added, "There's something else I shouldn't tell you about. The DA should notify you, so don't let on that you know about it. We found a second phone, a smart phone. So far it has provided no information that would help Jake either. We are checking for any information from deleted messages."

Kim was shaking her head and spoke firmly, "Well I hope you find something helpful or an innocent man is going to be maimed for life and might even lose his life."

Kim realized she was speaking out of her frustration and Gunny was doing what he could. It was even risky for him to be talking with her.

Gunny offered, "I know the chaplain there and have called him. I asked him to do what he could to help Jake."

"Well thanks for that."

Kim started asking Gunny personal questions about how he was doing with life. Gunny responded by saying, "Maybe another time. I've got to get back. I have little time to help your client get out."

Gunny was not sure why they had met and headed back to the office.

*******

A voicemail greeted Gunny when he got back to his desk: "Gunny, this is Virginia. I was able to get one thumbprint and two partial prints from the e-mail paper you sent us. Call me when you can."

He punched in the number for Virginia at the fingerprint lab.

"This is Virginia, how can I help you?"

"Hey, Virginia. You do that so nice. What do you have on the fingerprints?"

"Let's see," she said as she pulled up her report. "I found one full thumbprint and two different partial prints. I compared the prints to the victim's and the thumbprint belongs to Janice Meredith. The two partial prints are another thing. I found one matched a guy that has been arrested several time for public intoxication, a Paul Walker. I compared the other partial print to the fingerprints of Doctor Brantley on the glass you gave us. They do not match. Probably it belongs to the person who printed the e-mail. We do not have anything on who that might be yet. Any suggestions?"

"No, not yet. Thanks for the information. It's helpful."

"OK, I sent the report to the DA and a copy to you. Let me know if there is anything else we need to do."

Gunny thanked her and hung up. His mind processed the new information. What did this mean? If the professor's prints were not on the printed e-mail about abortion, did he just not get them on the paper, or was it someone else who gave Jan the paper? If so, who could that be? Time was ticking and he did not need more questions. He needed some answers.

Gunny remembered that he had written down who had sent the e-mail and he had not checked that out yet. He took out his notebook and looked back to when Doc gave it to him. The only note was that the name on the sent line was "Sheela"—no last name and no e-mail address. It would be available on the electronic e-mail, but not on the hard copy. It did not include the name of the abortion place. He wondered if Sheela knew about the place because she was an employee or had been a patient. He knew there was one women's clinic in the city that did most of the local abortions. If she was a patient, they would tell him nothing—patient confidentiality.

He called the clinic. After the receptionist answered he asked, "Could I speak to Sheela, please?"

He lucked out. "Sure . . . but she comes in later to clean up. She will probably be here about 4 p.m."

"OK, thanks. I'll try back later."

Gunny made a mental note to swing by the clinic a little before 4 p.m. to catch Sheela before she went inside to work. He was not sure how to recognize her, but hoped she would be the only one to enter the employee entrance about that time.

*******

At 3:45 p.m., Gunny pulled into the clinic parking lot and parked where he could watch most of the lot. He figured other men probably waited in their cars for their wives or girlfriends when they went there for an appointment. He doubted he would stand out.

At 3:55, an old Chevy Blazer pulled into a parking space. A thirtyish thin woman with brunette hair got out of the Blazer. Gunny moved to cut her off before she entered the employee entrance. He noted that she wore a housekeeping type uniform.

Holding out his badge, Gunny asked, "Ma'am, are you Sheela?"

She was taken aback! She looked at him and his badge and began to shake. "I've got to go to work," she said. "What do you want?"

"Several weeks ago, you sent someone named 'A' an e-mail giving information about coming here for abortion counseling. I want to know who 'A' is and how to reach him or her."

Sheela turned pale. She looked around nervously. She was in a jam. She did not want to give any information about her drug dealer, and she definitely did not want to give the cop a reason to look in her purse, which held some crystal. She needed to get to work. How could she get out of this? She finally said, "I don't remember that…and I really need to get to work. How about if I talk with you in the morning, when I am off?"

Gunny figured she would be gone by morning. He pressed her. "Sheela, I know you sent the e-mail. I have no beef with you, but I really need to know Ace's real name and how to reach him, and I need to know now—or we can go to the station to talk about it."

Sheela felt flushed. She looked around again and saw no one, so she said, "I don't know any names, but Ace. I can give you a phone number, but you can't tell him where you got it." She pulled out her phone and looked up Ace's number in her contacts. She had two numbers for Ace. Once, he gave her a different number than the one she usually called for drugs. She thought that might be better than giving a cop the drug number. "Here it is," she said as she gave Gunny the number. "Can I go now?"

He let her go inside with a warning not to leave town in the next few days.

She looked up at him and then turned and walked quickly toward the clinic employee entrance.

Gunny called the phone company, identified himself, and requested the name of the owner of the phone number Sheela had given him. The name was Franklin Jaimison, with a billing address on East Valley Drive. Gunny drove by the house. It was a middle class house; nothing particularly attention-getting about it. A privacy fence closed off the back yard. He called the city waste department to check for when garbage was collected in that area. He made a note on his calendar to check the garbage before the crew picked it up to see if he could find something that might have Ace's fingerprints.

Gunny called John, the DA, to update him on the status of tying up the loose ends. John was not available, so had asked his secretary to give John an update note. Gunny knew that John thought his efforts were a waste of time, but he was trying to work with him.

Gunny got a call from a New Orleans police detective, Frank Maury. "Hey buddy, thought I'd give you an update on your missing person. A fisherman found a body yesterday in one of the bayous. It turned out to be Brad Jones. Since he had a prior arrest for drugs, we identified him by his fingerprints. He had been shot in the back of the head, execution style. Fortunately, they found the body before the gators did. We also found someone who works for the bus company who saw a guy pick Brad up at the bus station. He has given us a description. We issued a BOLO (be on the lookout) for anyone meeting that description."

"Thanks for the info, Frank. Happy New Year. I guess you guys celebrated it in a big way."

"It isn't Mardi Gras, but we don't let a reason to party get away. Happy New Year to you, and good luck with that case." The call ended with Gunny thinking he needed more than luck to get to the truth on the student's murder.

When He headed home he still felt edgy over his inability to come up with something strong enough to support his idea that someone other than Jake had killed Jan Meredith. He looked forward to being with his family and relaxing a little.

*******

Wednesday morning, Gunny drove to Franklin Jaimison's house on East Valley Drive. He saw one garbage container out on the street. A light snow had fallen during the night, and car tracks in the snow suggested Jaimison had already left the house. Gunny parked his car, got out, and moved quickly to the garbage can. He opened it and was met with a rotting garbage aroma. As he looked at the contents, the garbage seemed typical. He moved some trash around with his gloved hand until he found what he was looking for: a beer can that might have Ace's fingerprints on it. There were two cans, so he took both to improve the chances of getting a good print.

Back at the office, Gunny turned in the cans for fingerprint analysis and asked them to compare any prints to the prints on the e-mail. He told the lab tech it was important for him to get the prints ASAP. "Good luck with that," the tech responded. "Don't you know the holidays put us behind?"

*******

Jake kept surviving. Unfortunately, Jake got into it with one of his cellmates and ended up in the emergency room. They admitted him overnight to observe him for a concussion, since he had blacked out after his opponent shoved his head sharply against a wall.

At church that Sunday, the chaplain told Gunny about Jake's situation. "They moved the guy who hurt him to another cell. I'm sure they would have separated Jake from the others if they'd had the space," he added. "You know that voters are not interested in paying more taxes for jail space right now, and jails are crowded. It's worse this time of year with all the excess celebration that went on at New Year's and the increased domestic dispute arrests during the holidays."

# Chapter 24

*Gunny decided to drive to Covenant College to pay the professor a visit and confront him over the affair and the late night meeting with Jan.*

Gunny was dragging, so he asked for a double shot of espresso in his coffee at the drive-through Thursday morning. He checked, but had received no new reports. They still did not have the drug screen or any DNA tests reports back from the Tennessee Bureau of Investigation (TBI).

Gunny evaluated what he could do to move the case forward that day. The professor was intriguing. Gunny did not like him because of his misbehavior with students. The professor picked Jan up just before the murder. Though his prints were not on the e-mail, this did not eliminate him as a suspect. It bothered him that Brad was murdered in New Orleans. He could not bring himself to believe that he had it in him to arrange that kind of disappearance, but stranger things had happened.

There was also the drug dealer. Gunny wondered about him, but had nothing concrete pointing to him as the murderer. If his fingerprints were on the e-mail, things might heat up on the drug dealer. He was more likely to have set up Brad's disappearance.

Gunny decided to drive to Covenant College to pay the professor a visit and confront him over the affair and late night meeting with Jan.

*******

It was difficult to find a parking space, and he had to walk a distance, but he found Doctor Brantley's office. He knocked on the closed door, hoping he did not have an early class. A man Gunny assumed was another professor walked by, turned around, and inquired, "You looking for Brantley?"

"Yes, sir. Is he in class?"

"No, no. He's teaching a seminar at a small college in South Carolina. He should be back on Wednesday. Are you a parent of a student?"

"Oh, no. Why do you think I am a parent?"

"Well, he has a reputation for personal involvement with some of the female students. I thought maybe his reputation had caught up with him."

"Yeah, I have heard about that. Do you think that girl that was murdered, Jan Meredith, was one of those students?"

"I would not know, but he did act a little sidetracked right after it was in the paper. Is that what you want to see him about?"

Gunny did not want to reveal too much to this guy, so he simply said that he had some business with Doctor Brantley and thanked the fellow professor. He headed to the office feeling a sense of helplessness while he waited for others to do their work. He hoped to at least hear the results of Jaimison's fingerprints sometime that day.

# Chapter 25

*"He said that Brad saw a professor pick that student up close to campus just before the time of her murder. He said he was with Brad and saw it too."*

Doc went with Angel to the mission on Monday night. On the way, Angel told Doc about a conversation she had with Gunny at church on Sunday. "It seems Gunny is close to finding one or more other people who could be suspects in Jan's murder, but it's not going anywhere fast."

Doc said when they got out of the car, "I may see what the street is saying about the case. Homeless people are often invisible to others, so they sometimes see or hear things most others might miss."

Doc ate supper with the guys. After supper, Cookie came over with his coffee cup and sat down across from Doc, who was nursing his own cup of coffee. "Don't see you much anymore since you hooked up with Angel."

Doc reacted with a bit of anger, saying, "I've not hooked up with anybody. I was blessed with a place to live, and it is in the duplex next to Angel's. We are friends. Nothing more is going on."

"Okay, okay, I hear you. I guess you heard about Jake's troubles in jail."

"Yeah, I heard. It makes me mad that he is not separated from the other prisoners."

"Huh, not likely. But it would be good to do." Cookie said sarcastically.

"I wish that detective you know could come up with enough evidence to show that someone else killed that girl. So far, it is going slow."

"He's a good one. He'll do it if anyone can. I heard someone talking about it the other day. He said rumor has it that Brad knew too much. Brad had seen a professor pick that student up close to campus just before the time of her murder. So he was sent to New Orleans to disappear for a while. The guy talking said he was with Brad and saw it too."

"Who said that?" Doc queried.

"Oh, you know. He was probably just bragging about something he made up to make himself look important."

"Maybe, but it could be he does know something. Who was it?" Doc asked again.

Cookie realized he had said too much and he did not like giving up anyone's name. Paul realized Cookie's struggle and spoke up, "Come on Cookie, this could help Jake. I won't tell anybody where I got it from."

Cookie thought that Doc was as trustworthy as anyone he knew, so he decided to reveal the name and lowered his voice. "It was Jeff, Brad's friend. He eats here once in a while, and he was up here last night for supper. He had enough alcohol to be loose with his tongue without being sloppy drunk. Don't you tell anybody where you got that information."

"It's safe with me, Cookie. Thanks." Doc stood to leave and Cookie headed back to his kitchen. Doc soon heard him yell at the cleanup crew. Doc's thought shifted to the comment about Jeff. He would go see Gunny on Tuesday morning and give him this information.

Doc marveled at the change in himself, from not wanting to talk with any policeman and fear for his own well-being to wanting to talk with Gunny out of concern for another homeless man. He did not hesitate to want to do the right thing. He was not as concerned about himself as he was for Jake's well-being. He realized this was a genuine change and improvement in his life. He then realized he had not thought about having an alcoholic drink in many days. It was not attractive to him. He thought he would talk about this with Angel on the way back to the duplex.

*******

Gunny walked into the Bristol bus station later in the afternoon on Monday and saw the clerk finish a ticket purchase for the bus that evening. He waited until the man walked away from the small counter and approached the clerk. He noticed the ID tag on his shirt said, "Jimmy Wiley".

The clerk was finishing data entry into his computer. He commented, "Be with you in a minute."

In a couple minutes, the clerk looked up at Gunny. "Can I help you, Mister?"

"Jimmy, I'm Detective Gunny Hawkins." Gunny held out his police badge. I need to know about a ticket to New Orleans you sold several days ago. Do you remember selling one to New Orleans recently?"

"Let me see," Jimmy said slowly as he turned to his computer and searched the recent ticket sales history. "Oh, yes, here it is. A slender, blond-headed man bought it. He was a little demanding. He bought it for a passenger named Brad Jones, who got on the bus at the right time."

"Can you tell me who bought the ticket?"

"Let's see . . . no. It looks like he paid cash."

"Did you notice anything else?"

"Yeah, I saw him get into a nice car. It was a black or dark blue Caddy."

"You do a pretty good job remembering details about your customers, Jimmy."

"Yeah, I saw a movie one time where the train station clerk was key in identifying a guy and a gal that took the train to try to escape the law. So, when I got this job, I thought I should make an effort to notice things about people. I guess it paid off if this helps."

"Thanks, Jimmy," said Gunny. "You have a good evening." He handed Jimmy his card and said, "Give me a call if you remember anything else, or see him here again."

"Sure will."

Gunny stepped back into his car and realized the clerk had come very close to describing the professor. When he saw the professor on Wednesday, he would tell him the clerk at the bus station described him, to get his reaction.

Gunny usually left his car radio on and tuned into the local contemporary Christian station. Within seconds, a weather bulletin on that station caught his attention. Here it was, February, and two lows were converging on the area: one from the northwest to provide the cold, and one from the southwest to provide moisture from the Gulf. This was a recipe for a snowstorm in the Appalachian are. The bulletin predicted six to twelve inches of snow, starting Wednesday, around noon.

# Chapter 26

*"This guy, Jeff, is likely a key witness in a murder case,
and I think the killer is after him to stop him from telling
what he knows."*

Gunny had a good day on Tuesday. It started with doc sitting in the chair next to his desk when he arrived.

Gunny teased Doc, "Well, you are becoming a regular here. Are you getting comfortable around us cops?"

Doc was beginning to tell when Gunny was joking versus being serious. He joked back, "Yeah, you know what they say, 'feed a homeless person and he will follow you around all day.'"

"Yeah, well, good luck getting anything but coffee out of me. Want any?"

Doc answered, "No thanks. I'm here for only a minute to tell you about something." He continued before Gunny could speak again, "I talked with a friend at the shelter and he told me there had been a guy there that was loose tongued and said he and Brad had seen the murdered girl meet with a professor from the college along a street near the campus the night of the murder. The guy's name was Jeff and he's a friend of Brad, the guy that works at the Borderline."

Gunny pulled out his pen and pad and wrote for a minute before saying, "I'll follow up on that. That information could be helpful."

"I'm trying to do what I can to help Jake. I don't know quite why, but I think it is because he seems to be unable to defend himself and he's a fellow street person."

Gunny looked Doc in the eyes and said, "Thanks for your help, Doc, but please do not get yourself in trouble trying to help someone else. Leave the heavy lifting to me."

Doc agreed with Gunny and stood to leave the office.

Gunny watched Doc leave the room. Once clear, he took out his phone, looked in his notepad for the number. He realized as he was dialing the first part of the phone number that he had confiscated Jeff's phone.

He grabbed his jacket and coffee on the way out. He knew where Jeff lived so he headed to Moore Street.

A girl answered his knock on the door, "Who is it?"

Gunny spoke authoritatively, "This is detective Hawkins with the Bristol police. I need to talk to Jeff right now."

The door opened and the scantily clad girl said, "He's not here. You can call him."

"I took his phone. How can I call him?"

"Oh, I heard about that. He was really mad about that. He got a prepaid phone."

"Okay, what's the number?"

"Umm, he doesn't like me giving out his number."

Gunny held up his badge and said firmly. Lady, you do not have a choice. Give it to me now!"

She stepped back from the door and returned a moment later with a small slip of paper. The girl read off the number on the paper.

Gunny said, "Thanks. If you see him, tell him Gunny needs to talk with him urgently."

The girl closed the door and Gunny walked back toward his car. He dialed Jeff's new phone number.

The phone range three times and Jeff answered.

"Yeah."

"Is this Jeff?" gunny asked.

"Yeah, who's this?"

"It's Detective Hawkins. I need to talk with you. Can you meet me for lunch at noon at the pawn shop café on State Street?"

Jeff did not answer right away. He cleared his throat then asked, "What's it about detective?"

"I need to ask you something about Brad and I do not want to do so over the phone." Gunny thought that Jeff slurred his words like he was under the influence.

"You buying?"

Gunny answered, "Sure. See you there at noon."

"Yeah, I'll be there."

*******

What Jeff did not say was that someone he did not know had dropped by with an envelope a half hour before Gunny's call. The envelope contained a bus ticket for that evening for New Orleans. A note with the ticket said that Jeff would be wise to get on the bus and take a vacation for several weeks. It said someone would pick him up at the bus station in New Orleans and arrange for a place for him to stay, probably with Brad. The envelope also contained a $50 bill the note said was for expenses.

Jeff did not trust whoever sent that note, since he had heard the rumors about Brad. He grabbed his backpack and loaded it up with some warm clothing, a small camp stove, a water camel, and lots of dry and canned food. It was heavier than he liked, but he had to carry more than the usual amount of food. He attached a small, one-man tent to the top of his pack, and a cold weather sleeping bag to the bottom. Jeff pulled the chip from his phone and destroyed it, throwing the phone in the trash. After putting on his boots, gloves, and a knit cap, Jeff caught a ride to Hickory Tree, near the Holston Mountains. He would hide out in Cherokee National Forest until the air was clear, or until he figured out another place to go.

*******

Later in the morning, Gunny got a call from the tech at the fingerprint lab.

She stated, "We found several prints on the beer cans in the Meredith case. One of them matched the half-print on the e-mail.

We found a matching print in the national data base. It was for a man with the name Franklin P. Jaimison. There was no address given in the Bristol area. That's it.

"Thanks, that's very helpful. Have a great day." They hung up at the same time.

Gunny thought about the report, *Wow, I did not see that coming. The guy Jan argued with behind the restaurant was likely her drug source. The matching print was good evidence that Jaimison was the man that argued with Jan behind the restaurant. He had given her information on getting an abortion. However, it did not prove anything related to Jan's murder—it only complicated the picture. After all, he was Jan's pusher, not her lover. Her lover was the one seen with her just before her death. She may have argued with Jaimison that night, but that did not make him a murderer. Still, he could not eliminate Ace now. In the meantime, Gunny would keep the professor as his most likely suspect.* Gunny glanced at his watch and realized he needed to head downtown to meet with Jeff.

*******

Gunny waited at the café at noon. No Jeff. He ordered a bowl of soup and a cheese sandwich. No Jeff. He ate the soup and sandwich and had a slice of apple pie. No Jeff. He called the DA's office and left a message about the fingerprint match on the e-mail. Forty minutes had gone by and Jeff was a no-show. Gunny called Jeff's number. A familiar voice said, "This phone cannot be reached at this time."

Gunny, knowing what had happened to Brad, was suddenly anxious about Jeff's welfare. He drove to the address Jeff had given him. There was no answer to his knock on the door or his call. He tried looking into the windows, but sheets and blankets covered them. There was no light inside that he could see. He tried the doorknob and was surprised to find the door unlocked. He pushed open the door and entered cautiously, calling out, "Bristol police. Jeff, are you here? Bristol police." Gunny was taking a close look all around while walking through the front of the apartment calling out "Bristol Police."

It looked as if someone had packed up fast and left. Unwanted clothing and other things were scattered around one of the bedrooms. He found an empty package for AAA batteries and an empty Ramen Noodles package on the kitchen counter that would have held several of the individual packets. The hallway closet door was open, and some camping gear was strewn across the floor, including cooking utensils, an old pair of gloves, and a set of hiking maps.

Gunny was getting the idea that Jeff had flown quickly, with backpack loaded. The question was, who was he running from, Gunny . . . or someone else? The second question was where? He noticed a wadded up piece of paper in the trash. When he reached for it, he found the bus ticket to New Orleans. It was no wonder Jeff had taken off for his own safety, if he knew anything about what happened to Brad. Gunny packed the items in evidence bags and returned to his office. He wondered if the professor was cleaning up anything . . . or anybody who might implicate him.

Gunny called Doc. One of the benefits of Doc's part-time job was that he now had a cell phone. Doc answered, "This is Paul. Can I help you?"

"Good afternoon, Paul. This us Gunny. I see you are using your given name at work instead of Doc."

"Yeah, the boss said I needed to. What's up?"

Gunny jumped in, "I had a lunch meeting with Jeff and he did not show up. I am at his apartment now, and it looks to me like he has flown the coop—and did so in a hurry. He took his backpack with him. Any idea where he might have headed?"

Doc paused a moment before answering, "This is not good. I don't know Jeff that well. I do remember him talking about growing up in Hickory Tree, and how often he liked to hike in the Cherokee National Forest. I think he said he really liked to go where Roaring Fork emptied into South Holston Lake. He said that it was quiet there and he could think. Don't know if that's where he went, but I heard him talk about it more than once."

"That's good, Doc. I will get the forest rangers to look for him in that area. Could you see if Cookie knows where he might have gone?"

"Sure thing. Do you think someone is after him to shut him up?" queried Doc.

"I am afraid so. I found a bus ticket to New Orleans in his trash. Looks like someone was trying to get him to disappear like Brad and he chose to run instead. Give me a call after you talk with Cookie."

They ended the call.

Gunny called to put out a BOLO for Jeff, and he got a phone number for the ranger station from dispatch. Gunny called the forest ranger station to ask them to check for Jeff in the Roaring Fork area, where it empties into South Holston Lake. The ranger complained about being understaffed, especially given the bad weather forecast. He agreed to try to get someone into that area. "What do I do if we find him?" asked the ranger.

"Nothing, yet. Just let me know when you've located him. He's possibly a key witness in a case I'm working on and I think he's running from someone. He grew up in Hickory Tree and likes that area."

"Okay, we're getting ready for that storm coming in, but I'll give you a call when I know something," said the ranger.

*******

Gunny dropped by the bus station to see if the clerk knew who bought the ticket for Jeff. It was a small station, so only a few buses came through each day. But it was an important means of getting around for people without cars. It meant slow going in most cases, as the buses stopped at many medium sized or small towns.

When he entered the station, Jimmy was reading a magazine. He looked up just as Gunny spoke. "Looks like things are a bit slow, eh Jimmy?"

"Uh-huh, but I don't mind. It lets me get caught up on my reading."

"That's a good way to look at it. I'm looking for someone who bought another ticket to New Orleans today or yesterday."

"Oh yes. After we talked last time, it caught my attention right away when the purchaser wanted another ticket to the Mardi Gras city. He said he was giving it as a gift to someone else. We have to have the passenger's name on the ticket. Let me just look here on my computer and see what name he gave me."

He took a couple minutes complaining about how slow the old computers were, and that he had asked for a better one without success. Then he exclaimed, "Here it is. It was purchased yesterday—late in the day. I remember him. I think it was the same guy both times: blond hair, slender build, and he drove that dark-colored Caddy."

"He insisted on not giving me his name, and he paid with cash. So I just put 'John Doe' in for the purchaser's name."

"Anything else?"

"Oh yes. He had a slight scar on his…umm…left cheek area just below his eye. It did not show up much, so I almost missed it."

Gunny wondered if the professor had a scar. He would look for that when he met with him on Wednesday. He thanked Jimmy and headed back to the office to check for messages before he headed home.

On his way to the office, Gunny's cell phone rang. "Gunny here," he answered.

"Gunny, this is Ranger McElroy—just call me Rob. We have been looking for the guy you said might be in the Roaring Fork area."

"Yes, have you found him?"

"No, not exactly. One of our local residents who knows his family saw him heading into the forest with his backpack this afternoon."

"I guess he is trying to hide from someone. Rob, would you mind going with me tomorrow if I wanted to hike into the Roaring Fork area?"

"I would not recommend that. We are under a winter storm warning expecting heavy snow and high winds about noon tomorrow."

"I could leave early in the morning. It is very important. This guy, Jeff, is likely a key witness in a murder case, and I think the killer is after him to stop him from telling what he knows."

"You don't make it easy. I guess we could get close on Big Creek Road. Be sure you bring winter gear in case we are out there when the storm starts. How about meeting at 7 a.m. at the corner of Hickory Tree Road and Morrell Creek Road?"

"Sure! Thanks, Rob. See you there at seven. I wouldn't normally ask you to do this, but I'm really worried about this guy's life."

"It's my job. His life could be at risk just due to the storm. See you tomorrow morning, bright and early."

Gunny thought about his cold weather training in the Marine Corps. It might come in handy now. He liked to hike on the Appalachian Trail which passes through the mountains in this general area. He thought it would not be difficult to pull his gear together. He hoped his wife had fixed a good supper so he would have plenty of calories to call on in the morning. Most of all, he hoped they would get to Jeff in time.

# Chapter 27

*Gunny shouted, "Police! Stop! Put your gun down!" At
the same time he saw something in the man's hand and
it was pointing his way. A firecracker type sound reverberated through the mountains!*

It was usual for Gunny to get up early in the morning. It was part of
his Marine training that he had maintained. He was up a little earlier this morning feeling excitement about hiking into the mountain-
ous forest with a snow storm on the way to rescue a key witness
that could clear up many of the loose ends he had been unable to
resolve. The weather forecast was unrelenting about this being a
dangerous storm.

He had packed up his gear the evening before, including a
down jacket with a hood that should handle the cold. He knew that
the key to handling the outdoor cold with wind was layering with
an outer barrier to the wind. He liked the new fabrics that held in
the warmth. He used to use wool, but the new fabrics wick away
moisture better and are not as heavy as wool. He always stuck in
a first aid kit. Karen handed him a thermos full of hot coffee she
had freshly made for him. He smiled at her, kissed her and headed
out the door.

Thirty minutes later, about six fifty-five, Gunny arrived at the
intersection of Hickory Tree Road and Morrell Creek Road. Ranger
Rob showed up five minutes later. Gunny parked his car off to the
side of the road and got into Rob's SUV. They greeted each other
and headed toward the forest on Morrell Creek Road. Rob turned
left onto Morrell Creek Lane. Bumping along the pot-holed road the

trees were taller and thicker in density. There was an occasional small house or mobile home on small farms along the way. Gunny wondered to himself how long some of these properties had been in these families and why people wanted to be so secluded.

Rob turned onto Big Creek Road. Now there were fewer signs of human life. He checked his GPS and determined that the next creek bridge would be Roaring Fork. When his GPS indicated they had arrived at the destination, Rob pulled off on the side of the road leaving enough room for another vehicle to pass. He called in to report that they were leaving the vehicle to hike along Roaring Fork toward the lake. There was enough static to let him know they had received his message even though the signal was very weak.

Gunny noticed another SUV had pulled over and was parked about thirty yards further up the road. He jogged over to it and it was unoccupied. He looked in. It was locked and he saw nothing to give away the identity of its driver. He made a mental note of the tag number.

Gunny jogged back and told Rob, "Let's get going."

Gunny already was wearing his Smith & Wesson. Rob grabbed his holstered gun out of the glove compartment, locked up and they headed into the woods along Roaring Fork.

The icy cold, gusts of wind burned Gunny's face and ears. It was twenty-eight degrees at seven o'clock and it was supposed to only get up to thirty degrees before the wind would blow in a cold front from the northwest that would meet a low coming up from the southwest. At that time the temperature would begin to fall and a heavy snow would begin to fall soon after. Gunny had a hood on his jacket and gloves in his pockets, but he felt that he did not need them since he would warm up as they hiked. He was right. The trail was rough and could hardly be called a trail. A storm in December had left tripping branches across what trail there was. There was some evidence of recent travel on the trail, a fresh boot print, broken small branches and a candy bar wrapper.

A hundred yards from the road, they saw fresh boot prints in a muddy section of the trail. Rob turned around to face Gunny and said, "That's what you were afraid of isn't it?"

"Yeah, that's likely the guy that wants to eliminate Jeff from revealing what he knows. We need to get there soon."

The distance from the road to the place where the creek joined the lake was two and a half miles. They picked up the pace. Gunny unzipped his jacket to avoid the dangerous sweat that would develop if he had too much clothing. That sweat would cool him down too much later and could cause hypothermia. He noticed Rob zipping open his jacket at the same time and had the thought that it was foolish to think a forest ranger did not know a lot about surviving in the forest.

About a hundred yards from the lake the crack of a gunshot echoed through the mountains. Gunny was already on high alert. The shot gave him a surge of adrenalin. He picked up speed. It was just one shot and that meant either the shooter hit his target and that was all that was needed to take out Jeff or Jeff got away and the shooter did not have a good second shot. They pressed on toward the lake. He hoped they were not too late.

Within sight of the lake, Rob saw a tent off to the left of the trail. It was almost hidden from the trail. They carefully moved toward the tent, Gunny now holding his Smith & Wesson in ready position with a round in the chamber.

When they arrived at the tent, it was obvious that someone had set up camp and was not there now. It had started to snow and that almost hid the boot prints leading from the camp. There were two sets of prints. About twelve yards along the path of these prints was a small amount of red in the freshly fallen snow. It looked like blood.

Gunny took the lead and followed the prints. He and Rob both had their guns drawn. Ahead of them another shot rang out followed by a noise ahead of them that sounded like a grunt and someone thrashing in the brush. It was a man struggling to get up after falling on a steep section of the trail.

The man was pulling his knitted cap back on his blond head when he saw Gunny. The man's face became distorted and he said something that Gunny could not hear over the howling wind and thought he did not want to hear anyway."

Gunny shouted, "Police! Stop! Put your gun down!" At the same time he saw the man's hand rise in Gunny's direction with something in the man's hand and it was pointing his way. Gunny dove instinctively to the ground for cover.

A firecracker-like sound reverberated through the mountains!

The man had taken a shot at Gunny. The bullet hit a tree next to Gunny throwing splinters on him. Gunny would have shot back, but he did not have a good shot and he did not know if Jeff was in the area. The shooter then took off through the woods in a direction that made Gunny think he was trying to get around the two officers and back to the trail.

Unwillingly, Gunny found himself in a different place and time. He saw before him his platoon of marines fighting in an attempt to rescue a hostage boy from the enemy. It was a brutal fight, He felt a sick feeling deep in his gut. Someone was yelling at him. He came back to present reality of stormy weather in Cherokee National Forrest and heard Rob yelling at him, "You okay, Gunny?"

Gunny pulled himself up. "Yeah, I'm okay. Let's move forward cautiously. Gunny felt the shooter had gone around them and was headed back to the trail head. He kept his gun out just in case the man wasn't gone. He saw a man lying on the ground about thirty yards further up the mountain. They rushed to him. It was Jeff.

They knew immediately Jeff was in a bad way. He moaned and gasped as he grabbed the right side of his chest. It looked like a bullet had gone through him. The bloody bubbling and wheezing told Gunny the bullet had pierced Jeff's lung, which had collapsed. Blood oozed out of his wound—too much blood for Jeff to last very long.

Gunny and Rob moved Jeff back to the tent area where he could work on him. He propped Jeff up a little to help him breathe better and Jeff blacked out.

"What about the shooter?" Rob shouted. "Should one of us go after him?"

"No," grunted Gunny as he worked feverishly on Jeff. "I can't leave Jeff, and I need your help here. We'll get him in time, but I need Jeff to live. Quick, get me a shirt or something I can tie around Jeff's chest."

Gunny grabbed his backpack and pulled out the first aid kit. He knew, that adrenaline had surged into his blood stream and he was beginning to feel the letdown that comes when the heat of the moment has eased up. His shaking hands quickly found two large gauze bandages, each with plastic on one side. He applied one to Jeff's back and the other to his chest, over the exit wound, and held them both tightly until Rob returned with a shirt. Gunny rolled it and tied it around Jeff so that it put pressure on the bandages. He checked to be sure the bandages were sealed and held in air. It was working.

"Rob, here is my phone. See if you can call someone on either of our phones to get a rescue team out here. You may have to hike up this mountain a little ways." Gunny knew it was difficult to get any reception in the forest, but more people were using the lake for recreation, and many now had cabins or houseboats on the lake. He hoped the cell towers had improved.

Rob reached for the phone and commented, "Your hand is shaking."

Gunny quickly responded, "Look at your hand." Rob looked at his own hand reaching for the phone and found it shaking too. He stated, "Oh, yeah, adrenaline effect." Rob moved out for higher ground.

Gunny checked for any other problems and found a laceration on Jeff's left leg. It had already stopped bleeding, so was ugly, but not a threat. He covered Jeff with a jacket and thermal blanket from the tent.

Jeff began coming to and immediately grabbed his chest and moaned. "Don't do that, Jeff," Gunny warned him sternly. "You've been shot in the chest and I have a bandage on you, but it may not hold if you grab at it. We are trying to get a rescue squad out here."

"Where's Ace?" Jeff gasped in a voice wracked with pain. "He's trying to kill me."

"The shooter is gone for now," Gunny reassured him, "The shooter's gone. Did you say the shooter's name is Ace?"

"Yeah, he knows I saw him with that girl the night—" his words interrupted by a coughing fit followed by groans before he continued. "It was the night she was killed. He's trying…" Jeff coughed again. "He is trying to get rid of me like he did Brad."

"I'm Detective Hawkins. You're safe now. Just lie back now and stay as calm as you can. You can tell me about it later."

Rob returned about twelve minutes later and said, I got through to 911. An emergency team is on the way. "Do you think we can move him to the road?" he asked.

"I would like to, but this bandage is barely holding, and it would be best to not move him until the EMTs can put a better bandage on and put him on a stretcher. Did you tell them he had a sucking chest wound?"

"Well, not in those words, but I told them he was shot in the chest through his lung."

"That'll work."

Jeff had passed out again. It was no wonder, considering the blood he had lost. His pulse remained rapid, yet was stringy not strong, like a thin thread about to break. It took about fifteen minutes, but they heard the distant siren of the rescue squad approaching the trailhead. It took them another forty minutes to get to the campsite. They went to work right away. The EMT checking Jeff's vitals called out to the other two: "His pulse is 130 and stringy. His BP is 70 over 50. Good thing we got here when we did. Much longer and we might have lost him. Let's start an IV and seal that lung better."

Within ten minutes they had started an IV fluid drip and applied a new lung seal and bandage. One of the EMTs reported, "His pulse is lowering, and now 105. The BP is up to 90 over 60. I think we can transport him now. I'll keep the BP cuff on him so we can monitor along the way."

Gunny was impressed with how capable they were to treat Jeff far off the road in the midst of falling snow. They strapped him onto a stretcher and started the trek back to the rescue vehicle. Rob and Gunny took turns with the EMTs carrying the stretcher on the trail back to the road.

Through the roar of wind in the forest, one of the EMTs said, "We would have been here a lot faster had we used the four-wheeler to get in and get him out, but this trail is not quite wide enough, so we couldn't use it."

"Hey, you did well," Gunny assured him. "We were really glad to see you guys when you did get there."

When they arrived at the road, Gunny saw the emergency rescue vehicle and he saw a four-wheeler next to it. He recalled hiking once with a group of men on the Appalachian Trail (AT), along the border between Erwin County, Tennessee, and North Carolina when one of the men started suffering weakness and chest pains. It took a while to get to a place to get a cell phone signal, but after three tries, the man's fellow hikers had finally got the information to the 911 operator. Three four-wheelers had made it up to them on the AT. The EMTs check him out, strapped him into a four-wheeler and gingerly made their way down the mountain to a rescue vehicle that conveyed the man to a hospital. The hospital would later find the man had a severely blocked artery and had suffered a mild heart attack. Gunny was impressed with the mountain trained EMTs. Those EMTs had been skilled and confident and so were these that got Jeff out and to the hospital.

*******

Gunny rode back to his car with Rob and thanked him for all his help. He then drove to the hospital in Bristol where the rescue squad had taken Jeff. In the ER, Gunny asked for Jeff's location flashing his badge. The nurse pointed to a row of treatment cubicles and said, "He's in number four."

Gunny said, "Thanks and walked over to cubicle four and entered. A nurse was working on him putting in another intravenous (IV) line. Gunny walked around to the other side of the emergency room bed. He looked down at Jeff and said a prayer asking God to help Jeff live.

Jeff returned to lucidity off and on. One time he began asking where he was. Gunny briefly explained to him that he had been shot and was now in the hospital emergency room. He also let him know that later in the day, he, Gunny, would visit again and ask him some questions. Gunny assured him the police would have a guard near him all the time. Jeff passed out and later came to again.

Jeff said weakly, "I'm thirsty."

Gunny looked at the nurse that was now making notes on Jeff's chart. She looked up and shook her head to say no. She added, "He is headed to surgery and cannot have fluids except by IV."

Gunny told Jeff, "Sorry, man, but you aren't allowed to drink. They are giving you water through that IV line in you. Can you answer a couple questions?"

Gunny noticed the nurse looked up at him with some disgust. She looked back down and said nothing.

Gunny asked, "Are you sure it was Ace?"

Jeff nodded to indicate a yes.

"Does Ace have blond hair?"

Again Jeff nodded to indicate yes.

"Is his name Frank Jaimison?"

Jeff paused on that question. Then a light seemed to come into his eyes and he nodded yes to that question as well. With a pained, raspy voice Jeff said, "He did it. I'm sure. He'll try to kill me."

Gunny barely heard what Jeff said. Gunny put his hand on Jeff's arm and said, "You are safe now." Gunny did not usually make promises he could not keep.

*******

Gunny stepped outside Jeff's cubicle and called in a BOLO (be on the lookout) for Ace, after giving dispatch a description of him. It struck Gunny how closely Ace and the professor resembled one another. It was not exact, but close enough to throw people off.

Gunny had hoped to talk with the professor on Wednesday, but events changed that, and he decided he might not need to after all. If he could interrogate Ace, he might have his man without upsetting the professor. Gunny thought about that and decided he did not like the professor and would not mind upsetting him.

Gunny waited in the ER near Jeff's cubicle until a replacement officer showed up to stay with Jeff. Gunny headed to his car. He gathered his thoughts while walking, *if that was Ace, he might have been the one who picked up the bus tickets. But what motive would he have for killing Jan? She was his customer. Why did he have such a problem with her pregnancy? Why was he so concerned that he suggested an abortion…or decided to kill her? It's time to pull Ace in.*

When Gunny got home, he took a hot shower and changed clothes.

Karen was not home yet from grocery shopping. He was glad. She would want to know the details. she arrived home about the time he was headed back out. She let him know she was relieved that he made it home. Gunny gave her an abbreviated version of what had happened and headed to the office.

*******

Ace was growing desperate. Very little was going his way, and it seemed he kept getting in deeper every time he tried to clean up the mess. As he drove to Elizabethton, Tennessee, his thoughts grew darker. *I don't think that cop at Roaring Fork could identify me for sure. I think the only one that can is Jeff. Somehow I need to get the cops off my back long enough to finish what I started. Then I disappear and start over somewhere else.*

A plan came to his mind. He drove to a parking space off the main road in town, East Elk Avenue. He grabbed his laptop and warily walked around the block and into the front door of The Java Place where he knew Wi-Fi was available. Once settled into a single booth, he started putting details to his plan. Ace knew his plan was not perfect, but it was the best he could do under the circumstances.

Ace brought up his Internet browser and went to a bookmarked location, delta.com. After making a reservation on a Delta flight out of Tri-Cities, he called a friend.

Joe Mac was the only person Ace had ever called his friend. Joe was known for doing dirty jobs if well compensated. Joe Mac answered the phone.

"Joe, this is Ace. I need your help . . . and I need it now, man. I'll pay you well, as usual."

"What you want me to do, Ace?"

Ace briefed Joe on what he wanted. It basically involved exchanging vehicles and Joe taking a road trip from Bristol to Knoxville.

"I'm going to get into trouble with someone if I do this, right?" Joe queried.

Ace was prepared for the question. "You might have some confrontation with the law, but you should only get your hand slapped since they can't prove anything, and you really haven't done anything against the law. Besides, I am paying you well enough for any suffering you might briefly incur."

Joe was not so certain about that but said, "Well, I can handle it. How are you going to pay?"

"I'll send half to you now by PayPal, and the other half after I'm safely out of here."

"You got it. I'll leave keys in my car out front. Leave your keys in your car when you make the exchange. I'll start the road trip twenty minutes after that."

"That works for me."

As soon as they ended the call, Ace sent the PayPal payment, went back to his SUV, and then headed to Joe's house, thinking, *this might work out well.* Then he thought of what Joe looked like and thought he lucked out since Joe had bleached blond hair, like his own.

# Chapter 28

*Gunny tried to think why Ace would want them dis-
tracted. His train of thought led him in a deeply disturbing direction: Why was he trying to get out of the area?
Or was he? Did he have unfinished business? If so,
what might it be?*

Gunny found out that he would not be able to talk with Jeff again until Friday. He called the Bristol, Virginia, sheriff's office and explained the situation to one of the deputies. A couple deputies met Gunny at Jaimison's (Ace's) house. They knocked on the door. No one answered. Then, with guns drawn, one of the officers busted open the door and they entered the house, calling out, "Bristol Deputy Sheriff" several times. The deputies rapidly cleared the rooms of the one story, small house. But the odor typical of a meth lab pervaded the air. The deputies found a door leading to a basement, probably the location of a meth lab. One closet held an inventory of what looked like meth, crack, and marijuana worth tens of thousands of dollars on the street. They assumed the meth lab was in the basement and called in a special team equipped to handle the meth lab due to the dangerous chemicals involved.

When the special team arrived, they carefully entered the basement in case there were people or rigged explosives waiting for a careless move. Determining it clear of people and rigged explosives, the team took pictures of the meth lab and began collecting evidence. Eventually, the lab would be disassembled. But the house would be quarantined due to dangerous chemicals that would make the house useless for habitation until contaminated materials were disposed of and replaced, an expensive renovation process.

Gunny had trailed the deputies into the house. His skill of observation allowed him to quickly look around and garner what information he needed. He noticed clothes strewn across a bed in one bedroom. He thought it was probably Ace's bedroom. He looked through the wastebasket, but found nothing helpful. In the living room he noticed a wireless printer. He found the last page of something that had printed, the page that just has identification data at the top and or bottom, but no useful information for the person doing the printing. Thus, it is usually thrown away. He read a company name across the bottom: delta.com.

It seemed obvious that Ace had packed in a hurry and planned on leaving on a flight. The only airport within an hour's drive was Tri-Cities Regional. Gunny called dispatch, gave the lady a description of Ace, and had her contact security at Tri-Cities Regional Airport. He told her to send a car to the airport to keep an eye out for Ace, should he already be there. Gunny thanked the deputies and headed for the airport.

*******

Gunny walked to the head of the line for the Delta ticket counter, showed his badge, and said he needed to talk with an agent in charge right away. The ticket agent paged someone named "Jackson" to the counter. Two minutes later, Jackson showed up.

"Hello, I'm the lead agent, Joseph Jackson. How can I help you?"

Flipping his badge out, Gunny spoke quickly. "I'm Detective Hawkins with the Bristol Police Department. We have reason to believe a fugitive has obtained a Delta ticket online, and is attempting to flee through this airport. I would like to see if you have anyone on this evening's rosters by the name of Franklin Jaimison, or possibly Ace Jaimison."

Jackson stepped over to a computer and began punching the keys. After several minutes he looked up and said, "I have a Joseph F. Jaimison leaving here for New Orleans via Atlanta at 5:30 p.m., on flight 8584, from gate six. It is 4:05 p.m. now. It looks like he checked in online and did not claim to have any baggage to check. He could have gone straight to the gate if he printed his boarding passes himself. That flight is not at the gate yet, of course, and," he paused to switch pages, "is expected to arrive a half hour late due to a snow delay. It will be at gate six and the departure time is likely to change to 6:00 p.m."

"Thanks, Jackson. That's what I needed. Here's my card Please call the cell number."

Gunny walked briskly through the relatively small airport. Ace was nowhere in sight. He met up with two officers that had been dispatched earlier. They had not seen anyone that looked like Ace either in the main airport or in the gate area. Gunny checked the public restrooms on the main floor and lower floor. No Ace.

Gunny went to the security office and found the supervisor, Bob Harrison, "Jaimison or Ace should be considered armed and dangerous. He is a white, five foot, eleven inches tall man, about one hundred eighty-five pounds, has blond hair and blue eyes, a slight scar on his left cheek. Here is my cell phone number. Call me right away if anyone sees Ace." Gunny asked the security supervisor to notify the TSA staff of the same.

At that moment he remembered the private passenger lounge in a separate building for smaller, private aircraft. "Oh, by the way," Gunny called to the security supervisor, "do you cover the private passenger lobby as well?"

"No. They have their own security. We work closely together, so I'll notify them right now," he said as he pulled out his cell phone and made the call.

Gunny returned to the entrance to the TSA security checkpoints. All gates of the Tri-Cities Airport were located in one wing off a main building. There was only one security checkpoint for all gates. Gunny tried to find an inconspicuous vantage point to keep an eye on the entrance. He ascended the stairs to the mezzanine level that seemed to be the perfect place to wait.

*******

When boarding started for flight 8584 to Atlanta, Ace had still not shown up. Gunny looked at his watch. It was coming up on 5:45 p.m., and still, no Ace. Boarding would end in a few minutes. Security had not identified Ace in the gate area, or they would have notified him. There was no indication he had checked in at the ticket counter. Ace would have to check any baggage at the airplane—unless he only had a carry-on. Gunny used a backpack himself for a carry-on, and all Ace needed for a sudden trip to New Orleans could easily fit in a medium sized backpack.

Gunny felt increasingly anxious, even thinking out loud, "Where is this guy?" He silently reviewed why he had determined Ace would be on this flight. He had purchased a ticket online for this flight, as verified by the agent. It bothered him that Ace had used his full name instead of trying to disguise it. Airlines required passenger names and verification by picture ID at more than one point at the airport. Either Ace was careless or had some other purpose in using his name. Gunny felt a weight like a dark storm cloud move in on him. He did not like his feeling, but he had the same feeling before when things were about to go bad.

The last call for boarding flight 8584 had been announced. Gunny could not escape the thought that the ticket purchase was a ruse to distract their attention from something else. He had a BOLO out for the SUV he had seen at Roaring Fork, with a description of Ace. Perhaps he had rented a car and was driving to New Orleans or somewhere else. He called Danny Harris.

"Hi, Gunny," Danny answered. "What's up?"

"Danny, Ace is a no-show at the airport. I need you to contact the car rental companies in Sullivan County and Bristol, Virginia, to see if anyone who meets Ace's description has rented a car in the past forty-eight hours."

"You got it, Gunny. I'll check the bus stations in Bristol, Johnson City, and Kingsport as well."

"That's good. I doubt he will use the bus because he knows we are on to his use of the bus for the other guys. But try it anyway."

After hanging up, Gunny had a chain of thoughts about what and why Ace was not at the airport, *why and how was Ace trying to get out of the area? Or was he? Did he have unfinished business? If so, what might it be? Ace had demonstrated the violent lengths to which he would go to clean up after himself. He sent Brad to New Orleans…where Brad was murdered. He tried to get Jeff out of the way. The fact that he failed was probably disturbing to Ace.* At that thought Gunny felt a horrible feeling overcome him. *Ace misled me to get me out of the way so he could finish what he started to get rid of Jeff.*

Gunny called the airport security supervisor and asked him to continue to watch for Ace. He let him know he had to leave the airport right away. He jogged to his car. He called dispatch and requested that the officer at the hospital assigned to protect Jeff be notified to be extra vigilant for Ace—a threat might well be imminent. He requested the dispatch of additional officers to the hospital for backup.

Gunny used his lights and siren to get to the hospital in Bristol as fast as he could. He estimated he was about sixteen minutes away. He was concerned that Ace might try to complete in the hospital the job he had started in the forest. If Ace used the airline ruse to get them off track, he was smarter than Gunny thought. He kicked himself mentally for not thinking about this earlier. His lapse might cost Jeff his life—and the loss of their only witness.

The lingering snow slowed the traffic on I-81. Finally, he saw the turnoff for the Bristol hospital. He pulled up to the west end entrance, parked his car at the curb, hopped out, and jogged to the entrance doors where he had called ahead and asked hospital security to meet him. He could only hope he was wrong—or at least not too late.

# Chapter 29

*Gunny pushed open the door. He was shocked to see a pool of blood expanding on the sheet covering Jeff. Jeff was not moving.*

Gunny met with Mark Butler, Chief of Security for the hospital. He brought Mark up to speed on the situation as they walked quickly to the elevator. Gunny was happy to hear no incidents had been reported. Gunny knew Mark, and had worked with him in a couple other situations. He felt he and his staff would handle things well, and backup was also on the way—might even be on Jeff's floor already.

They stepped off the elevator and headed to room 2010. Gunny looked up to see three officers talking in the hallway outside Jeff's room. Just then, a man wearing scrubs, surgical mask, and head covering stepped out of the room and into the hallway. Gunny noticed a dark red spot the size of a grapefruit on the front of his scrubs. The man had started to walk in the direction of Gunny but made an abrupt about face and headed the opposite way down the hall. To Gunny, something seemed familiar about the man.

The officer who had been standing guard spoke up to Gunny. "Nothing so far, Gunny. No one meeting that description anywhere around here."

Looking at the identification the officer wore, Gunny asked, "Officer Bell, who was the person who just left, wearing surgical garb?"

"Oh, he said he just needed to check on the bandages and would just be a couple minutes. He had a hospital badge and seemed legit, so I let him in."

Then Gunny remembered what was familiar about the man. A tuft of blond hair stuck out from under the surgical cap. Gunny glanced quickly toward the end of the hall and saw the exit door to the stairwell slowly closing. He told the two backup officers to pursue the man who had just taken the stairs at the end of the corridor. He told Officer Bell to go down on the elevator to the first floor to look for the man.

Mark went off to notify his staff to look for the man in the surgical scrubs.

Gunny pushed open the door to Jeff's room. He was shocked to see a pool of blood expanding on the sheet covering. Jeff was not moving. He pushed the button for the nurse station.

A monotone voice responded, "Yes, how can..."

"We have an emergency in room 2010," Gunny interrupted. "I need help here right now. This man is dying. Get someone in here, now!"

The clerk responded to the authority and urgency in his voice with, "Yes, sir!" She turned to the nurse in the station, but she had heard the appeal for help and was already on her way to room 2010. She yelled over her shoulder for the clerk to call a code blue for room 2010.

The nurse proceeded into the room and went straight to Jeff. She pulled back the sheet, handed Gunny a clean sheet, and told him to put pressure on the wound site. She checked his pulse and found none. She began alternating compressions on his chest with using a mask to force air into his lungs. She knew he had a pneumothorax that could be a problem, but felt she had to do the compressions anyway or he was gone. In less than two minutes the code team started arriving, including a doctor from the ER. A tech took over for Gunny, so he stepped back toward the door. Once he saw the professionals were doing their thing and he would just be in the way, Gunny headed down to the lobby.

In the lobby, he found Officer Bell and Mark.

Gunny asked, "Did you see him?"

Officer Bell reported, "The other two officers are chasing him. He ran out of the hospital using the fire exit. Once outside, he jumped into a blue car and got away before they caught up with him. They got in their car and headed out to chase him. They told me all this on the radio. The last I heard, the guy was headed into town on West State Street."

"Into town? He must be trying to get to a place he can ditch the car and try to disappear, on foot, if necessary. I'm headed that way. You get back up to that room, or wherever they take Jeff, and watch out for him."

"Yes sir! I'm really sorry about misreading that guy."

Gunny looked at the officer and felt ready to jump all over him for his error. But he rechanneled his anger toward Ace. He turned to go and said, "Just get back up there and don't let anything else happen to him. Just pray he makes it."

Gunny tracked the progress of the chase on his radio as he headed down West State Street with lights and siren going. At one point, he heard they had lost visual contact. Next, they found the car, but no Ace. He had ditched the car and was trying to evade them on foot, just as he predicted. Gunny reached the location where the car had been abandoned. He told the officers to call for a team to process the car. He instructed them to search the area for Ace.

It was only a couple blocks from the college. He drove up Moore Street toward the college. He saw a man on the sidewalk waving his hands and yelling for help.

Gunny got out of his car and approached the man with his badge visible. The man was babbling, unable to get the words out. Gunny grabbed him by the shoulders and said firmly, "I'm a policeman. Settle down and tell me what happened."

The man stopped talking and looked at Gunny. He seemed to come to his senses and began talking rapidly to Gunny. "I was just getting out of my car to go to class. This guy came up, grabbed my keys (he stopped long enough to take a deep breath) . . . grabbed my keys out of my hand and waved a gun at me. He got in the car and drove off, burning rubber. He just stole my car!"

"Give me your name, the name on the car's registration, the state it's registered in, and a description of your car and tag number."

"I'm Reginald Wiley and I own the car. It's a gray, 2008 Toyota Camry. Umm, I never can remember the tag number, but it is registered in Tennessee."

"Alright, just hang on here a minute."

Gunny went to his car, called in a BOLO for the car, and asked dispatch to get the tag number. He told her to have a car come by his present location to pick up a man named Reginald Wiley, and to then take him to the station to get a report on the theft of his car.

Gunny returned to Reginald and told him, "OK, a police car is coming by take you down to the station to get a report on your stolen car. I've got to go. Just hang on here. They will be here in just a few minutes. By the way, was it a guy with blond hair who took your car?"

"Yeah, he had blond hair and, and I noticed a scar on his cheek."

"Thanks. Just hold on here a few minutes, alright?"

"Yeah. I guess I'll missed my class."

"You have a good reason to miss it this time."

Gunny drove in the direction Reginald reported his car thief had gone. He thought about where Ace might go. He would need to change the vehicle again or change his mode of transportation. His phone vibrated and he remembered he had put it on vibrate at the airport. "Gunny here," he answered.

"It's Greg with airport security. We haven't seen anything of the guy you are looking for, but there is a recent online purchase of a ticket for a flight to Atlanta leaving at 8:30 this evening. The purchaser's name is F.P. Jaimison."

"That's him. Watch for him to check in for the flight. I'll be there in twenty-five minutes."

Gunny called in that he was headed back to the airport and needed backup. He took off for the airport again, wondering if Ace was really trying to get out of town fast by air, or if this was simply another ruse. He parked his unmarked car in a passenger pickup parking space in front of the terminal, and then moved quickly to the security office. It was about 7:30 p.m. Bob Harrison, security supervisor, told Gunny that the TSA had been notified, and he had a security guard in the gate area. Two backup officers arrived. Gunny assigned them each to opposite ends of the airport building, and warned them to keep a low profile. He walked to his position on the mezzanine level and waited.

*******

At the hospital, Jeff had been revived, but his pulse was rapid, his BP was very low, he was clammy, and continued to need assistance to breathe. He was in shock from loss of blood. He was headed to surgery to find out what damage had been done by the knife wound he had just suffered. It looked like the assailant had tried to stab him in the heart. The attending doctor told the nurses that it appeared that the knife glanced off a rib and missed the heart and major arteries but he had still lost a lot of blood. He had ordered a unit of blood to be started ASAP.

Jeff was immediately prepped for surgery and sent to the surgical suite. He coded in surgery, but the anesthetist saw it coming and reacted immediately. Jeff's blood pressure was waning and his pulse was waning. The surgical team were able to bring him back again. The knife had made a mess of Jeff's connective tissue, but he was one lucky guy in that no major organs were damaged, including his lungs. With one lung damaged, another lung injury might have taken him out. Jeff would need assistance breathing for a couple days.

The doctor came out after surgery and told the officer waiting outside the suite that Jeff had made it and would recover.

*******

Gunny thought about Jake sitting in jail even though he was innocent. He knew Ace had done the deed. He had not had time to tell the DA about the events of the day. He just hoped Jake would last long enough to be set free from the murder charge (though he still had to face a theft charge). He thought this experience might well cause Jake to make a change in his ways in the future. Gunny thought about how much he had learned from the many struggles he had gone through, and that God did some of His best teaching and training during our crises.

He thought about the book Doc had talked about. Doc had said, "The writer says we can't handle all our problems alone. Sometimes we need help from outside ourselves, and that is where the Spirit of God can do His work." Gunny realized Jake was not the only one who would need that help. He needed that help in dealing with his PTSD.

Gunny's attention was drawn to his phone that was toning a call from dispatch. Dispatch was calling to let him know that the Tennessee Highway Patrol (THP) officers were in a high-speed chase south on I-81, following a suspect who matched his BOLO description.

Just as Gunny thanked her, he saw a man walking toward the security checkpoint. He had a hoody on, and though Gunny could not be sure, he thought the man was Ace's build. He carried a backpack and was moving fast, often looking around himself as he made his way toward the TSA inspection station for the gates.

Gunny waited until he entered the queue. Then Gunny made his way down the steps and stood to the side of the security checkpoint where he could observe the man and stay out of sight. He could see that the TSA agents were letting the man go through the line where he placed his bag in a tub for x-ray check. In another bin he placed his shoes, belt, and some coins—no keys. Gunny thought he probably left them in the car he stole. If he went through the x-ray checks without alarm, it was not likely he would have a gun on him.

*What's going on?* Gunny thought. The stolen car that seemed to have Ace at the wheel was racing south on I-81, but an Ace lookalike was checking in at the airport. He did not have time to think about it. It was his responsibility to deal with the airport, and THPs to handle the chase.

A TSA agent held back the couple other people who had entered the queue. When he stepped through the x-ray machine, a security guard was waiting for him on the other side, and said, "Sir, please come with me."

The guard was taking the man out of the security check area to a less congested location. Just as he reached for his hand-cuffs, the man in the hoody coldcocked the guard and took off running out of the security area toward an airport exit. The hood slipped from his head just enough for Gunny to see a couple locks of blond hair.

"Franklin Jaimison!" Gunny shouted. "This is the police. Stop where you are!" He had to yell it to Ace as a matter of procedure. He expected Ace to ignore his words and keep on running, which he did. Gunny was reaching his stride in the chase to catch a killer.

# Chapter 30

*Gunny jogged between cars toward the scream. He
heard grunting, followed by a gunshot . . . .*

Ace sprinted for the exit door, knocking a girl to the floor. Her large
purse emptied its contents across the floor. Gunny used his radio
to call the officers he had assigned to opposite ends of the airport.
Already breathing heavily, he gasped into the radio instructions for
them to move outside to the parking area where Ace seemed to be
headed. Gunny sprinted thirty yards behind Ace, in hot pursuit. He
had been slowed by the fallen girl still scrambling to her feet. Two
cars moving along the drop-off road between the terminal and the
parking area slowed him again and Gunny lost sight of Ace when
Ace reached the elevated parking area.

Gunny moved rapidly, taking the stairs two at a time up to the
short-term parking lot. He glanced around and saw Ace sprint
away from a trash can and into the lot. Gunny immediately moved
more cautiously. He thought Ace might have dropped a gun into
the trash can on the way in, and had just retrieved it. Ace disappeared in the rows of parked cars. Gunny cautiously moved row to
row looking for something to give him an idea which direction Ace
had gone.

A head bobbed up and down three rows further ahead and to
Gunny's right. He cautiously moved in that direction with his Smith
& Wesson drawn and bullet chambered. Movement to the right
caught his attention. It was the last thing Gunny wanted to see.
An unsuspecting older couple walked toward Ace's last known

position, presumably looking for their car. He knew Ace would track them to their car, assail them, and steal it.

Gunny began jogging toward the elderly couple, yelling a warning to them to go back. It was too late. A woman's scream sounded across the sprawling lot of cars and SUVs.

Gunny moved faster between cars toward the scream. He heard grunting, followed by a gunshot. Gun ready, he stepped out from the shelter of a pickup truck. His eyes went quickly to a woman leaning over a man who was writhing in pain. He did not see Ace. A vehicle suddenly roared to life just two spots away to his left. He heard the gears shift into reverse and the Jeep Comanche began backing out toward the defenseless couple. There was just enough time for Gunny to drop his gun, grab the woman with one hand, and grab the man with the other hand and barely drag them out of the path of the Jeep.

A shot rang out from the Jeep and almost simultaneously Gunny felt his jacket tug to his left. Gunny did not have time to see what the bullet had done to him. He dove for his gun as the Jeep jumped forward.

The Jeep's tires screeched from the sharp, high speed turns on its way toward the exit. Gunny realized that Ace would have to make a couple turns to get to the lane for the exit gate. He pulled himself up just as one of the other officers arrived at the scene. Gunny yelled, "Check out this man and take care of them both." He picked up his gun and ran toward the exit gate, taking a shorter route on foot than Ace could take in the Jeep. If he could get to the exit lane, he might be able to cut Ace off. Gunny was still breathing heavily when he raced toward the exit lane. His adrenaline dumping into his blood was beginning to help. He reached the exit lane and heard the Jeep racing toward him immediately to his left.

The Jeep raced for the gate. Gunny took aim and shot several times at the front right tire of the rapidly moving target. He knew the new tires could handle one puncture and keep going so he was trying to blow apart the one tire. The damaged tire caused the SUV to swerve to the right just enough to crash into a ticket booth.

The ticket agent had seen it coming and jumped out of the booth, likely avoiding his death.

Ace's door opened with the impact and he fell out of the vehicle, having had no time to fasten the seat belt. He gingerly stood up, picked something up from the ground near him and took off running in the opposite direction from Gunny. Gunny sprinted after him, keeping in mind Ace might still have a gun. He noticed Ace limping, and it had slowed him down. Ace stopped, whirled around and took aim at Gunny with his gun.

Gunny dove for Ace to tackle him just as the gun went off. He felt a searing pain along his right upper arm. He drove Ace violently to the ground. Ace lost his grip on the gun and it fell a few feet away from them. Ace fought back like a madman, trying to get an advantage over Gunny. But Gunny's Marine training in hand-to-hand combat gave him the advantage over Ace's street training in New Orleans, where he spent his teen years in gang fighting. In spite of the surface wound, Gunny wrestled Ace to a prone position on the ground with his hands behind his back. Gunny took out his handcuffs and roughly placed them on Ace's wrists. Breathing heavily, Gunny gasped out to Ace, "Franklin Jaimison, you are under arrest for the attempted murder of Jeff Jones." He proceeded to state his rights while jerking Ace to his feet.

*******

Gunny saw Ace off with the two officers who were taking him to the police station. He walked back to the place where the couple had been assaulted. A rescue vehicle was pulling into the parking lot with lights and siren blaring. Gunny checked his own arm. It was only bleeding slightly from a surface would. He saw another hole in his jacket where the first shot at him had missed him, but not his jacket. He looked down at his hurting knee and found a hole in his pants. He realized he had hit it hard when he tackled Ace. He would take that to get this perp put away.

Gunny gave instructions to one of the officers about securing the scene. An investigation unit would be there soon, but he wanted to get back to the station to interrogate Ace.

The rescue squad arrived a couple minutes later, and the crew first attended to a through-and-through wound in the older man's shoulder. He would be okay. An ambulance had arrived to transport the man to the hospital. The man's wife was sitting in the back of the ambulance.

Gunny asked the EMT that was taking her blood pressure, "How is your patient?"

The EMT responded when he saw Gunny's badge, "Her blood pressure is a little high, but whose wouldn't be. She'll be fine. You want me to look at that wound on your arm?"

"Oh, no. I've got to get back to the station, but I'll get it checked later."

"Your choice."

The lady began telling the EMT about her hero husband who had stood up for her against that mean, terrible man.

Gunny chuckled as he left the scene and walked back to his car. It felt good to laugh again. It had been too long a dry spell. The crisp cool air felt good. He called home.

When Karen answered, Gunny responded with more emotion than was comfortable for him. "Hi, honey." He choked a little making him unable to continue right away.

Karen asked with concern in her tone, "Are you okay, 'Gunny?"

"Yeah. I'm just having one of those moments where I feel overwhelmingly grateful for you and that I am okay. I wanted you to be the first to know that we got the guy, the one who I think killed that student. You might hear some news about it. There was some shooting, and I took a graze to my arm, but I'm OK. However, you might not be happy about the hole in the knee of my pants."

"Oh, forget those pants. I'm glad to hear you are alright. I had not heard the news, so I am glad you called."

"Yeah, we were all over the place, and it ended up at the airport. I am certain the news is—or shortly will—report it."

"Did you get that wound and knee looked at?"

"Not yet. I will as soon as I finish questioning the perp at the station."

"Can't someone else do that so you can take care of yourself?"

"No, I need to do it. I'm most familiar with the evidence. I promise I will have my arm and knee checked out afterwards."

"You better keep that promise."

"Honey, you know a Marine always keeps his word. Besides, I love you too much to let you down."

"You always do that. Just when I am putting the heat on you, you say something that melts me and I lose all initiative. I love you too, and I want to see you at home as soon as you can get here, Okay?"

"You got it. Got to go. Love you."

"Love you, too."

Gunny remembered an earlier crisis in his police career in which he had been in a shooting incident and had not called home. The news showed lots of blood and said that a policeman had been critically wounded. Karen saw the news and was beside herself with worry. She finally called him and got his recorded "busy" message. Gunny came home late that evening and found her sitting on the couch in a very angry mood. They talked it out, and he agreed to call her in the future as soon as he could. That was a good thing that the Bible calls "iron sharpening iron."

Gunny was walking back to his car when he called Doc's cell phone thinking that he was not sure why he was calling Doc whom he did not know that well. He resolved his doubt with the thought that he knew how concerned Doc was for Jake and this news would help Doc feel some relief.

Gunny heard the response on his phone, "This is Doc."

"Doc, this is Gunny. I thought you might like to know that we just got the guy who I think killed Jan Meredith. Jake will have to spend a little more time in jail while the process to get him out is handled, but I think the judge will let him out soon. There will probably be bail money involved due to the robbery."

"Wow, that's great news, Gunny! Can you tell me who it was? Was it the professor?"

"No, I can't give you details, but it wasn't the professor."

Doc agreed to let Angel know. He finished with, "Thanks Gunny for keeping after it and for calling me with the good news.

I've been really worrying about Jake. I hope he gets out sooner than later."

Gunny said, "Me too. Got to go. Talk with you later." Gunny hung up and got into his car thinking about how to approach the interrogation of Ace.

# Chapter 31

*Could this murder have been an unbelievably careless,
ignorant act that was not intended to kill?*

Gunny arrived at the station and wasted no time getting to the interrogation room, where he found Ace slumped down in his chair with his hood over his head. Gunny started with a demand. "Take that hood off your head."

Ace slowly took the hood off his golden head and said with malice, "I want to call my attorney."

Gunny slid his cell phone across the table and said, "Call him. You will need an attorney."

After the call, Gunny put his phone away thinking he would check on the number Ace had called. Good chance the call was made to someone other than an attorney, but someone who would send an attorney to him. He sat down across a table from Ace and looked him in his eyes. "We have you nailed for two counts of attempted murder. I suspect we will tie you to the death of Brad Jones. And we are going to nail you for the death of Janice Meredith. We have plenty of evidence to put you away for good. I might understand why you went after Brad and Jeff, but why did you kill Janice Meredith? You know you killed twice. She was pregnant, so you will be charged with the baby's death too. Why kill her and the baby?"

Ace looked away. He was silent. He reached to pull the hood back over his head.

"You put that on your head and I will rip it off . . . and your head with it," Gunny threatened.

Ace dropped the hood back and stirred, still looking away.

"Come on, Ace. Get if off your chest. You messed up bad. No attorney's going to get you out of this. So just help me understand why you would kill one of your customers after she turned to you for help. Why kill her when you knew she had a baby?"

Ace mumbled something with his chin in his chest.

"I didn't hear that. Speak up so I can hear you."

Ace looked up at Gunny and said, "Why did she have to go and get pregnant? I was not ready for that. A kid did not fit my life or plans. She messed it all up."

"You thought she was carrying your baby?"

"Might have been. I did it with her one time for payment for her . . . well, for something she wanted."

"For her drugs, you mean?"

"I just wanted her to get an abortion, that's all. Why wouldn't she do it? Everybody does that today. But no, she could not break a promise to her mother. She just couldn't get it through her head that an abortion would solve it all."

"I have an idea she did not see her baby as the same kind of problem you did. So, why kill her over a kid?"

For the first time, Ace showed some emotion and, in broken phases, blurted out, "I didn't mean...I didn't want to...to kill her. I heard about someone else who had taken a bunch of crystal and then drank a bottle of wine, and she lost her baby. I thought it would be a good way to get Jan to naturally abort." He paused for a couple moments and said, "I'm thirsty. Can I have some water?"

Gunny sent the officer outside the door for a cup of water.

After the officer returned and Ace had a couple sips, Gunny pressed further. "Are you telling me that you forced her to take crystal and drink a bottle of wine to try to make her abort the baby?"

"I've said too much already. I want my attorney."

Gunny went outside the room and sat down at his desk. He had to think over what Ace had said, *could this murder have been an unbelievably careless, ignorant act not intended to kill the mother, just the baby? The autopsy had shown that the marks on Jan's throat were not typical of someone trying to strangle someone.*

*That finding by Jerry would support an effort to force Jan to drink the bottle of wine laced heavily with meth.*

Gunny had done online research on what happens with that combination. He knew that a heavy dose of crystal and a bottle of wine would not likely kill someone unless they had another problem that contributed to the death. The combination could cause problems in pregnancy, however, including premature delivery. His line of thinking lead him back to Jan, *The bad news for Jan was that she had a congenital heart defect that the combination of meth and wine resulted in her death. In any case, Ace intended to kill the baby.*

Fifteen minutes later, an attorney showed up to represent Franklin Jaimison. Gunny briefed the attorney on charges and that Ace had been given and understood his rights.

The attorney responded, "We'll see about that."

Gunny said, "He has already confessed to giving Jan Meredith a heavy dose of meth mixed with wine just before she died. He said he just wanted to force her to abort the baby."

The attorney looked at Gunny and said with a hint of malice, "He won't be saying anymore. You probably intimidated him into those words. Where is he? I want to see him now."

Gunny and the attorney entered the interrogation room together. The attorney advised Ace that he did not have to say anything or answer any questions at that time. He added, "I advise you to say nothing more."

"But I didn't mean for her to die!" Ace blurted out. "I just wanted to get her to abort the baby. If she had just gotten an abortion…"

The attorney cut him off and instructed him not to say anything more.

"You didn't abort a baby!" Gunny responded intensely. "You killed that baby when you killed the baby's mother with drugs and alcohol. Then you tried to cover your tracks by sending Brad to New Orleans for your connections there to do him in. Oh yes, Brad was found dead and the New Orleans police are talking to your family there in regard to Brad's murder. Then you had to try to get rid of Jeff, but he outsmarted you and fled your vile plan to send him to his death in New Orleans as well. When that did not work, you went after him when you learned he had gone to his favorite getaway in Cherokee National Forest. I showed up at Roaring Fork just as you shot Jeff and tried to kill me. You fled that scene when I showed up. Then you tried again to kill Jeff in the hospital. You blew that too. He's alive and will live to testify against you."

Gunny paused to get his breath and settle down. His anger was rising fast and he did not want to do something stupid in front of Ace's attorney.

He spoke again—this time to the attorney. "The DA likes slam dunk cases. He has one here. The evidence and eyewitnesses make it a slam dunk. You might want to find a case you have a chance of winning."

Gunny stood up and walked toward the door. On the way out, he instructed the officer in the room, "Book Ace for the attempted murder of Jeff Jones, the murder of Janice Meredith and the murder of Baby Doe Meredith. I doubt there will be any bail for him."

He looked back at Ace and said, "By the way, we are not sure that was your kid. We will know when the DNA comparison comes back."

With an empty feeling of satisfaction, Gunny called the DA's cell phone. John did not answer, so Gunny left a message saying he had in jail a man named Franklin Jaimison who had confessed to acts that lead to the death of Janice Meredith. He told him there was more. Gunny included, "I will complete a full report in the morning and get with you then. I think you will have plenty to get Jake out of jail before he suffers more abuse."

Gunny's next call was to Karen, his wife, "I'm headed to the ER to get my arm checked out. It is just a flesh wound and should not take long. I will be home for a late dinner."

Karen responded, "Thanks, I was wondering. Call me when you leave the ER so I can get your food ready."

Gunny said, "I'm not too hungry right now, so don't fix a lot of food. It has been a tiring, eventful day. I will tell you about it when I get home." They ended the call.

Gunny leaned back in his chair. It was a good day, not an easy one, but he had gotten somewhere. He had stuck with it until he found the truth. That is why he liked his job. His cell phone vibrated. He looked at who was calling. It was Kim. He silenced the phone and headed home.

# Chapter 32

Friday morning came too soon. Gunny had work to do, so he got up and did his usual routine. Gunny was driving to the coffee drive-through when he noticed a feeling of satisfaction he had not felt for weeks. The DA called Gunny just as he was leaving the drive-through.

"Gunny," John Erickson blurted over the Bluetooth, "you almost let me put an innocent man away. I need to get with you right away to sort things out. Can you come to my office now?"

Gunny had several thoughts about smart retorts, but just enjoyed the moment of knowing that John really knew Gunny had saved his bacon, even if John would never admit it. "Sure, John," he said, "I'm almost at the office. I will check in there and head your way. I should be there about nine o'clock. I don't have the written report yet, but I can give you an oral report."

"Great. Get here as soon as you can. The reporters are already calling."

Gunny took his time and still got there in about forty-five minutes. The secretary waved him on in. Gunny noted he had never been waved in before.

John asked the secretary to get them coffees. Then, with relish, Gunny told him about the events and findings of the past couple weeks, especially Thursday's events. John assured Gunny that he would submit to the judge that very day a motion to absolve Jake from the murder charge and recommend letting him out of jail on a $500 bail. John wanted a $10,000 bail, but Gunny talked him into the lower amount because Jake could not even pay $500. Gunny felt Jake's friends might come up with the smaller amount.

When he had all the information, John told Gunny to put it all in his report, and complimented him on his good work. "After all," John said, "I love slam-dunk cases!"

Back at the office, the Major walked over to Gunny's cubicle. Gunny was working on his report. The Major spoke up, "I'm looking forward to your report, but what I hear is that you have done a great job getting to the bottom line on the Meredith case. I like the way you stick to your gut beliefs. Good job, detective!"

*******

Friday morning's buzz was the newspaper headline: "Student Murder Case Takes Big Turn." The trial of Jake Worley had been canceled and Jake Worley would be eligible for bail.

That morning, Doc caught Angel for breakfast and filled her in on what little he knew that had happened. He shared, "I am sure Jake will be cleared of the murder charge right away, but I am not sure what will happen with the theft charges."

Angel encouraged him, "I think they might be more lenient about that since he had been in jail for so long and had such a bad experience there. I hope that the bail, if any, will be a lot less."

"Angel," Doc looked seriously at her, "I've been saving some of my money. How much do you think the bail might be lowered?"

"I'm not sure, but maybe $1,000, though it could be even lower."

"I have about $400. We have to get him out of there," Doc spoke with a mixture of urgency and hope.

"Well, I have some savings." Tongue in cheek she continued, "Do you think he is a good risk?"

Doc looked up with surprise and then caught the sparkle in her eyes. "I think he is not such a great risk, but maybe we can talk to him about the Lord. I think the Lord is a good risk."

"Well, I'll have to agree with you on that. I can probably come up with $500."

"You know, Angel, we agreed to pray over this when it seemed nothing else would work. Guess prayer does work."

"I've found it does. I prayed for you a lot, and look at you now. You have been through some trying times lately and yet you have stayed away from the bottle as far as I know," Angel said with her winning smile.

"I was sorely tempted a couple of times, but that book you gave me, umm, *The Key to Triumphant Living,* made a difference. I am living a triumphant life that I did not know existed before."

"Me too. I've got his next book, if you're interested. It is entitled *Much More.*"

"Yeah, I'd like that."

Doc turned toward Angel and took a couple steps closer to her. He reached down and took her hands in his, "Angel, you have been a change agent in my life. I want you to know that I, um, I mean I, um, love you for that. I have never felt so inspired by any woman or anyone since Angela. But you are real and I can trust you when I felt I could not trust anyone anymore, especially myself."

He looked deeply into Angel's eyes, and she into his, and ever so slowly, they moved their faces toward each other, their lips almost touching. Doc's phone rang. He wanted to ignore it. There were too many important possibilities for the call, so he reached for his phone. Angel pulled away.

Doc caught himself about to speak harshly into the phone for interrupting the moment, but heard Gunny say, "Doc, can you come to the Sullivan County Jail? They are going to let Jake go today with just the theft charge pending if he can come up with $500 bail."

"Oh, yes. I think we can help him come up with that. We have to get the money, and then we can come down there."

"I'll see you there in about forty-five minutes," said Gunny.

They ended the call and Doc told Angel the news. Doc got $200 from the bank and Angel got $300, and they headed to the jail.

On the way, Doc and Angel talked about Jake's beat-up condition.

"Would you consider letting me keep him in the duplex just long enough to help him heal?" Paul asked.

"Huh? You want me to take more risk?"

"Sure, I can keep him straight and have time to talk with him about getting his life in order. You know, talk with him about the Bible and the Lord."

Doc looked over at Angel thinking that maybe she was joking again and he had missed the joke. She was just laughing.

"Okay, you got me again. Go ahead and laugh. But I am serious," Doc appealed.

"Since you put it that way, I guess I have no choice. How can I fight God?" Angel, who was driving, looked back to the road with a smile on her face…and on her heart.

Gunny got to the jail shortly after Doc and Angel arrived. They posted the bail money and waited a few minutes for Jake to be processed out. When the door opened and he stepped out, both Doc and Angel caught their breath. He was a mess, with bruises, cuts, and stitches. He walked with a limp. But he was still able to get a few key words out: "Hey Doc, I knew I could count of you. You got a light?"

"No, Jake, I don't have a cigarette or a light. Let's get you out of here. We have a place for you to stay that will be safe and let you do some healing. You can stay with me in my duplex. How's that?"

"Yeah, that sounds great. You got some decent food there?"

"Sure I do, but we will have to talk about some things like that smoking."

"Oh, no. I thought there might be a catch."

They took him home and Jake slept all afternoon and night until about 8 a.m. the next day.

# Epilogue

Franklin Jaimison's (Ace) trial for the murder of Janice Meredith and baby lasted five days, including jury selection. The most time was spent arguing over whether the baby was a person or a fetus. The jury deliberated for only an hour before returning a verdict of guilt for murder in the second degree. Additional trial dates for attempted murder of Jeffry Jones (Jeff), Detective Richard Hawkins (Gunny) and the older man at the airport and a request by New Orleans for his extradition still remained to be determined. Jaimison would spend most of the rest of his life in the courtroom and in prison.

Jeff Jones healed and agreed to testify about what he saw the night of Jan's murder, and about Ace's (Jaimison's) attempts to kill him. It turned out that Jeff and Brad were cousins. Doc tried to reach out to Jeff, but Jeff lost interest in a short time.

In New Orleans, two of Jaimison's relatives would soon be tried for first-degree murder in the slaying of Brad Jones. That trial had not yet started. Extradition of Ace from Tennessee to Louisiana was being sought so he could be included in the murder trial there. Louisiana would have to wait in line.

The e-mail with its fingerprint was admitted as evidence, but the clincher for the jury was that Ace's recorded confession to Gunny in the interrogation room was admitted as evidence. Paul Walker, Doc, was pleased that he had done the right thing turning over the email to Gunny. It turned out that the observations of several homeless men (invisible witnesses) had helped get to the truth of what had happened.

John Erickson eventually ran for State Attorney General in Tennessee, He lost the first try, but succeeded several years later.

Dr. Brantley, the professor, turned out to be Jan's baby's biological father. That little bit of information made its way to the media somehow. The professor resigned rather suddenly from Covenant College and moved somewhere (location currently unknown). Rumor had it he was facing divorce as well. He never found out who had blackmailed him, but he suspected Jaimison or maybe Brad or Jeff.

Although arrests for drug dealing were made in the general area of the campus, the drug business continued to be `a problem. Meth labs were a scourge in Tennessee and southwest Virginia even though law enforcement worked hard to stop them.

Gunny loved his family, loved his job and enjoyed his church. He wondered why he was so blessed in a world that was going amuck in so many ways. He did get back on the protocol for PTSD with the VA and went a long time without the more disturbing symptoms.

Gunny saw Doc (Paul) and Angel at church every so often. They did not meet again as a group to talk about their PTSD. Karen and Angel talked about it together occasionally. They talked about starting two support groups at their church, one for fellow PTSD sufferers and the other for PTSD sufferer spouses.

Gunny and Doc started getting together for coffee at the Sweet Tooth Bakery early every Thursday morning. Gunny encouraged Doc to freshen up on his EMT skills training, and consider going to work again in that field. Doc seriously considered the idea. Occasionally, they talked about their PTSD, but it was some time before their friendship grew close enough for either to be openly honest with each other. Even then, there were some things Gunny could not talk about and did not fully understand himself.

Doc continued to live in Angel's duplex next door. They frequently rode to church together, went to other events together, and were a popular topic of conversation among several groups in town, including the street people and the staff at the shelter. People thought they belonged together. It is still not known if they ever got back to that kiss. Time will tell.

# About Wayne Sheridan

Wayne Sheridan is a writer/speaker who draws his writing from his four years of experience as a Navy corpsman in the military, twenty years in hospital administration, six years as a small business owner, fifteen years directing a homeless shelter ministry, and a lifetime of service and leadership in the church. He and his wife Alice have been married for more than forty-five years and have two godly, successful sons, and nine grandchildren. Wayne writes in various genres to challenge Christians to be sincere—even radical—as they walk their trails of life in the power of the Holy Spirit, characterized by integrity, love for God and others, and love for God's Word. He believes the current times require committed Christians to share the message of Jesus to a world in turmoil through how they live their lives and through vocalizing their testimonies.

Watch for Wayne's next book entitled *Wisdom from the Trail*, a compendium of devotional, inspirational lessons he and his son, Keith, have learned from the many miles of hiking on the Appalachian Trail and other trails.

www.ingramcontent.com/pod-product-compliance
Lightning Source LLC
Chambersburg PA
CBHW050349190726
48284CB00007BB/2215